M000314379

A rustle came from behind the door. "Whaddya want!" came a shout, more a demand than a question.

"That you, Lucky? It's Red Maguire from the Bugle."

"Ease in, boy. I ain't in the mood."

Maguire turned the knob. Behind the door, he found a burly man slouched behind a desk. The man clenched a tall glass bottle of brown liquid in one hand and a menacing silver gun in the other. Maguire figured him capable with both.

MYSTERY OF THE PURPLE ROSES

Introducing Red Maguire,
crime-solving ace reporter

BOOK 1

Kevin S. Giles

BookLocker
Saint Petersburg, Florida

Copyright © 2020 Kevin S. Giles

ISBN 978-1-64718-651-7

All rights reserved. No part of this publication may be reproduced, stored in a retrieval system, or transmitted in any form or by any means, electronic, mechanical, recording or otherwise, without the prior written permission of the author.

Published by BookLocker.com, Inc., St. Petersburg, Florida.

Characters and events in this book are fictitious. Any similarity to real persons, living or dead, is coincidental and not intended by the author.

Library of Congress Cataloging in Publication Data
Giles, Kevin S.
MYSTERY OF THE PURPLE ROSES by Kevin S. Giles
Fiction | Mystery & Detective | Hard-Boiled
Library of Congress Control Number: 2020910351

Printed on acid-free paper.

kevinsgiles.com 2020

First Edition

Cover graphic © Helen Vonallmen | Dreamstime.com

To Don and Buggs
True Butte Rats

Yet another cold body

Clouds over the mountains felt close and heavy. Rain streamed off the windows. What a dreary day for a man to die but die he must. Six bullets, only one needed. The killer set aside the gun and caressed the photograph. Sorrow, what a regrettable thing.

Maguire nudged the door open. The man's body sprawled on the living room floor, his head resting on glass shards from the busted coffee table. Maguire looked around. The room otherwise appeared orderly and smelled of fresh coffee. A newspaper lay neatly folded on the table next to a plate of buttermilk pancakes barely touched. That morning's *Butte Bugle*, the August 11, 1954, edition. His eyes turned back to the body. The victim, shaved and dressed for business, appeared respectable enough. Below the single bullet hole in his chest his smooth hands clutched a purple rose.

Maguire dialed a number into the rotary phone on the wall. "Butte police. What is your emergency?" inquired a woman's no-nonsense voice.

"Hello, Betty, it's Red Maguire calling in a murder. I came to this address, 1242 Copper King Lane, to interview a source for a story. I found him dead."

Betty asked Maguire several questions just like he knew she would. Did Maguire know the man? How did he know a murder occurred? Was anybody else in the house? Was Maguire armed? The cops would want to know. Maguire had covered crime for twenty-one years for the *Bugle*. He knew the drill. He also knew Betty. Old as dirt, for sure, but nimble enough to stay on top of it. He pictured her speaking through caked red lipstick as a cigarette smoldered in the ashtray. She told him police were on their way and advised him to step outside the house. Disturbed murder scenes make cops grouchy. Not that Maguire meddled in evidence. He knew better than to dirty his hands with the dead.

He said goodbye to Betty, to a silent line because she hung up without notice. He went outside to wait. Rain poured from the eaves of the covered porch. Two, three minutes passed before he heard approaching sirens. A prowl car rolled up. Soon a second prowl car, its tires splashing water, arrived from the opposite direction. Maguire knew most cops on the Butte force but not these two. They walked toward him cautiously in the pouring rain. The younger cop took his hand off his holstered pistol. He had that crisp fresh look that would disappear after a few years of hard drinking in Butte's bars.

Maguire took note as he always did whenever someone new crossed his path. Such descriptions became useful in news stories. He had filed a million of them in his brain. The younger cop fidgeted with his silver badge, reaching across

2

his chest to oddly pinch it between thumb and forefinger. Maguire knew the subconscious gesture meant the man lacked confidence in being a cop. Or, he fretted over how to handle himself at a murder scene. Either way, he had much to learn. Maguire set his square jaw and looked hard at the men.

Crime reporters, Maguire had learned on the job, became amateur psychologists. Every cop and crook he met had a back story. The baby-faced badge-fidgeting cop stood as tall as Maguire, alert as taught in the academy, somewhat naive to the ways of the street. He would learn. The older one, gripping his gun, remained suspicious of Maguire. Shorter, duty belt straining under a sprawling paunch that screamed late-night pizzas, his red face spilling considerable cynicism from beneath the shiny bill of his police hat. Wearing a badge would do that to a man. Maguire had worked the crime beat long enough to know how it went. Butte had a surplus of ex-cops who told long stories in bars.

"You called in a dead guy, bub?" the older cop asked.

"He's in there flat on the floor, took a round, skin turning blue as the shirt on your back. Pretty sure he's not getting up." Maguire smiled at his joke.

"Come off the porch with your hands up until we figure out what's going on, OK?" Maguire complied. As he eased down the steps, arms in the air, a car flashing red light from the roof braked to a stop. Detective Harold "Duke" Ferndale jumped out. He held a clipboard above his balding head to catch the rain. Maguire knew well how Duke's cheap brown suits hid the cannon for a sidearm shoulder-holstered under his coat. Ferndale called it "the rib tickler" because the barrel of it hung a good three inches from the leather. Ferndale scowled at the scene before him. "Ease up, boys, that's Maguire you're holding up. No need to waltz him around like he's on the most wanted list. Hands off the heat, will you? Where the hell's the stiff?"

The older officer, hesitant, turned to Ferndale. "Who's Maguire? I don't know this guy, Captain."

"Manny, read the *Bugle*, will you? You're holding up the best crime reporter in Montana. Don't tell him that. Got a big enough head already. How long you been working the force, anyway? Put away the sidearm. If Maguire became a wild-eyed killer we'd let him write a big damn front page story to tell all about it after we pitch him into jail with the lowlifes from the Saturday night fights. Wouldn't that be something, Maguire in the slammer, eating stale bread for breakfast and making boyfriends? Now, where's the dead guy?"

Maguire dropped his hands from their "don't shoot me" position. "Living room floor, Duke. He called me at the paper about an hour ago. Said he knew something about the murders I wrote about. When I got here the front door stood partly open. I went inside and found him all dressed up with no place to go."

"You get a good quote from him, Maguire?"

Load of laughs, Ferndale. Rangy pugnacious sort, medium height, arms swinging freely as a man would expect of a southpaw light-heavyweight boxer of some repute in his day. His face showed it. Ferndale figured as the ugliest cuss on the Butte force. Not only his nose, pushed out of place to the left, or the drooping right eye that had taken too many hits. Scars covered his cheeks and chin from bare-knuckle fights. His face read like a road map of early Butte brawls. Ferndale owned a reputation as the toughest cop in the city even though his best years vanished somewhere in the past. Maguire saw him knock a man cold as they drank beer in an uptown bar one night. The drunken fool danced around, promising a beating and feigning jabs, until Ferndale tired of him. One smashing punch from a left fist put the man on the floor, lights out. Maguire knew enough about Ferndale's reputation as a fighter to play him straight. Anybody who gave him lip wound up like the goon on the floor, bleeding teeth. Soon after Ferndale hung up his gloves, he became Maguire's best source for crime news. Maguire's best stories, the ones that got readers howling when they saw his byline on the *Bugle* front page, usually started with secret tips from Ferndale.

The detective led Maguire and his fellow cops into the house, a fashionable one-story estate in a grove of weeping willows, miles away from the old-brick mining portion of Butte. The house sat on the plain known as the Flats. Ferndale walked to the kitchen table where he grabbed a pancake off the plate. He took a savage bite as he looked out the window above the sink. "Needs heating up but I ain't got time. No breakfast for the third time this week makes an old dick grouchy. You uniform boys, check around the house for anybody else, will you? That shed out back, too."

Ferndale gulped the last of the pancake. After wiping his maple syrup-stained hands on his pants, he knelt at the body, feeling the man's throat for a pulse. "Like you say, Maguire, he won't be needing no ambulance. Stiff as a board by lunchtime. The undertakers will stand him in the corner for the embalming. Like my humor this morning, Maguire? Now don't he look pretty as a peach with the flower adorning him? Wanna bet he'll sit up any minute to say, 'How's she go?' "

The detective shifted for a better look at the bullet hole. The slug left a neat red circle on the man's white shirt. Straight shot to the heart, all right. Just like the others. The stiff's eyes stuck wide open as if disbelieving at whatever he last saw.

"Maguire, let's kick this around before I go yapping to the chief. His name, you figure?"

"David Fenton, confirmed. He sells real estate is what he told me. Somebody around Butte, I suppose, but nobody who darkened my door. First time I heard of him was this morning when he rang my telephone."

"What did he want, anyhow?"

"He read my stories in the *Bugle*. Had the makings of another good scoop, he said, a clue to these murders being committed this summer. Refused to say more on the phone. Didn't sound particularly anxious or scared but he asked me to come over quick."

"When?"

"About ten minutes after nine. I drove up about nine forty."

"So in that thirty minutes somebody knocked him off and left a familiar calling card. Now ain't that sweet?"

The two officers reappeared in the living room. The younger one spoke first. "Nothing, Captain, except for the back door standing open. Seems odd. Killer left that way, do you think?"

"Fair guess," Ferndale said. "You new to Butte, junior?"

"Came over from the Three Forks force a week ago, sir. We never had a murder in the four years I've been a cop." The officer stared at the corpse. No more than an instant in time stood between a breathing thinking person and a lifeless body. Maguire, a veteran of crime scenes, nearly smiled at the stricken cop.

"Save the sir for the chief," Ferndale said, scratching a ragged fringe of gray hair that suggested he cut it himself. "He's the big deal here in Butte. Anybody named sir warms chairs in the office. Cops like you and me are the dicks on the street who mess with dead bodies so get used to it. That purple rose, boys, would you say it's fresh?" Maguire fought the impulse to touch it. The delicate petals, spattered red with the victim's blood, otherwise looked straight out of a flower shop. "I'm no florist, Duke, but it sure looks fresh to me. Just like the others."

"Like the others, Maguire. This one makes four. Hell, we got us a serial killer in Montana. Suppose I'll read all about it in the *Bugle* tomorrow morning?"

"Chances are." Maguire took a long look at the stiff sprawled before him. Fenton came from wealth. Black Oxfords freshly shined, check. Black dress trousers neatly pressed at a dry cleaners, check. Navy blue bullet-nicked necktie with stripes, check. Black suit coat dropped casually on the couch, check. Curly brown hair, newly barbered and combed with a part on the left, check. Face peaceful in death, check. Maguire had seen too many dead faces contorted into masks of fright. Lips curled, eyes bulging. Fenton greeted death like another business deal. A murderer had ruined his morning. His face didn't show it.

"You think he knew the killer, Duke?"

"That's what I make of it," Ferndale replied. "Except for his eyes stuck open and a hole in his heart you'd think he ain't had a care in the world. No sign of a struggle that I can see. What do you suppose, Red Maguire?"

Maguire pushed his hands into his pockets and leaned his tall frame against the door jamb. White pinstripes on his dark suit suggested a serious man. He tipped back his fedora and crossed his arms. That's what he did at crime scenes. Ferndale had seen Maguire do it dozens of times. Maguire didn't spill whatever crossed his mind like some people. He took his sweet time to consider details. He thought like a cop. He had learned that much from Ferndale. Savvy cops and news reporters shared one crucial talent. Observation. They watched for details that told a story. A dead man's tale. Almost everybody else missed those details. They reacted to murders emotionally.

Maguire squinted at the orderly death scene. "Looks to me like David Fenton opened his front door to somebody he knew, Duke. Invited the killer into his living room. Only natural, you see, a friend or acquaintance stopping at breakfast time. Maybe Fenton offered a cup of joe. 'It's no trouble at all,' he told the killer. The killer met his offer with an obliging smile. Of course, Fenton never made it to the coffee pot. I see only one white cup on the counter. He attempted hospitality but the killer had other intentions. Raised the gun right away. Death came quick. Happened soon after Fenton opened the door. That quick. Betting the killer left no clues. That's what I suppose, Duke."

Ferndale belched. "Not bad for an Irish mick from Dublin Gulch, I'll give you that. Gotta dust for fingerprints just in case."

Maguire glanced out the door at the downpour. "Call me if you find any juicy details, Duke? I've got to write my story with something more than finding a well-dressed man holding a rose."

"Ain't bad for a start," Ferndale growled.

Maguire ran outside to his Pontiac. Rain fell in buckets. Water dripped off his chin as he slid behind the wheel. He cursed his bad luck. Had he arrived even five minutes earlier he might have seen the killer. He tried to remember automobiles he had passed as he drove to Fenton's house. A gray two-door sedan, a Ford, had a blue right front fender, from a wrecking yard, that had replaced a damaged one. He recalled a chugging Studebaker pickup, a '47 model, ancient man and woman riding still as statues in the cab. Then came a tan Chevy four-door sedan, he guessed a '52, driven by a young mother in a red headscarf as two young children, boy and girl, stood on the seat beside her. Of the three Maguire could remember, the Ford with the mismatched colors seemed the most suspicious, but he knew better than to jump to conclusions. Sometimes killers drove the best cars in town. Maguire cursed his bad luck. Catching the killer in the act would have ensured newsboys screaming his story on uptown street corners. It never crossed his mind that he might be stretched out dead beside Fenton. With or without a rose. Maguire never thought that way.

Gloom fell over the neighborhood. An old woman in a full-length apron ignored the rain while she stared at the prowl cars at Fenton's house from beneath a black umbrella. Maguire reached for a notebook on the floor of his car. He rustled through the inked pages as if looking for answers but he already knew the facts. Three purple rose murders in Butte, all men. But why the woman, forty miles away in Deer Lodge, shot dead in the alley behind a laundromat? Work of a copycat killer? Maguire had written stories about all four cases. News of it reported on the *Bugle* front page attracted eager readers in Butte. He dutifully reported details of each murder. Why did somebody knock off four people who evidently didn't know one another? Every crime committed remained a mystery waiting for someone to figure it out. Maguire knew how it went. Someone got the itch to kill, did the deed, fled the scene, hid the secret. The cops worked night and day to find the damn fool who did it. Taxpayers paid the price of the hunt. Finally the killer blabbed the truth to strangers during a night of drinking. Guilt, sometimes, after the third or fourth beer. Bravado, sometimes. Maguire kept his ear to the ground, making acquaintances all over the bar district, because he wanted the first call when a killer made a barroom confession. He had solved crimes, big and small, in the *Bugle* news columns. There would be more. Red Maguire, news reporter and amateur detective. People knew his name in Butte.

As Maguire sat in his car, a lime green two-door hardtop, Police Chief Donald Morse drove up to Fenton's house. He splashed through the rain in a billowing blue overcoat. Morse and Ferndale talked on the covered porch. The men waved their arms and pointed. Thunder rumbled. The noise disguised what they said. The grouchy detective never liked explaining things to the front office. He despised political types. The governor would call from Helena to turn up the heat. Already he had complicated the investigation with premature public promises about catching the crook. The chief by nature became the first cop caught in the line of fire. Maguire knew how it went. In writing hundreds of newspaper stories about Butte crime, maybe thousands big and small, he had crossed paths with the state folks in Helena too many times. Ferndale had no use for them. They tried to put a happy face on stiffs shot all to hell, he said. Maguire couldn't disagree.

Maguire thumbed through his notebook as the rain hammered on his car. That morning, during his brief phone conversation with David Fenton, he had scribbled an observation. It said, "DF says killer might be closer than you think." Maguire kicked himself for not pressing Fenton for more answers before agreeing to meet in person. He should have known the killer would beat him to Fenton's house. In murders, his experience told him, take nothing for granted. Desperate people wait for no one. How futile to pry the truth off the lips of a dead man.

~ 2 ~

Red Maguire, crime newsman

When Maguire was a boy his father divorced his mother. They lived in Chicago where his father killed wailing cows with a sledgehammer at a slaughtering plant. His mother, perpetually married to alcohol, hit the bars by noon. She had little interest in being a housewife. Lily married Sean at fifteen years old. By seventeen, she gave birth to Kieran, the boy destined for newspaper crime reporting. He remembered his red-haired mother as being sufficiently beautiful to turn heads. Sean called her "my calendar girl" and sometimes made curvy lines in the air with his hands. Young boys know more than they should. Kieran recognized that his mother appealed to men other than his father. He watched her flirt when she took him to the grocery store and post office. The drink held power over her. A whiff of it lured her, seduced her, stole her away on impulse. At least a half dozen times, Kieran stood nervously outside Eddie's Bar down the block, peering into the dim interior to watch his mother toss beers with men who just came off shift at the munitions plant.

Even as a grown man, Maguire never understood what led her to a life of drunkenness. Maybe the young Lily lacked the strength to face life as wife and mother. Because of her, Kieran knew cops early in life. They came to his family's South Side house to bring his mother home from whatever trouble she had found. She reeked of cigarette smoke and beer. She also smelled of something else, something carnal, which he later knew as the lingering scent of her flings. Sean noticed too. After the divorce, Maguire came home from school on a September afternoon to find their meager furniture, including his bed, lashed with clothesline rope into the back of his father's pickup. "Get in. We're going to Montana," Sean told Kieran, who didn't know anything about Montana. Sean stayed silent until the next morning when they crossed the border into Minnesota. "Going to a city named Butte. Fair distance yet, Kieran. I hear they got copper mines out west, deep as a trip to Hell, that pay union wages to any man not afraid of hard work."

"What about school, Pop? What about my friends?"

"I'm sure Butte has schools. Your friends, they'll get by. You'll make new ones soon enough."

"But what about Mommy?"

They rode in silence for five miles before Sean answered. "What about her anyway? We go our own way, now, son. If you're thinking of crying over her, it don't do no good, hear me? Never forget that she left us. She don't want us, understand? Your mother, I can't control her, never could." They followed endless narrow highways that wound through tall corn. Somewhere in western North Dakota the corn gave way to red and orange valleys and mesas that billboards described as badlands. Then, in Montana, came oceans of sagebrush and forests of pine. Never had Kieran imagined vast empty prairies and mountains that loomed beyond them to the West. Kieran marveled at a land devoid of honking cars and skyscrapers. He had known only the urban bustle of Chicago.

On the third night Sean steered his coughing old pickup onto a mountain pass named Pipestone. Twice the radiator boiled over. Sean pulled off in the gravel at the edge of a canyon. Kieran held the brake hard to the floor as his father poured water into the steaming radiator. "You been wondering all along what we use this canvas bag for, boy?" He slung the strap over the antenna on the side of the hood. Night fell by the time they crested Pipestone. A few miles later, they left the canyon and saw their first glimpse of Butte. Its lights glittered on a mountain of torn earth. Looming towers, silhouettes against the commotion of lighting, stood protectively over their mines. Kieran would learn later that those towers, known as gallows frames, lowered hundreds of miners far below ground. They hoisted tons of ore to the surface with mighty steel cables. Sean and Kieran spent the first night in a rooming house where he got his first taste of Butte. Two drunken men, swinging clumsily, fought over a painted woman in a pink dress. The owner of the place, a thick crabby matron swathed in a green apron that hung to her knees, ended the brawl with a vicious arc of a broom handle that slammed one combatant on the ear and rendered him whimpering in a corner.

"What a town!" Sean marveled later that evening as he watched Butte's churning industry, always in motion, from a window of their dusty bedroom. Kieran, young and bewildered, listened to rumbling machinery and blowing whistles. He heard sirens and barking dogs. Even in the dark, the sidewalks coursed with people, many of them yelling. Maybe Butte resembled Chicago after all.

Sean and Kieran soon learned that newcomers gathered with their own kinds in neighborhoods such as Corktown, Centerville, Finn Town, Dogtown and the Cabbage Patch. Many, like Sean Maguire, were born to parents from Ireland. Kieran and his dad moved into a ramshackle Irish neighborhood known as Dublin Gulch. A smoky stretch of shacks and boarding houses, between the Kelley and Steward mines, teemed with immigrants. Boys earned their reputations on the street. Kieran grew up fighting. He made new friends and new enemies. The boys of the gulch threw insults and punches as readily as they threw baseballs.

Soon, Chicago became a distant memory, except for Lily Maguire. Kieran never forgot his mother. Sean found a girlfriend, Aggie Walsh, who lived in a flat full of Irish families four doors down. She doted on Sean and Kieran. His mop of red hair earned him an obvious nickname. She took to calling the boy "Red" in a motherly way. Soon everyone in the district knew him by that name. At St. Mary's school, where Sean enrolled him, he remained Red. Kieran became a distant identity as lost as the mother who had named him.

Two weeks after he graduated from Boys Central High School and the day after his eighteenth birthday, Red went searching for his mother. Sean turned over the keys to the pickup, handed Red a half-empty bottle of foul whiskey and five cans of motor oil, and sent him east. "Don't figure you'll find what you're looking for," his old man said and left it at that. Sean Maguire wasted no time on words.

As Red drove through Chicago, realizing his foolishness at trying to find his mother in a huge city, he stopped at his old house. Abandoned, shutters hanging askew, windows broken. Someone had started a fire in his bedroom. He felt no emotion at the decay of his neighborhood. Down the street, on a block of sagging boarded-up buildings, he found a phone booth. He tore through the pages searching for his mother's name. He found a LaVonne Maguire, and a Lucy Maguire, but no mention of Lily. Maybe she remarried. Maybe she died. The young man hoped his mother would show up in Butte. The Maguires would be a family again.

As Red scoured Chicago, tragedy hit in Butte. An explosion half a mile below the surface at the Kelley Mine killed his father and three other men. He returned to Butte three days later to find Aggie crying on the front porch. "I have sorrowful news, me boy."

Sean Maguire lost an arm and half of his face. A doctor determined that internal injuries from his crushed chest caused his immediate death. The undertaker put Sean on public display during the wake despite his shocking appearance. A parade of men in dusty coveralls set glasses of beer beside his broken body to honor him. Sean, forty-seven years old, looked like an old man. Hard labor has taken its toll. Sean departed the mortal world no different from hundreds of miners before him. Underground work claimed his life. That's how it went. Nothing more to say about it.

After the funeral, Red searched for a job to pay the bills. He knew the quick answer. Walk up Anaconda Road to the Kelley. The mine's gallows frame, two hundred feet high and swarming with ravens, loomed over Dublin Gulch as a constant reminder of Sean Maguire's death. The union men, sympathetic to Sean's untimely departure, told Red he could take his father's place. Sign papers in the union office. Find a peg in the dry, the changing shack, to hang his clothes. Squeeze into the chippy hoist with five other men and descend into a life of hard rock mining. Red feared going underground after Sean died. He couldn't bear the compressing loneliness of dark shafts and drifts.

Instead, he hustled billiards games in uptown bars to pay rent on the shack. Maguire had learned a thing or two about putting spin on a cue ball from Aggie Walsh's son Patrick. The older boy fed off the considerable vice in Butte's saloons and gambling parlors. Patrick taught Red how to play billiards, but also how to play a man for a fool, making jingle from it. Red learned how to invite drunks to play, men much older, because they jumped on the temptation to whip an Irish kid on the green felt. His opponents slammed their sticks in disgust when they lost. The dollar Maguire bet on a game usually stayed in his pocket. Aggie Walsh, never happy with Patrick's nocturnal prowling and his influence on Red, clucked her disapproval to neighbor women as they hung their wash behind the shacks. "Me boy Red would be better off working shift," she told them more than once.

Red tired of hustling two years later when Aggie finally convinced him that respectable men worked honest jobs when they could find them. It was 1936 in the heart of the Great Depression. Maguire had watched newsboys on street corners calling out headlines. A *Bugle* crime reporter named Peter Sullivan wrote most of the big stories. Red admired Sullivan's colorful tales of heroes and villains. He wondered how Sullivan found out so many details about people mentioned in his stories. Red Maguire decided that someday, somehow, he would become a newspaper reporter. One morning he saw a classified advertisement in the *Bugle* seeking someone to hang out at the police department on nights and weekends. The job required reading crime reports at the police department and listening to conversations between cops for news tips. He went to the *Bugle* offices for an interview with the editor, Clyde Stoffleman, whose piercing eagle-like gray eyes bore into him. The man scared Red. Opinionated, inquisitive, wicked smart.

"So you were a basketball hero over at Boys Central," Stoffleman said. "I read about that big crosstown game with Butte High when you scored eleven points and took a punch to the eye."

"Eighteen, Mr. Stoffleman, and punches to both eyes. One during the game and one after."

"You're no stranger to fighting, Maguire?"

"I ain't never backed down, for a fact."

"How tall are you anyway?"

"Three inches north of six feet last time I measured."

"Ever married, Maguire?"

"I'm too young for that, Mr. Stoffleman."

"You didn't get one of those cheerleaders in trouble? A dashing sports star like you? Don't all girls like redheads?"

"Never crossed my mind, sir. See I —."

Stoffleman interrupted. "The *Bugle* is no place for a personal life, Maguire. Unlike your possible inclinations toward romantic entanglement. You would be married to the job. Know what that means, sonny?"

"That you would own me?"

"In a manner of speaking, yes. Being a reporter at a newspaper means the job never ends. Fast as a reporter writes one story, another awaits. A reporter who fails to report the news, all of the news, is of no use to me. I want a constant flow of stories told with drama."

"Like Peter Sullivan?"

"Cream of the crop, that man. Glad you brought up his name. He writes stories that sell papers. You know what the word 'sensation' means?"

"Making people want to read the *Bugle*?"

"Well, sonny, you might have some promise after all."

"Why is *Bugle* the name of the newspaper?"

A quick smile flashed over Stoffleman's lips. "Curious, are you? That's one feather in your cap anyway."

"Why a feather?"

Stoffleman shook his head in impatient dismay. "Never mind. The *Butte Bugle* has been around since the turn of the century. You heard it right, our beloved newspaper is a piece of history, a compendium of knowledge. As the story goes, the founder of the *Bugle* grew fond of the notion that his new paper would blare out the news, much like a bugle stirred troops to action on a battlefield. He wanted a forceful newspaper. One that appealed to the working man in Butte.

When the price of beer jumped in Butte he wanted to shout the news to his readers. He wanted the unions represented in his paper. He considered any murder committed by knife, gun, rope, and bludgeoning instrument ripe for the front page. He wanted stories that attract readers, not put them to sleep, which is too often the result when a newspaper quakes at its own shadow. Name of this crusading man? Barclay Cole. His photograph hangs in the *Bugle* city room as a reminder that the paper we print every morning has a broader purpose than to soak up ink. My job, as editor, is to carry on his legacy. Now, no doubt you wonder why the *Bugle* wants to hire somebody while people out of work stand in lines all over this country for a bowl of soup. This nation has unemployment approaching 25 percent. You've noticed, I would hope."

The boy nodded. Stoffleman shook his head. "I expected an articulate answer, sonny. Hearing none, let me explain. Our crusading founder, Mr. Cole, made it clear that even in hard times the *Bugle* would sustain as the working man's paper in Butte. He wanted news reported that caught the eye of any man down on his luck. Therefore, as President Roosevelt tries to straighten out the financial disaster throttling this country, we do our part by pricing the *Bugle* accordingly. In other words, we sell it cheap in hopes of recovering our cost with more sales. The more news we report, the more papers we sell. Follow me?"

The young Maguire, bewildered at the fancy language, attempted a compliment. "It's the paper that gets my attention on street corners," he said.

Stoffleman snorted. "Big difference between hearing headlines shouted out and reading the stories behind them. Even bigger leap between reading the news and reporting it. Now, tell me, how come you never joined the Army? A strong boy like you would make President Roosevelt proud. The recruiting depot is a block from here. Didn't you see Uncle Sam in the window? Despite all the isolationist talk we might need to send troops to Europe someday to reason with the German socialists."

"Who are they, Mr. Stoffleman?"

"Your ignorance astounds me, Maguire. You apparently know every alley and gulch in Butte but seem to understand nothing about international affairs. Disappoints me, in a way, considering you earned a high school diploma from a fine Catholic high school. Are you a practicing Catholic?"

"Only when required," Maguire said. "I go to confession once in a while."

"Any confessions I should know about, sonny? Rob anybody, kill anybody, slipping it to somebody's young wife on the sly?"

Maguire failed to hide a smile at the line of questioning. The *Bugle* editor took no prisoners. Stoffleman's relentless personality reminded Red of the priest at the elementary school who liked to spank boys with boards. He smacked their bare bottoms in a windowless room behind his office. Red got it once after offering a cigarette to a nun. The priest kept hitting him like he enjoyed it. "None of that, Mr. Stoffleman. No terrible crimes in my background. I tapped my old man's hooch until I got caught. Aggie Walsh didn't stand for misbehavior."

"Who's she?"

"Aggie is my stepmom, or close to, seeing that she never married my pop before the explosion killed him."

"Kept you on the straight and narrow, did she?"

"Best as she could," Maguire replied.

"Who's Montana's new governor?"

"Elmer Holt."

"Why is he new?"

"Because the other guy died."

"Who was that?"

"Frank Cooney. He had a heart attack."

"I suppose you know Governor Cooney's home city?"

"I know that one. It's Butte."

"Let's try another. Who's the mayor in Butte?"

"I don't know."

"Who's the police chief?"

"I don't know."

"What do police do in Butte?"

"Crack heads, near as I can tell."

"You aren't far from the truth although I had hoped for a more universal answer."

"I ain't old enough to know," Maguire said in his defense, smiling at Stoffleman's persistent questioning. The boy recalled similar interrogations from the Irish Christian Brothers who taught at the high school.

"I doubt you've written nary a coherent sentence in your life despite the very best diligence by the brothers over at

Central," Stoffleman continued. "It's clear that except for your cursive recollection of Cooney you don't possess the vaguest idea what goes on in Butte, at least among adults, and you know nothing about journalism. I encourage you to subscribe to the *Bugle*, not any paper but the *Bugle*, and do it today. You can't expect to amount to anything in journalism if you don't read the news. You're likable, I'll give you that, but I caution you to listen to me and listen close if you want to succeed. Here's some more free advice, sonny. Work on your grammar. The word 'ain't' doesn't belong in my newspaper."

"I'm hired?" Red asked, mystified.

"Pay attention to what's going on," the editor said. "That's the first lesson in newspaper journalism. Yes, you're hired. We'll pay you twenty-five dollars a week provided you earn it. Remember you work for the *Bugle* and not the cops. Stay sober. Come to work on time. As long as you do your job, the way I expect it done, you get paid. Show me what you can do."

Stoffleman told Red to make notes on little crimes, phone in big crimes to the paper, and watch for anything unusual. Some weeks into the job he began contributing minor tips to the city desk. Sometimes a hotshot reporter, usually Sullivan, used Maguire's tips in his big murder stories. Predictably, Sullivan whipped up a tale for the morning paper that could make madams on Mercury Street blush from ear to ear. One of his stories read: "She wore nothing, naked even of the bedsheet-scented perfume that wafted off her customers in uptown saloons after their ten-minute inspections of her womanly ways." Sullivan once advised Maguire, "Dull descriptions don't sell newspapers in Butte. Find somebody in bed with the mayor's wife and then write the hell out of it as if you were watching."

By the time Stoffleman had taught Red Maguire how to report news, Sullivan's legendary *Bugle* career came to a drastic end. He died when an ore train crushed him as he wandered home from a midnight drinking binge at Babe's Bar in Finn Town. What a pity Sullivan's obituary lacked colorful insinuations as if he had written it himself. The reporter in charge of such work, Calvin Claggett, did his best. Sullivan's death silenced the *Bugle* for a week or so. The news columns seemed boring and mournful without his seductive descriptions. After the funeral, Stoffleman declared his interest in finding a new crime reporter. Maguire got the job after Stoffleman told him, "Don't screw up this job or you'll find yourself mucking ore four thousand feet down and they tell me it's no picnic." Maguire never understood how he could mess up a murder story in Butte except for missing it altogether. Ferndale and other sources at the jail made sure he didn't make that mistake. Maguire learned he had a way of getting along with cops. Cops got a kick out of seeing crime in print. They put him on to good stories. Because of Duke Ferndale, his most reliable source, Maguire often knew of a murder before police arrived at the scene. Ferndale never wanted his name in print. The detective felt more comfortable telling stories on bar stools. "Just keep me out of it," Ferndale warned Maguire more than once. "You burn me, no more gravy."

On the day David Fenton died, Maguire drove back to the *Bugle* city room on the third floor of the Hirbour Block. True to Barclay Cole, the *Bugle* never faltered in its reign as Butte's independent newspaper. The Hirbour Block commanded the northeast corner of Main and Broadway. Maguire looked down on the busy streets from his desk near a front window. The people scurrying below him knew hard work. Butte impressed him as a city built on sweat and dirt.

A dozen reporters and editors and a solitary photographer named Stu worked from mid-morning to midnight in the long city room. *Bugle* journalists were rebellious sorts, molded in the image of Stoffleman, a fierce newsman. An odor of ink and old wood mingled with the stench of cigarette smoke. The *Associated Press* teletype machine clattered all day long, spitting out a slithering tongue of yellow paper that reported the latest news from around Montana and the nation. Reporters wrote their stories on typewriters atop their brown wooden desks. Some of them worked on those newfangled electric machines suddenly advertised in the catalogues. "Why not? It's 1954, for god sake," Stoffleman told Maguire one day.

Maguire tried to slide into his chair without catching Stoffleman's attention. When the springs creaked Stoffleman's head swung around. He wore a corny green eye shade and rectangular eyeglasses that resembled a windshield on a bus. He smiled a crooked grin. A nasty scar trailed from his jaw to his left eye. Stoffleman said little about his wounds from the Allied invasion into Germany during World War II. "Damned Krauts," he responded predictably to questions. Except for the war, he had lived in Butte most of his life, a bachelor married to the *Bugle*. Stoffleman's absence from the city room for nearly four years led to a quieter *Bugle*. Older men such as Calvin Claggett avoided the rush to join the Army or Navy. Maguire remained out of uniform as well but not by choice. The government exempted him from military duty to cover important mining news in Butte as the mines churned out copper ore for the war effort. Some days at the *Bugle* he helped Claggett write stories about Butte men and women killed overseas. When the war ended, and Stoffleman returned to the *Bugle*, he revealed nothing about his combat ordeals as an infantry sergeant. He barked orders at his reporters as if he had never left.

Now, as Maguire hurried into the newsroom, Stoffleman sensed a scoop. "How's she go, Maguire? Got another stiff for us? Waiting until tomorrow's paper comes out to tell me? Or until I read about it in the Company papers?" Stoffleman hated the Anaconda Company press. It marched to corporate orders from the suits on the top floors of the Hennessy Block farther up Main Street. The *Bugle*, a working man's paper, chased crime and labor stories with glee. Maguire fit right in.

"Don't go raining on my parade, boss. I've got a purple rose saying my story goes front page." Stoffleman, suddenly all ears, said nothing as Maguire described David Fenton's murder. "The killer shot him dead during breakfast. None of the neighbors admit to seeing or hearing a thing, maybe because of the distance between houses out there in that country club estate."

Stoffleman smirked. "Hell, in this town, half of everybody might cover for the killer. You think of that, sonny?"

Maguire leaned back in his chair. "Anybody who's lying to me can kiss my Irish butt." He pulled off his fedora, pushing his thick red hair into place with long fingers. Maguire, although pushing forty, looked ten years younger. He had his father's strapping physique and his mother's chiseled features. "You're an attractive man any sensible young woman would want," Aggie told him in her lilting Irish accent, "but you're too shy around the girls and they think you're not interested. You seem aloof, Red, too wrapped up in your work to find love." Maguire knew he echoed Stoffleman in that respect. They were men who invested their lonely lives in the daily paper.

"That's my boy. Before you go out looking for more news, write everything you know. Dress it up in some purple prose, get it?" Stoffleman, laughing over what passed for humor at the *Bugle*, went back to where editors worked at the other end of the long room. Maguire glanced outside at the brick buildings in uptown Butte. Near noon. Shoppers filled the sidewalks. Down the street, doors at the M & M bar were flung open to the wet day, men gathering with glasses of beer. He turned back to his desk to insert a sheet of paper into his typewriter. Nobody gave him one of the experimental electric ones and he felt glad for it. The keys had a mind of their own, he heard, automatically typing letters like nobody's business. He began writing:

"David Fenton started his day with the Bugle and a short stack of pancakes, but in the minutes before he ate the first bite, he became Montana's fourth victim in what's become known as the Purple Rose Murders."

Maguire lacked Sullivan's gift for colorful prose. Instead, he wrote the news in a concise style all his own. He continued:

"Fenton, a real estate man of some repute, was found slain in his south Butte residence on Tuesday morning by a Bugle news reporter. The killer fired one bullet into his chest and placed a purple rose on the wound."

Maguire then wrote more details about the scene. He included a quote from Chief Morse who vowed to find the killer in a matter of days. Maguire recognized the chief's comment as intending to pacify fearful Butte residents rather than represent a true declaration of crime fighting. Solving a murder took time. Solving several crimes at once took longer. Newspaper reporting sometimes depended on luck. Maguire opened the city directory and began dialing the telephone in search of someone who knew Fenton. Half the calls rang and rang. The few people who answered had little to say. One man described Fenton as a responsible resident who kept his property in good shape. Another had seen him carrying groceries into his house. It appeared Fenton avoided neighborhood conversation. Nobody knew him personally. He had no office, no staff, no obvious trail of civic accomplishments. Fenton, it seemed, hid much of his life from public view despite his apparent wealth. He worked long hours selling houses. He otherwise lived in relative isolation in his well-furnished house on the Flat. Fenton had friends, surely, but they evaded Maguire for this story.

After Maguire exhausted his notes, he realized how little he knew about Fenton's background and the circumstances of his murder. Why did the Purple Rose Killer target a middle-aged real estate salesman? He ripped the last page of his story from his typewriter and walked it over to Stoffleman. The editor waited happily with his blue pencil. Nothing gave him more delight than to put a reporter on notice that a story failed to meet expectations until it had the Stoffleman touch. He moved paragraphs around, crossed out some sentences, wrote others into the story and occasionally corrected factual references. "It's what we call editing," he reminded Maguire again and again. Stoffleman loved his work.

Maguire looked around the city room. Smoky rays of light from the dirty windows revealed a jumble of desks. Claggett, the sour old obituary reporter, slumped as he pestered someone over the phone about yet another heavenly departure. Deep in his work, his lips clenching two glowing cigarettes, he scribbled notes between questions. Claggett resembled an ancient mortician. He looked as dead as the people in his stories. Antonio Vanzetti, who covered local government and city politics, lived in Meaderville, the Italian enclave farther up Butte Hill. Vanzetti spent hours combing his hair, black and slick, between bursts of clacking on the typewriter. A pretty boy, yes, but also a crack reporter. Vanzetti's news judgment, Stoffleman often said, ranked with the best in the business. At the desk next to him sat labor reporter Ted Ketchul. He straddled his chair like a lumberjack. Unlike the black suit crowd around him, he wore overalls and heavy boots and a plaid shirt calculated to blend with miners and unions. Ketchul wrote stories about safety violations and mine accidents that never appeared in the Company press. He had covered the closing of the Travona mine, one of Butte's oldest, and he dug deep into the Company's plans to abandon underground mining in favor of a yawning open pit. "They'll dig it a thousand feet deep and swallow up half of Butte," Ketchul told Maguire one day. The Pit would cost Butte jobs. Everyone knew it, the unions deplored it, but the Company embraced the Pit as the sensible next generation of metals mining. Behind Ketchul, near a windowsill decorated with potted plants, sat the *Bugle*'s newest reporter. Mary Miller wrote feature stories about Butte history. She covered tea parties and other social events for the society pages. Miller brought visual relief to the drab personalities in the black and brown city room. This day she wore a cream-tinted dress and, around her neck, a bright blue scarf. Mary's hair, brownish-red like honey, didn't go unnoticed either. Her way of shaking it when she smiled aroused some life into even the cadaverous Claggett. Maguire knew nothing about her. He vaguely remembered her coming to work at the *Bugle* during the winter, when snow drifted in the recesses of the windows.

How unlike Maguire, a journalist wedded to detail, to ignore a pretty woman. He typically took note of personal characteristics at first glance. He would have remembered that Mary walked like she meant business. He would have seen her tall elegance, her penchant for necklaces, her dainty gold watch, her even white teeth flecked with orange lipstick. He would have wondered what brought her to the *Butte Bugle*, to a city room inhabited by rough men like himself who never got around to shining their shoes. Maguire watched her for a minute, admiringly and even longingly, before feeling some guilt at neglecting more urgent matters. Pressing news awaited a diligent crime reporter who had a name in Butte. A name associated with dead people and drunks and domestic assaults and the like. Maguire knew of his reputation. "Never think you're anything special, me boy, just because you hang your name on every ugly crime in Butte," Aggie Walsh told him time and again. "A responsible man knows the difference between right and wrong, Red. Do the right thing. That's how you'll be remembered, aye." Nobody commanded more influence over Red than Aggie.

Maguire thought of these things as he reached for the telephone receiver. "Get me Helena, Luverne, you sweet adorable thing," he cooed to the older woman working at the switchboard across the hall. "Yes, I know you'd marry me if I were twenty years older. But, Luverne? How would you break the news to Howard? Your poor suffering husband, what would he do without you to keep him from gambling away your life savings down at the Board of Trade? No, I won't tell anyone. ... Yes, I know, you can't wait forever for me. ... Yes, I'll remember to let you know when I'm ready for some loving. ... Thanks, Luverne, I appreciate your compliments. ... He said what? Well, tell Howard that if every man in town is after you, he had better shave once in a while and change his underwear like he means business. ... Helena, you have that right, connect me with the state crime bureau, Luverne. Yes, I'll wait."

Meanwhile, Stoffleman put down his pencil and yelled across the city room. "Damn fine story, Maguire. We might find a place for it in the back of the paper with the classified ads." That led to a storm of guffaws from everyone, even Claggett, who barked his approval through a cloud of blue smoke.

"Bastards," Maguire said to himself. As he waited for someone to answer his call to Helena he reached for his notebook and began scribbling. "Purple rose, purple rose," he wrote. "Flower of enchantment ...."

3

Crime sells newspapers

The photograph, old and cracked, remembered a family. It remained the killer's fondest possession. To see it jarred deep grief. Evil people rob others of their dreams when they take life. For that, they must suffer.

Close to dusk, Ferndale dropped onto a bar stool beside Maguire at the M & M. "Wish I could tell you that after busting my balls all afternoon on this dead guy that I had something new, Maguire. Ain't got nothing but a whole lot of nothing. You?"

Maguire wiped beer from his lip. "The state folks tell me they're all over these cases but can't comment because it's an open investigation. I couldn't get a straight answer when I asked why the state got involved when Butte cops already had the case."

Ferndale smirked. "Bet you never saw a response like that coming."

"I ask them why I see no state dicks working the street in Butte? Undercover, they tell me. What do you make of that, Duke?"

"I know how to spot them. Hell, any dumb cluck could spot them guys. They ain't around. Politics, Maguire. Make people think something is happening even when it ain't."

"Well, Duke, then I asked for comment on the meaning of the purple roses. Know what they told me?"

"To get lost?"

"That nobody grows purple roses in Montana. How do they know that? Do they think we're making it up?"

"Sounds like the experts in Helena ain't got a green thumb."

"You thought about that, Duke? Where is the killer finding purple roses?"

Ferndale burped. "Beats me. We checked with every florist in Butte. They grow red, white, blue, yellow, you name it. You mention purple, they look at you like you're some dumb lost dog. Not the Montana way, I guess. What do you hope to get from Helena anyway?"

Maguire signaled the bartender for two more beers. He dropped a silver dollar beside his empty glass. "Sure as hell I thought somebody in high places might have a notion about this string of murders. This kind of business comes along once in a blue moon in Montana. You know, I hoped to find somebody up there in Helena who can put these murders in perspective."

"Hopeful, ain't you? The chief told those white-collar bureaucrats to stay the hell out of Butte. He told some jackass trying to pull rank, we run our own show in the Mining City. Those suits in politics demand answers right now. That's their whole deal. We ain't got answers. Not yet."

"I know this, Duke, I can't write many more cops and robbers murder stories from the cheap seats. I need more insight, more of something, hell, anything that will help solve these crimes."

"No confidence in cops, huh?" Ferndale belched again. "Secret between us? Me neither."

They sat silently for a few moments, thinking, until a drunk began pestering Ferndale for jingle. His friend pulled him away toward the door. "Jesus, Sam, you're messing with Ferndale." They shot a look at the cop before scampering into the night.

"Know what, Maguire? Someday I'll be a dried-up old fart in suspenders sitting here and they won't give a damn whether I could ever throw a punch."

"I'll be right here beside you, holding a purple rose."

"You damned fool, Maguire. Why the hell do you care whether we ever solve these murders? Crime sells papers. Isn't that what you've told me a thousand times?"

"You can take that fact to the bank. It's something different this time. Guess I'm feeling some civic responsibility at solving them."

Ferndale wiped beer from his lip. "Then run out and join the Good Samaritans club."

"Help me out, Duke. I need more."

"How did you report those other purple rose stories?"

"Except for hanging out with you at the murder scenes, pretty much by phone, from the stately offices of the *Bugle*. There wasn't much to go on."

"Not exactly your cup of tea, Maguire, is it? Since when did you become a desk-bound office boy? Get on your feet and do some digging. That's what we do in Butte, right?"

"Shouldn't cops be doing that?"

"Let me tell you a story, Maguire. Remember the time that crazy lady shot up her old man in Centerville? Twice to the chest with a twelve gauge?"

"Hard to forget that one. Station One washed the blood away with a firehose. We hoped those boys wouldn't run out of water."

"And you saw the murder scene because I took you there against the chief's orders. You got a hell of a story out of that case, played big as the mayor's ass in the *Bugle* as I recall. The chief threatened to can me over it. Not the first time, let's say."

"But you did it anyway."

"My point is that every time I toss you a scoop I get kicked for doing it. Payback ain't a bad thing."

Maguire turned toward Ferndale. "You saying I have a better chance of cracking these murders than you? Than any of your cops?"

"You've known this for twenty years, Maguire, so why rub it in? People around here already know that crime stiff writer Red Maguire is a better investigator than the cops, I'm sorry to say."

"That's staff writer, Duke."

"Whatever. Who did that guy Fenton call this morning before he got knocked off? Sure as hell no police dick like me. So yeah, hit the road, see if you can find something useful for me, will you?"

"Glad to be of service. You never told me how much you cared."

"Knock it off, Maguire. I still have a wicked left. You ain't had the pleasure yet."

"Hope I never do. So when will you tell me more about today's murder?"

Ferndale held up his hands. "Under investigation. Now you've heard the official answer. You already know I'll give you something when I've got it."

"You think Lucky Finero might know something?"

"Cops ain't supposed to consort with bounty hunters."

"What can you tell me about him, anyway?"

"I figure we've got three people in this town who have their ears to the ground like it matters. Me, you, and Lucky. Watch yourself around him. He ain't nobody to mess with. Some years ago he shaved a fugitive's ears off with a knife. When the judge asked Lucky why he did it, know what he said? 'Judge, that old boy, he didn't listen when I told him to stop running so I figured he didn't need them ears.' Lucky spent a year swamping the cell house in Deer Lodge over that. When they paroled him, he came back to Butte like nothing happened. Still carries that big knife sticking out of his belt like he's Jim Bowie fighting Injuns down on the Yellowstone. I'll tell you this, and it's a fact. No criminal escapes from Lucky. Not more than twice. He chases them down, lashes them with a roll of electrical tape he carries around, throws them in the bed of that '47 Ford pickup he drives, hauls them to jail to collect the reward and walks away with jingle in his pocket. Not bad work if you can get it."

"Is it true he catches half of his bail jumpers in the tenderloin?"

"Confirmed, Maguire. Waits until they have their pants down, which don't take long at the Dumas. Hell of a brothel, that place. Anyway, what does a young cuss like me know? Old Lucky, when he shows them that big knife when they have their jewels hanging out, it's over. Now the other half of these bad boys, they put up a fight. Ex-cons, case-a-night drinkers, wife beaters, gunslingers, that sort. We arrest them and throw them in jail and some shyster springs them out on bail and away they go on the run. Not a one of them has any common sense. No law says they have to kiss the judge in court. Just need to show up when the summons tells them to be there. When they skip, they work up a head of steam and get nasty. Lucky, when a younger man, he cornered one of them boys in a drug store reading magazines. Partial to *Ladies Home Journal* as I recall. Figure that, Maguire. This particular upstanding citizen beat up a whore in the Copper Block. He jumps bail. Lucky catches him reading recipes for lemon meringue pie. Figure that, will you? The mug jumps through a plate glass window when he sees Lucky walk in the door. Bled like a pig at slaughter. Lucky brings him down on the sidewalk with that sap he carries around. Nearly killed the mug with a blow to the head. Whole crowd gathers to watch the fun. I arrive on the scene in a prowl car. "Finero," I tell him, "when you catch the hoods you can't kill 'em. Tape 'em and bring 'em in, that's within the law." I considered that practical advice. Know what Lucky says back to me? 'Officer,' he tells me, 'what I done here ain't nothin' more than a good

38

attitude adjustment.' Can't argue with that line of reasoning when it comes right down to it, even if I do wear a badge."

"Even if beating suspects breaks the law, Duke?"

"That's the problem, ain't it?"

Maguire wiped a froth of beer from his upper lip. "Good story, Duke. Belonged in the *Bugle* if you want to know the half of it."

"I weren't exactly on speaking terms with the *Bugle* before you came along. Peter Sullivan didn't need no facts from me. He made them up. Know what a police chief once said about this city? 'Butte is an island of easy money surrounded by a sea of whiskey.' He hit the mark with that one. Sullivan could have wrote those words himself."

"Which chief?"

"Guy named Jere Murphy. Went by the nickname 'The Wise,' like wise guy. He told it how she goes. No disputing him even if he was another damn mick."

"You and your distrust of the micks, Duke. Finero is a wop and you don't like him either."

"Knowing where the bodies are buried in this town is a heavy burden for an old Cornish cop," Ferndale said.

"You're a Cousin Jack? I thought you said you were Scottish."

"When the mood suits me, Maguire."

"Long as I've done this job, Duke, I never had a run-in with Lucky. Think I'll find him, see what he knows."

"Watch out for that knife in case he takes a disliking to you. Lucky, he don't play by the rules. Or the law, for that matter."

"How did he get the name Lucky anyhow?"

Ferndale pushed his empty beer glass aside and climbed off the bar stool. "How does anyone get a nickname in Butte? I'm Duke, you're Red, he's Lucky. Probably because somebody ain't killed him yet. Somebody hangs a label on you in this town and you wear it around for life. Lucky ain't a bad harness to wear. How about Leaky Nose Larson at the meat shop? Buying a pound of hamburger when he's dripping like a faucet weren't a pretty picture. Anyhow, I got to run. Go find some news that I can investigate, will you?"

"You sound like Stoffleman, Duke."

"Somebody ought to straighten you out, you damn Irish mick."

The next morning, a Wednesday, Maguire announced his intention to drive the thirty-nine miles to Deer Lodge to investigate the single Purple Rose murder that occurred outside of Butte. Stoffleman ranted about the cost of mileage and how he it hurt him to let the Butte crime beat go dark for a day. Maguire assured his editor he found nothing new to report on the Butte murders and that driving to Deer Lodge wouldn't blow a hole in the *Bugle* budget. By mid-morning he aimed his Pontiac west on Highway 12. An hour later he coasted on fumes into the Texaco station a few blocks north of the state prison. While the pump jockey filled his tank, Maguire asked for directions to the alley where the woman died a month earlier. "Nothing much to see," said the man. A patch sewn above his shirt pocket said, "Happy." He pointed farther down Main Street. "You'll find some mud puddles and a whole lot of garbage cans back behind the laundromat down there by City Hall. That's the spot. I heard they found a flower on her body. What kind of a killer does a thing like that?"

"An artistic type, I guess. What else did you hear?"

"She moved to Deer Lodge a month ago is the word. Nobody knew her. Strange, that, because everybody knows everybody else in this town. She didn't live here long enough, I reckon."

Maguire drove down Main Street. The cafe looked busy. The fire chief polished his truck at City Hall. Three boys raced down the street on their bicycles. A bearded man barreled out of a bar, screaming at a meter maid ticketing his pickup truck, while a drunk friend tried to calm him. Maguire parked his Pontiac near the laundromat and headed to the alley. Just as Happy predicted, he found nothing unusual. Maguire figured everybody in town had cruised the alley in hopes of seeing some remnant of the murder. They drove away disappointed. The laundromat's back door stood open. An odor of detergent and hot clothes washed into the alley. He knew the town's overnight police officer had discovered the woman's body when he noticed light from the back door spilling into the alley. Linda Danvers, nature photographer. Shot up close, just like the other victims. People in town often saw her alone with her camera clicking on sunsets and wildflowers and mountain ranges wrapped in rain clouds. Maguire remembered how the Deer Lodge police chief, Sam Williams, described an inconvenient murder. Maguire asked what he meant. In Maguire's book every murder meant inconvenience for the victim.

"The killer didn't allow the poor woman to finish her laundry. She had two loads in the washer when the killer gunned her down," the chief told him. "We know for sure because her daughter identified her clothes."

"How long you been on the job, chief?"

"Six months and counting, Mr. Maguire."

"What did you do before that?"

"City hired me as part-time dogcatcher. Worked at the grocery, too. Do you know they have a sale on cantaloupe this week?"

Now, back in Deer Lodge, it occurred to Maguire that he missed interviewing the daughter. He walked into the laundromat. A few machines turned clothes. The only person present, an old man buttoned into a gray cardigan despite the heat from the dryers, waved at him. Maguire introduced himself. "Call me Mack with a k," said the man, who owned the laundromat. Yes, he knew the dead woman's daughter. "Name is Louise, lives over on Cottonwood Avenue. Nice gal but not too sharp, turns out. I stood right here working the morning she came to get her mother's clothes. Sad, I'll tell you. We don't get murders in Deer Lodge. Hell of a thing that it happened right here at my laundromat. Took a bit of scrubbing to clean up the blood out back. Thought business would drop off but no, people came. Morbid curiosity, I guess. You'll find Cottonwood Avenue over that direction. It's a bright blue house. Only blue house on the street."

Maguire thanked Mack and looked around. The ordinary laundromat had wide front windows on the street. Anybody passing would witness trouble inside. Even in this sleepy valley town. He stepped back into the alley. One more look before finding Louise Danvers. As he bent near the garbage cans, looking for clues in the gravel, he heard a roar. A gray sedan raced toward him. He heard it kick into passing gear. Maguire instinctively hugged the wall of the laundromat. The car swept past him by inches. It squealed rubber around the corner and disappeared from sight. Maguire slid to the ground, trying to calm his pounding heart. He missed the plate number. He couldn't even describe the driver. A drunk leaving a bar? A kid joyriding in the old man's car? What if the incident amounted to nothing more than a coincidence? Maguire slapped dust from his suit and stood up. What a big target for a barreling automobile. Maguire had a feeling someone tried to award him a purple rose. "You all right, son?" he heard from the doorway. Mack, his arms full of wet laundry, stared anxiously. "I heard the commotion. Sounded bad news. You'd think we live in Butte for all the ruckus around here."

Maguire inspected a tear in the elbow of his suit jacket. "Far from, I hope, but for sure nothing good comes from this alley. I'd keep the door locked if I were you. There's no telling who's next." Maguire left Mack, color draining from his creased face, to find the dead woman's daughter. She let him into the house reluctantly. Maguire saw the interview going south the moment she opened her mouth. Words came disorganized and confused from a feeble mind. Louise smiled through crooked teeth. She expected her mother home any minute. Did Maguire know she had found her mother's clothing at the laundromat? Louise offered her mother's bra size at least five times. She went into the bedroom to retrieve her mother's pink blood-flecked pedal pushers. Maguire noted they were trim as if worn by a high school girl. Murder victims wore all sizes of clothes. Louise said she and her mother had moved from Nevada. She couldn't remember why, or from what city, or when.

Maguire looked around the living room. Amid unpacked moving boxes, color photographs of valley vistas and old mine cabins adorned the walls. A magazine folded open on an end table showed elk grazing in a mountain meadow. Maguire looked closer. The name under the photograph said Linda Danvers. So that's it, Maguire thought to himself. She earned jingle by selling photographs. But what now of her daughter? Louise said she would pour him a cup of coffee. She swept aside stacks of dirty dishes on the kitchen counter. The coffee, pale and cold, looked weeks old. Maguire suspected Louise's mother had made it the morning she died. He set the cup on the counter. "You got a daddy? Anybody coming over to help you?" he asked her. She shook her head, confused. "Please, mister. My momma, where did she go?"

Maguire stopped at the Presbyterian Church on the way out of town. The young minister, puzzling over his Sunday sermon, nodded his understanding. "I've read your stories in the *Bugle*. Terrible loss of life, so contrary to the Lord's teachings. So many in this town continue to wonder when the police chief will catch the killer. People are scared, you know. Now the daughter of the deceased, what a pity she's light in the head. We'll go to her house to see how we can help. I promise. It's hard to understand why the young woman's relatives haven't come for her."

As Maguire drove back to Butte, he checked his rearview mirror to make sure nobody followed him. He watched with alarm as a gray sedan speeded toward him. It passed harmlessly. Middle-aged couple on vacation, top carrier covered with a tarp, Idaho plates. He ran the day's events through his mind. The murder in Deer Lodge seemed as mysterious as the others. Why did Linda Danvers die? Who pulled the trigger? Back in the *Bugle* city room, Maguire briefed Stoffleman on his slim findings. "Hell, boy, that speeding car drama gives you another front-page story. Purple roses sell papers, right? No point in discounting the magic of having a dab of color in these drab surroundings. Killer has an artist's imagination, no?"

As Maguire hammered out his latest story, his telephone rang. He nearly ignored it but pushed the receiver to his ear. "Maguire, *Bugle!*" he belted out. A woman's voice purred in his ear. "I've been reading your stories about the murders, Maguire. What's with the roses? Can you tell us more? Somebody's got style, would you say? Are you having fun, Maguire? Living your dream? Catching criminals? Trouble for you is, you're not even close. I had hoped for better reporting from the *Bugle.*"

Maguire managed, "And you are ...?" before the caller hung up. He shrugged. News reporters got too many calls like that. Some malcontent complains about coverage and hangs up. They never identified themselves. Bitch a little, slam the paper, hang up. He wondered for a moment whether this caller had anything to do with the murders. Not even close? Something about the woman's voice sounded vaguely familiar. Maguire threw out the notion as quick as it came to him. Sometimes an angry caller stretched a sock over the phone to disguise a voice. No way to trace it anyway. Complainers had all kinds of crazy fears that they might be quoted in the newspaper if the reporter knew who called. Most of it was fantasy, not knowing how journalism worked, but people played that game all the time.

Maguire finished his story, handed it to Stoffleman, and headed home to the Logan Hotel. A wave of exhaustion flooded over him. He flopped into bed still wearing his suit. Water dripped in the sink. Rain pelted the windows, again. Early evening but already dark for a summer night. Maguire knew things could be worse. He considered himself lucky he wasn't stretched out in the morgue with Ferndale standing over him, stating aloud, "Now ain't Maguire a pretty picture all shot up."

~ 4 ~

A story like no other

The fourth Butte murder came overnight. A hard knock came at Maguire's door as he slept. He stumbled out of bed and searched for his pants before remembering he already wore them. Ferndale, looking impatient, stood in the hallway's dim light. "Get your ass out here if you want a scoop. Another body turned up. This one ain't as pretty as the last one." Ferndale waited as Maguire threw on a clean shirt and slipped into his shoes. He grabbed a notebook from the kitchen counter and headed outside where he slid into the car with Ferndale. The detective gunned the automobile down the steep streets. A rare quiet hour in uptown Butte, between bar closing and day shift at the mines, nobody around. "So some overnight workers at the Orphan Girl find a guy dead," Ferndale said. "Don't look like he belongs there. Nobody heard a ruckus. Lost his head, too."

"How so? You mean he went crazy?"

"No, not like out of his mind. I mean it's missing. Can't be found."

Ferndale pulled into the mine yard. Red flashes from his car illuminated a cop holding a flashlight and two grubby men dressed in bib overalls. The three of them looked at a muddied object on the wet ground. Ferndale slammed the shift lever into park and jumped out. Maguire followed, stepping around piles of rusting metal, feeling water seep through his shoe leather. Lightning flashed in the eastern sky. The uniformed cop shone his flashlight on the dead man. His upper torso, what a garish sight. Only a few inches of his neck remained above his shoulders. Ferndale whistled. "Looks like somebody took an axe to him in one clean swipe, don't it?" He reached for the flashlight and waved the beam around the mine yard. The officer, a graveyard Irish cop Maguire knew as Jimmy Regan, spoke. "Me and these boys searched all over, Cap. No trace of the other part. Guy up and lost his head." Laughs all around. Cop humor, usually disrespectful, never got old.

"He ain't no miner," said one of the grimy men. "Nobody comes to work prettied up like he's ready to go dancing." Ferndale turned the light again to the dead man. He wore black slacks and a yellow shirt. They were soaked to the bluish-white skin from the rain. Odd wardrobe to wear to a mine sure enough. Beneath the purple rose, a bullet hole visible in the victim's chest. Ferndale frowned. "I'm thinking he's a younger man, too, like the other dead guys. Hard to make sure with no face, but that's how I'm figuring it. You, Maguire?"

The *Bugle* reporter stared at the body through bleary eyes. He took a moment to think. Having no door jamb available for leaning, he crossed his arms, another signal he was combing his mind for clues. "Something doesn't look right, Duke."

"You mean that his head's missing?" More laughter.

Maguire stepped closer. "No, not that, although I admit the sight of him gives me a jolt. It's his build. He reminds me of someone. I guess he could be anybody after all."

"That's all you've got, Maguire? Some buddy of yours you figure?"

Maguire shook his head. The rattling Orphan Girl hoist nearly drowned out his voice. "Why a mine with workers coming and going on night shift? Makes no sense. Why chop off his head after he's shot dead? No bullet casing found, same as the other murders?"

"Scoured the grounds. No casing, no bloody axe or saw or whatever the killer used," Regan said. " 'Course, the light ain't too good. The boys here say anybody wanting to hide a murder weapon could find a million places around here."

Ferndale looked around. "Call the coroner and the mortuary, Jimmy. Clear the body before we get a full shift of workers tromping this way to see these here remains. At first light we'll get some uniforms up here to check high and low for weapons. You boys union?" he said, turning to the two workers.

"I'm a steward in electrical," said one who offered his name as Merl.

"Being that murder is a serious matter, I need the union's cooperation that if anybody finds evidence of this killing, don't touch it and call me at the cop shop pronto. Name's Ferndale."

"We know who you are. Seen you fight," said the other worker. "We know your pal too. Everybody knows Red Maguire."

Ferndale looked at the night sky. "Going to pour again real soon. You boys watch your backs until we find the killer. No reason to spread panic. I got a feeling this here killing had nothing to do with the Orphan Girl except it's noisy and dark enough that nobody hears a gunshot. Maguire?"

"That's how I figure it, Duke."

Dawn broke when Ferndale and Maguire drove uptown to the Silver Star for coffee. The cafe on Broadway Street had a sign in the window that said, "You Got a Dime? We Give a Damn." Underneath, in smaller letters: "Best Coffee in Butte." Maguire made regular visits to the Silver Star. Soon after he joined the *Bugle* a cook went berserk with a butcher knife. He stabbed and wounded a customer eating bacon and eggs at the counter. Before he could finish the job, he slipped on spilled coffee and took a tumble, driving the knife clear through his throat. The spectacle offered no small novelty to dozens of curious onlookers who leaned over the counter to witness the bloody tip sticking three inches out the back of his neck. Spurred on by Stoffleman, Maguire spared no details. One of the best quotes came from the stabbed customer. "Damn fool should have mopped the floor if he intended to kill somebody," the man told Maguire. "I ain't doing nothin' but sittin' there eating breakfast when he drives that knife into my right arm. Now I gotta hold the fork with my left."

Maguire and Ferndale settled in a back booth, their usual. Maguire flipped through a menu but tossed it aside. "No appetite for anything needing ketchup, Duke, which in here is most everything."

"What's the matter, Maguire, weak stomach? Never seen a head sawed off? The hash special sounds good. Say, Marie?" Ferndale shouted to a waitress. "Two hash specials and coffee. Bring me a new bottle of ketchup, will you? Biggest you got."

The waitress bowed to Ferndale in mock surrender. "Anything else, your highness?" Marie came to the booth to fill their cups. "You been coming in here what, twenty years, Duke? Never seen you this early. Another dead one?"

Maguire smiled. "Read all about it in tomorrow's *Bugle*, Marie. What goes on while the city sleeps."

"It ain't a pretty picture," Ferndale added.

"Never doubted it for a minute," Marie said, pushing a pencil into tangled iron gray hair. Maguire figured she combed it with an eggbeater.

After Marie stepped away, Maguire asked, "Why the decapitation, Duke? You ever see anything like that?"

Ferndale pulled out a handkerchief to wipe lipstick off his cup. "What the hell, don't they wash dishes in this joint?" he bellowed, throwing a dirty look in the direction of the kitchen. Then, quieter, "Nobody goes around cutting off heads unless they're itching to send a message. What the killer is trying to tell us escapes me right now, but I know this, it's an escalation. I figure the killer wants us to pay closer attention. We need to get this thing handled in Butte or we'll have everybody and his brother barreling into town trying to take control of our case. Five murders, four of them on my turf. One head missing. Evidence room full of dried up purple roses. Wish I knew more." Ferndale exhaled in exasperation.

"I did some research, Duke. Went through a few books about flowers at the city library. Turns out a purple rose is a symbol of enchantment. Love at first sight, that sort of thing."

"So we have somebody killing lovers? That doesn't explain the woman in Deer Lodge."

"Not her, no, but there's more. I read that purple rose enchantment is often one-sided. Maybe it's unwanted, like a bad crush. It's all sunshine and rainbows at first but can quickly die off."

"Die off. Interesting choice of words. Hell, Maguire, you might be on to something. Suppose now that the killer, if there's only one, is a spurned lover. You ever read those pulp fiction crime stories? First comes love, then comes murder, then comes a body even before marriage and a baby carriage? Maybe what we have here in Butte is some sad sack who can't find a date to save his soul, all worked up over lost love. Sounds like you if you want to know the half of it."

"Can't deny it," Maguire said.

Ferndale smirked. "Maybe the killer is a woman. I romanced a few that I swear would rather kill me than look at me."

"Hard to figure, a woman chopping off a man's head."

"Usually it's a penis. Happened one time down in the Cabbage Patch. He dipped his line in the fishing pond one too many times and his old lady got wise to it. But these purple roses? Our boys checked every florist and greenhouse within fifty miles of Butte. Nobody admits to growing them. You going to write about this enchantment stuff in the *Bugle*?"

"Tomorrow's story, Duke. It's a theory but enough to keep our readers interested until you find more evidence."

"Maybe it will kick up some dust, Maguire. Couldn't do no harm."

"Know what, Duke? I can't shake that picture of a headless body."

"Ketchup goes good on hash, you know that, Maguire?"

"Need to get my mind off it, I guess."

"Try to imagine some doll whispering in your ear down at the Board of Trade. Rich type with jingle. Ideas for how you might spend it. Tight sweater stretched over the biggest knockers in Butte. That ought to keep you busy for a while." Ferndale looked at his watch. "Gotta run soon as Marie brings breakfast. Don't forget to ask the doll if she has a sister."

That afternoon, Chief Morse held a news conference at City Hall. Reporters packed the room. Maguire saw a few familiar faces among many strangers. The series of murders had become a big story, bigger than Butte and bigger than Montana. Some of the reporters drove from Spokane and Salt Lake City. They pushed to the front. A few of them interrupted the chief as he tried to read a statement. One of them elbowed Maguire aside. "This is how we do it in Butte," Maguire whispered to him. He knocked the man to his knees with a hard blow in the kidneys. "Man fainted here," Maguire called to the chief, who looked at him suspiciously.

Little news came out of the event, as Maguire knew would happen. The chief described his illusion of "a full court press" in search of the killer. The chief liked basketball. He played for the Bulldogs at Butte High. He repeated the usual "under investigation" denials until the reporters took over, firing questions at the beleaguered chief until he threw up his hands and left the room. Despite four murders in Butte, and the fifth in Deer Lodge, police couldn't claim any progress in catching a serial killer. Ferndale stood in the corner of the room. He motioned to Maguire as the other reporters filed out. The out of towners would head home soon enough.

"Saw you give that other fella an attitude lesson," he said. "In any other city that's assault."

"And in Butte?"

"In this city you went easy on him."

Ferndale looked impatient. He waited until the room emptied. "We found something that ain't any prettier than what you saw this morning. Let's go for a ride."

For once, the rain had stopped. The sun felt hot. Ferndale cranked down the window in his old Dodge. It shrieked with every turn of the handle. "Damn thing sticks," he said. He pulled over to force the window down with his hands. He kicked the gear shift lever into Drive and they rolled down Butte Hill, away from the mines, onto the Flats. Sagging brick buildings huddled together as if trying to hold each other upright. The ground looked bleached and oily. Ferndale turned onto a rutted dirt road that wound through piles of mine tailings and rusting metal. Maguire saw a prowl car. A lone cop stood beside it. Ferndale pulled to a stop. "Your stomach ain't got any weaker since breakfast, Maguire?" He didn't wait for a response. Ferndale walked to a place in the weeds. He pointed to the ground. "Here's the rest of the story," Ferndale said. There, covered with dust, rested a severed head. Neck cut cleanly, eyes squeezed open, lips frozen in an otherworld grin Maguire had seen on many dead bodies. Seeing a head all by itself looked ghastly enough. Something else alarmed Maguire more. He peered through blood and dust caked on the man's face. "Good God!" Maguire cried out.

"I thought so," Ferndale said. "Damn shame, ain't it?"

"Stoffleman spit fire when he didn't show up for work. Figured he went on another bender. He did that a few times a year, you know. Drank up half of uptown Butte when he worked up a thirst. Had a snout for the hard stuff. But this?"

"You know for sure it's Antonio Vanzetti? He got a wife and kids?"

"No family to my thinking. Just a humble working man when sober."

"City Hall reporter, right? Broke that story about embezzlement in the police pension fund? Damn thieves."

"He's the one, yes. The man had skills, Duke. Antonio rarely made a mistake in print. Now this. How do we break the news to Stoffleman that he's got a crack reporter out here, dead? At least the top of him. You think it matches the other piece?"

"I imagine. We ain't got any other calls for missing heads this week," Ferndale said.

The detective leaned against the prowl car. He reached into his suit jacket for a cigarette. Up on the hill, a few miles away, the late afternoon sun cast shadows over the broken land. "Here's the thing, Maguire. We got to keep this quiet until tomorrow morning when you break it in the *Bugle*. You're the only reporter we talk to anyway. The official story until then is that we don't know the victim's identity. Imagine if the chief had spilled the beans this afternoon that we found a cut-off head on the Flats. Picture those out-of-town news crews parading down Montana Street like some sideshow out of St. Paddy's Day."

"Bigger than the event itself, no doubt. How did you know to come here?"

"Truck driver from one of the mines drove to dump junk. Puked his guts out when he saw the head. Doubt he'll get over it anytime soon. I guess it would give a man a start, finding a pair of eyes staring at you from the weeds."

"I'll write it for the morning paper then."

"Make sure my shop gets credit, will you? 'Butte police identify the headless victim,' something like that? How about, 'Antonio went out of this world smelling like a rose.' "

"Black humor, Duke, but not bad. That's the way Sullivan would have written it."

"Maybe you ought to try your hand."

Ferndale went with Maguire back to the *Bugle* to tell Stoffleman what had happened. The editor kicked his chair, knocking it over, drawing stares from around the city room. "Damn fine reporter! You're sure it's Vanzetti?" he asked, hope in his eyes.

"Confirmed," Ferndale said. "Maguire made a positive ID."

"Now the killer is after my reporters? Vanzetti didn't write a lick about the murders. It's been Maguire all the way. Explain this to me, will you?" Stoffleman, usually decisive, looked worried.

"Wish I could, Mr. Stoffleman."

The editor stared at Vanzetti's empty desk. Stoffleman seemed, for the moment, sequestered in a rare moment of surrender. "What is it about this town that would allow such brazen disrespect for a human body? To insult the honor of a man whose stories in this newspaper kept the city honest? A dark place, Butte. Remember that book that came out in '43 that got Butte so riled up? Joseph Kinsey Howard's 'High, Wide and Handsome?' Remember what he wrote about Butte? 'Black heart of Montana, feared and distrusted.' Can we think of any reason to disagree with his conclusion? Maguire? Ferndale?"

"No argument here," Maguire said.

"Seems right on point with his reasoning," Ferndale said.

Maguire realized the conversation had caught the full attention of the city room. The night editors had arrived at work to assemble the paper before the midnight deadline. Claggett and Miller and a few other reporters sat motionless at their desks, listening intently. Clicking and clacking of their old typewriters had stopped. Stoffleman turned to Maguire. "Report the hell out of this story for the morning paper. I want every graphic detail that is fit to print in Butte, which we already know is most of them. Ferndale, I hope you police boys are more forthcoming than what we saw at the news conference today. Give us something new, will you?"

Ferndale exhaled a whiff of impatience. "Already did that. Maguire was the only reporter who saw Vanzetti's head."

Stoffleman sat on the edge of his desk. He pulled off his eye shade. Maguire rarely saw him without it. In fact, he rarely remembered being in the city room without Stoffleman. The editor never missed a chance to take charge. "Know what bothers me, boys? What do all these victims have in common except for the purple roses?" He rubbed his balding scalp and tugged the eye shade back over his head. "You find out that answer, Maguire, and someday you'll be back in Chicago working the crime beat for the *Sun-Times*. Imagine, Red Maguire covering gangland murders in the big city, a million readers hanging on every word. Now wouldn't that be something?"

5

Lucky the bounty hunter

Dead men need a voice. Someone capable of sharing their stories, someone knowing of the ways of sharing details with strangers. Did Red Maguire see himself that way? He brought dirt to print. That's what crime reporting dug up, dirt and spit and blood. Maguire revealed secrets. A true story lurked behind every crime. Most of the time, people closest to the crime hid the story. No, the killer thought, how wrong. Report the details. Unveil injustice. Red Maguire will know what to do.

Headless man identified as Bugle reporter

Fifth person found dead
in Purple Rose Murders;
victim Antonio Vanzetti
is fourth one in Butte

The morning *Bugle*'s banner headline blared the news.

True to expectations, Maguire played his scoop to the hilt. The story filled two full columns on the front page. He spared no grotesque details but avoided any hint of how he came across both murder scenes. The other papers and broadcast stations looked silly by comparison. None of them had news of the severed head. They ran with canned comments from the chief, the mayor, and other city officials who dressed up for work. Maguire took no pleasure in his scoop. He felt bad about the bitter irony. Only in death had Antonio Vanzetti, a steady and reliable *Bugle* reporter, figured in the most sensational news story of his journalism career.

The *Bugle* hired twelve newsboys to work the streets in uptown Butte and posted two others on the broad concrete steps to City Hall. They sold five hundred papers by mid-morning. Stoffleman loaded them up with five hundred more to prowl the bars and cafes. A few hours later, every single paper had sold. The newsboys poured out bags of coins as the clerks at the circulation desk downstairs strained to count them. The *Bugle* also sent a hundred extra papers to Deer Lodge to stock news racks and restaurant counters. Eager readers snapped them up like free ice cream cones. Nothing sold better than news of a severed head. Many outraged readers clucked their criticism of Red Maguire for describing the grisly scenes where both parts of Vanzetti were found. Then they read every word.

Maguire's phone rang repeatedly that morning in the *Bugle* city room. A few callers complained about his lack of restraint. Others were amateur detectives seeking to involve Maguire in conspiracy theories about the Purple Rose Murders. Finally, he had heard enough. None of the callers had yielded anything useful for his next story. He decided he would answer one more call, one more jangling intrusion, before heading over to see the cops. When that call came, he barked into the receiver, "*Bugle* city room, Maguire!"

A woman's voice came on the line. "What a big day for you, Maguire. I see you've got an inside connection with police, but you have a problem, don't you? Nobody knows what's going on with these murders. Surely there's so much more. Have you found the real story, Maguire? Can you figure it out?"

The line went dead.

Maguire looked at the phone for a moment before replacing it in the cradle. "That really is the problem, isn't it, Maguire? Plenty of gore, no evidence of motive," he said to himself. He looked over at Vanzetti's desk. The man had never said much about his personal life. He did his job, did it well when sober, and left the city room each night without saying much to anybody. Vanzetti's parents were dead. He might have a sister in California. Nobody knew where to look for her.

Over at the Forever More Funeral Parlor, both parts of Vanzetti were laid out on a slab like pieces to a puzzle. Maguire pictured it. In cellars under mortuaries he had seen naked dead bodies, including his father's, being stitched together the way a seamstress would assemble a rag doll. Hard to know which was more urgent, grieving for Vanzetti, or watching his own back. The killer probably walking the same streets in uptown Butte, finding a way to inflict suspicion into every Butte resident. Maguire could feel it. Nervous people hurried up and down the sidewalks, avoiding shadowy alleys, while flower shops struggled to find customers. The murders dominated talk. People wondered who would be next, who would be found headless, who would receive a purple rose. Maguire had no reason to blame them. He had the same worries. He hoped it wouldn't be him.

He thought about the woman's phone call. Did she know something? She had a distinctive alluring voice, almost sexy, but Maguire knew she disguised it. She might be an attentive *Bugle* reader. She might be a witness. Maguire thought about telling Ferndale about her. He also knew the crusty old detective would respond with something like, "You ain't got more than that, Maguire?" Cops, like journalists, were paid skeptics. So was Lucky Finero.

Intrigued what the bounty hunter might know, Maguire leafed through the phone book until he found a listing on East Galena Street. He donned his fedora, buttoned his suit and walked to the street. Fat dark rain clouds swarmed over the mountains. It was the wettest August in all the years he'd lived in Butte. The air reeked like a wet cellar. Maguire hurried along before the rain hit. He knew nothing about Lucky Finero, like Vanzetti, a denizen of Meaderville. In all the years Maguire had reported news for the *Bugle*, hustling the Italian district for scoops as much as anyplace else in Butte, their paths hadn't crossed. Because Finero preferred working in the dead of night, people thought of him as a ghost, hovering in the dark to catch fugitives and deadbeats when they were sleeping.

Maguire found a paint-blistered door to Finero's office between an empty grocery store, where the awning hung in tatters, and a hardware business. He pushed it open. Creaking narrow stairs led him to a musty landing illuminated by a single yellow lightbulb hanging on three feet of frayed electrical cord. Stenciled on the door in front of him were the words, "Finero Bail Recovery." He knocked.

A rustle came from behind the door. "Whaddya want!" came a shout, more a demand than a question.

"That you, Lucky? It's Red Maguire from the *Bugle*."

"Ease in, boy. I ain't in the mood."

Maguire turned the knob. Behind the door, he found a burly man slouched behind a desk. The man clenched a tall glass bottle of brown liquid in one hand and a menacing silver gun in the other. Maguire figured him capable with both.

In one sweep of his eyes, Maguire took in details useful to a newspaper reporter. Curly gray hair, no balding. Bushy eyebrows that would shame a bear. Steel-gray eyes rimmed in red, hardened and searching for weakness. Rumpled gray suit, torn at the right elbow, far out of fashion. Gnarled fists big as dinner plates. Scarred knuckles. Maybe from dragging, Maguire thought with amusement. A supposed office that consisted of nothing more than an empty room with a five-year-old calendar hanging behind Finero that said, "Sundberg Plumbing and Electric, 1949." Coil of half-inch brown rope, at least fifteen feet long, stashed in the corner. On the wooden desk, a cascading stack of apparent court papers, a black telephone with dried blood on the receiver, handcuffs with key protruding, rolls of electrical tape, black leather sap for clubbing. A glistening knife big enough to gut a shark sat on top of the jumble.

Finero eased back the hammer on his pistol and laid it on the desk. "We finally meet, Maguire. The husky Irishman everyone knows as Red. So I'm looking at the *Bugle* hero who shines light on the dark criminal underbelly of this city. Sounds damn poetic, don't it?"

Maguire leaned against the door jamb. He struck a match to light a cigarette. As a trail of blue smoke rose around his face, he studied the brute, an unpredictable sort from the looks of him. "It's been said, Lucky. You and I both know what lurks in the shadows."

Lucky snorted. "It's how we make our jingle, ain't it?"

Maguire gestured to Finero's weapons. "Expecting trouble, are you?"

Finero sighed. "Long night. I wrestled a bail jumper to the ground in the Cabbage Patch. His buddy clubbed me from behind. Got a grip on both of them when a third punk jumped in. They landed a few punches until I pulled my knife. No concern to me what part of them I bring to the jail. Get paid all the same."

"What was their trouble, Lucky? They want to put you six feet under?"

Finero shrugged and took a swig of the brown stuff. A strong odor of whiskey hit Maguire's nose. "Hell, every one of them. World owes 'em a living, don't you know? Butte's got so many goons on the run they could form a club if they had the sense. Ain't no problem for me. I make my jingle from their foolishness all the same."

Maguire gestured to a chair in front of the desk. Finero nodded. "You read my stories about the Purple Rose Murders?" Maguire asked, settling on the wobbly chair.

"Every damn one twice if you want the truth of it. People commit crimes, I read their names, know what I'm up against when I chase their sorry ass down." Finero wiped a hand over his tired eyes. "Shame about Vanzetti. Any attack on a wop in Butte is an attack on us all. If I find who cut his head off, I'll put my knife to good use so he knows how it feels. You can quote me on that, Maguire. I ain't afraid of speaking my mind. Lucky Finero, do-gooder. About time I read my name in the *Bugle* on occasion as somebody who's doing favors for this town. Just quote me straight, that's all I ask."

"Remember that when the time comes, Lucky."

"You think I might know something about these murders?"

"Being a man who hears things, like me, yes," Maguire said.

Lucky reached for the handcuffs. "I can start asking these boys when I hunt them down. Usually they have plenty to say after I cuff 'em. You ought to hear them sing when I show my blade."

"How's that, Lucky?"

"I tell 'em I like a little tongue with my coffee in the morning."

"You're a legend in this town from what I hear," Maguire said. "I'm beginning to understand why. That knife does your talking, does it?"

Finero reached for the knife. He held it, blade up, while pulling his ratty tie away from his ample belly. He laid the tie over the blade and with a snap of his hand, sheared off a chunk of his tie. "Get the idea, Maguire?"

"Never doubted you, Lucky. A man in your line of work needs persuasion to get his point across, I'm thinking."

Finero dropped the knife back on his desk. "Tell me, Maguire. From where I sit your line of work ain't much different from mine. I read your stories, know the messes you step in, hell, I know everything. Unless you've got Ferndale hanging over you around the clock you're an easy mark with nothing but a notebook for protection. I figure you right? You're a big man, I'll give you that, and I hear you hold your own in a fight. Word to the wise. Guns outmatch fists. You packing heat under that coat? If not you're a damned fool."

Maguire pulled open his coat lapels to show he had no weapon. He had left his .38 tucked under his mattress at the Logan. Few people bothered with entering the old building. The two-story brick affair on East Granite Street stood in a row of half-empty nondescript rooming houses.

"Figured," Finero said. "Why do you cover the news anyway? Reporters and bounty hunters wind up drunks. I could tell you stories about Vanzetti that would curl your hair. Damn, never mind, I see it's curly already. Vanzetti, he liked to run with the boys. Know what I mean? Let's say I caught Antonio in a compromising position. Never saw him pinching my ass in print, now did ya? I know secrets about most everybody in this town. So do you, far as I know. Take my free advice. If you won't carry a gun, at least arm yourself with a knife before somebody figures out what you know on them. You never know when you'll find yourself in a tight spot. Say, where are my manners, Maguire? Want a gulp of the hard stuff?"

Maguire stood, pushed his fedora back, and crossed his arms. He looked down on the older man. Finero watched him closely. "Thanks, but I stick to beer when on duty, which is most of the time. Newspaper work keeps me out of the mines. Pays for a room at the Logan and meals at the Silver Star, too. I'm living on Easy Street, Lucky."

Finero gulped from his bottle and belched. "Sure as shootin' we both are, Maguire. That's if'n we don't get shot."

Maguire shivered when he left Finero. He didn't want to encourage the bounty hunter to cut on bail jumpers again. Ears, fingers, who knows what appendage Lucky would sever next. Finero relished his line of work.

Meanwhile, over at the police department, Ferndale stood in front of Chief Morse's desk behind a closed door. Mayor Fred Ticklenberg fumed. He had stuffed his fat body between the arm rests of a wooden chair. The chief pulled on a crooked pair of reading glasses and unfolded the *Bugle* front page on his desk. He motioned to Maguire's story. "This headless guy isn't the only one getting killed, Ferndale. Our city is taking a beating from uppity politicians in Helena. Everybody and his brother have a theory about these murders and want to know what we're doing about it. Bodies stacking up by the day, Maguire over at the *Bugle* riling people up with this drama, state crime bureau dicks threatening to come and take over our investigation, and me without a pot to piss in. Get my meaning?"

The mayor leaned over, eager to pile on his own complaints, pink-purple jowls quivering in anger. The belt he wore surrounded his girth like a hula hoop. "We're a city in crisis, Ferndale. Anxious residents have our phones ringing off the hook. I had to put three more ladies on the switchboard to keep up. Three! First time I ever had to do such a thing. Everybody in Butte wants to know when our cops will arrest the killer. I've got an election coming up next year. Can you hear it now? Ticklenberg let Butte go to the dogs. Ticklenberg let a serial killer run loose. We can't afford to lose voters who think we're not protecting them. If they kick me out of office, the chief's out of a job and maybe you too. Why, I —."

"Here's the thing, Ferndale," the chief said, interrupting the ranting mayor. He placed his glasses neatly on the desk. Morse, meticulous in his manner, put on his serious face. "You and I go way back, Duke. I promoted you to detective all those years ago because you are the best damn copper I've got. Still are, as far as I know, but here we sit, idling in neutral. We need answers and need them fast."

Ferndale raised his hand to calm both men. He showed no worry at their reaction. They were at the front end of the police operation, dealing with an angry and worried public, while he worked the streets. A detective did the gritty work. Sifted through gore at crime scenes. Dirtied his hands with suspects. Took heat from everybody looking for someone to blame. Ferndale had seen plenty of death over thirty-five years of wearing a badge. Until the Purple Rose Murders he had prided himself at finding killers. Usually they were husbands, wives, even third-party lovers with jealousy motives. Some victims died in fights over money, some in drunken fits of rage, others for perceived wrongs.

Evidence stood out like red fire hydrants in most of those murders. Sometimes police caught a killer standing over the body. Sometimes, but less often, a remorseful killer showed up with bloody hands at the cop shop to confess. Many killers he had arrested had no explanation for why they pulled the trigger. Most of them were dumb as rocks. By comparison, the Purple Rose Murders were more, well, sophisticated. Not a word often used in Ferndale's vocabulary. He had scoured the murder scenes for clues. The killer left no fingerprints or other telltale evidence. The cops had no eyewitnesses. They knew of no prior disputes involving the victims. If Butte had typical murders, these weren't it. None of the four Butte victims shared anything in common except being men. The first two, Mike Kelly and Rodney Townsend, were young men in their twenties. They worked deep underground in separate mines. By all accounts they didn't know each other. What about David Fenton, the real estate agent, and Vanzetti? And how did the dead woman in Deer Lodge fit in?

"It's a puzzle, chief," Ferndale said. "I wish I had more. You've seen the evidence reports. Forty-four-caliber slugs in every murder. Shots expertly placed to the heart."

Ticklenberg looked worried. "Expertly placed? Like a cop would do?"

"Like a conniving killer would do," Ferndale said. "These ain't crimes of passion where the killer shoots recklessly at the victim until he runs out of lead. In those cases we see people shot in the face, arms, legs, even in the ass. People not accustomed to handling guns get jacked up with emotion and blaze away. What we got now is someone who knows how to shoot."

The mayor sighed. "With deadly efficiency, it appears. We've ruled out ex-cops, soldiers, people like that? Talked to the gun shops?"

A flash of resignation crossed the chief's face. "We have, yes. Can't fault how Ferndale and the rest of my boys checked everybody out. Unlikely a rogue cop would go chop off someone's head. Know what sticks in my craw, though? Those damned purple roses." Then, to Ferndale, "You're telling me nobody grows those things?"

"Can't find evidence of it. Checked everywhere in western Montana."

"So ask around eastern Montana, will you? Idaho? Wyoming? Canada?"

Mayor Ticklenberg jumped in. "I've got another bone to pick," he said, pointing to the newspaper on the chief's desk. "What about that screamer in the *Bugle* this morning? Every damn bloody detail of the guy's head chopped off revealed. Since when does that reporter Maguire own stock in our police department? He's sure enough a bona fide Butte boy but sometimes I wonder if he knows too much. Nona Leary from the Chamber of Commerce tells me we'll never see new stores opening in Butte with a reputation like this. I'm hearing from every service club in town that nobody wants to spend money. All those folks, hunkered down hoping they won't be the next victim, and now we've got Red Maguire exposing police business to all of Butte."

"Ferndale ran it by me," the chief said. "I made the call to let Maguire see the head. Without Maguire reporting the facts, the rumor mill would kick into high gear. No, seeing details of a chopped-off head in print pretty much ruined my breakfast this morning, but he got them right. Besides, his story might kick a suspect out of the bushes."

"If he don't get himself killed first," Ferndale said.

Chief Morse straightened the badge on his crisp blue shirt. "If that happens," he said, "make sure everybody understands you gave Maguire the headless murder story, not me."

6

Tough boys of Dublin Gulch

Saturday morning. Behind a cabin high on the Continental Divide, far from any road of consequence, sunlight streamed into a homemade greenhouse built of boards and plastic sheeting. The growing season would end soon. Only an accomplished gardener knew how to keep flowers alive in dry air at a mile above sea level. A few roses remained. Down in the valley, nobody sold the purple ones. No matter. Bought in town, they would be easy to trace. These were genuine roses, deep purple and breathtakingly beautiful, grown with loving care. They were especially symbolic. Circumstances required cutting so many of them. What a shame. Soon summer would fade. The first snow would come. The temporary greenhouse would bend and tear in the winter winds. No matter. Only a few more roses would be needed to finish the job. Handy tools, these purple roses. Without them, Red Maguire would never understand why the murders had a common purpose. One more rose. It would be clipped soon enough. Give it time to bloom. How beautiful to caress its delicate petals with a lover's touch. Soon.

Finally, Ferndale found an important clue. Maybe no more than a coincidence. The young miners killed earlier in the summer, Kelly and Townsend, had something in common after all. The names bothered Ferndale from the start. He had a long memory, dusty as a forgotten attic, that wandered through often dark and disturbing alleyways of time. He rustled through the storage room where cops stashed records, searching for those names. An hour later he found a file that confirmed his suspicions. Fight in the Helsinki Bar in 1930. Men named Kelly and Townsend punched a business owner several times during an argument. When he fell to the floor they put their boots to him. The victim, Harvey Addleston, died three days later at Silver Bow Hospital. Doctors said his fatal heart attack came about from the severe beating. Ferndale, a younger cop then, had worked the case. He found notes in his handwriting in Addleston's file. "Motive not known but perps drunk and disorderly and resisted arrest," he had written. "Kelly and Townsend cuffed and taken to jail. Confessed to beating. Pleaded guilty and sent to state prison in Deer Lodge."

It took more digging before Ferndale confirmed that the younger Kelly and Townsend were sons of the convicted men. The older Kelly died in a car accident in 1941 after his parole. Drunk, he careened into a power pole at fifty miles an hour after sounding off at Babe's Bar about being railroaded to prison. Witnesses said the more Kelly drank, the more details he divulged about his attack on Addleston. A miner walking to work found him pinned in the wreckage of his '37 Plymouth with a quart bottle of Butte's cheapest lager, drained of its contents, jammed halfway down his throat. He lost control of his car as he tipped the bottle behind the wheel. "If the crash didn't kill him, drowning in beer did," the coroner told the *Butte Bugle*. The older Townsend died of silicosis, a common fate of Butte miners, soon after his release from prison. The cops knew little else about him. Ferndale wished he had taken thorough notes. He wasn't a detective then but a street cop. He doubted anyone else of higher rank had spent much time investigating Addleston's death.

File open on his desk, he telephoned the mothers of both young men, hoping for fresh clues. They hated him for nosing around their husbands' criminal pasts. Lenora Townsend, although audibly feeble, accused Ferndale of killing her husband by sending him to prison. She swore and slammed down the phone. Maud Kelly, inquisitive, wanted to know more. "Do you think me son's murder has anything to do with that trouble me old man got hisself involved in? A drinking son of a bitch. Always wanted to fight anyone who got in his way. Knocked me around every time he got a snoot full. Me boy, I raised him to stay away from the drink. Good boy, he worked hard you know, now he's gone. Me only child, you know."

On a hunch, Ferndale called Maguire at the *Bugle*. The reporter picked up right away. "Figured I would catch you there," Ferndale told him.

"No rest for weary cops and news reporters," Maguire said, sure Ferndale would ignore his turn of the proverbial phrase. Ferndale shared what he had discovered about Kelly and Townsend. "You think the *Bugle* has anything more on this deal back in 1930?"

Maguire said he would look around and hung up. An hour later, he called Ferndale back. "I found a lot of dust and mold in the basement. Can't say the *Bugle* kept the best records morgue known to newspapers. I can see other people turned the place upside down trying to find things. Nobody keeps the place up."

"I don't need a tour of the damn basement," growled Ferndale, impatient. "Find anything or no?"

"I'm getting to that, Duke. Found a clipping of the murder story. Way back, long before I carried water for the big shot reporters on weekends. The story says Kelly and Townsend were jawing at this guy Addleston in the Helsinki before punches started flying. Appears we didn't report what caused the fight. So I found nothing new, except that it says here the perps had a beef over some bad business in the miner union. Story says Addleston had a family. The bottom of the clipping soaked up water from leaks in the basement. The rest of the story is indecipherable."

"Indy what? Speak English, will you?"

"I can't read it, Duke. Type is washed out. I also looked around for stories we wrote about the trial. I found a file. Trouble is, when these mugs pleaded guilty, they never had to tell a jury what went on that night."

"Maguire, I don't need no schooling on how the courts work," Ferndale said.

"I had my suspicions the fight had something to do with jingle, Duke. You know how it is when a man wants jingle filling his pocket and he thinks the other guy has more. Isn't every fight over love or jingle? I looked and looked but that's all I've got. Who knows what happens to our records over the years with reporters rummaging around for background on every story under the sun?"

Ferndale sighed at the other end of the line. "Wish you had more, Maguire. Whatever family Addleston had here is long gone. I looked in old Butte city directories but found no listing of a phone number for anyone named Addleston within a year after the murder. Not surprised. Families tend to hike out of town after a loved one gets snuffed." Maguire heard rustling over the phone. "Wait! I wrote on the back of the file the dead guy had a relative named Martha Addleston. Lived in Finn Town. Wife, maybe?"

"What's the address? I'll go look her up. Maybe there's a story in her."

"No point, Maguire. The houses on that block fell to the wrecking ball a few years ago. They were in that area near the Berkeley Mine where the Anaconda Company wants to dig that big damn pit."

"We're at a dead end?"

"Except for one other thing. The senior Kelly and Townsend both worked at the Orphan Girl. Same place we found the lower piece of your buddy from the *Bugle*. No idea what that means. Crime investigations are full of coincidences that lead nowhere. You tell me."

Maguire said he would keep looking and hung up. The political heat over at City Hall must be hot to the touch. Ferndale leaned on him to help solve the Purple Rose Murders more than he had done with other crimes in the past. Maguire felt inclined to help the old detective. Without Ferndale taking him to murder scenes and sharing clues, he would be writing the same slop other reporters served up to their readers and viewers. The *Bugle* built its fortunes on crack crime coverage. Peter Sullivan wrote flashy stories that long would be remembered. Dead now, six feet under, his bylines yellowing and forgotten. Maguire had taken his place. Maguire knew he never would be as eloquent as Sullivan, flowery with the language, but he knew how to dig for stories and verify facts. He also trusted Ferndale. He could take that trust to the bank.

Across the city room, Stoffleman hunched over his desk, penciling changes into stories for the Sunday paper. *Bugle* reporters knew he would work eight days a week if he could. Stoffleman preferred a city room to the outside world. When Maguire stood from his squeaky chair to leave, Stoffleman lifted his bent face, squinting at the big Irishman. "You there, Maguire! Got anything for tomorrow's paper? Don't tell me no. I hear the Company is hiring muckers to work a couple thousand feet down."

"Nothing, boss, but looking hard. Don't send me up the Hill yet."

Stoffleman motioned Maguire into the hallway. "I've been thinking, Maguire. You're damn good, but this murder story is big, too big, for one reporter. I'm giving you some help. I thought of Vanzetti as the logical choice until, well, his funeral is Tuesday, right? Still can't believe what happened to Antonio. Then I thought of Ketchul but the way the Company is putting the squeeze on underground mining, he's turning too many stories off his labor beat. Well, you're getting Miller, the new gal. Put her to work, will you?"

"Miller, boss? Mary Miller? You're giving me a society writer who wears lipstick to work?"

"Look around, Maguire. We're a vanishing staff as we speak. She's no shrinking violet, pardon the pun, and she can turn a phrase. I doubt that she knows a lick about covering a murder or any crime. Miller will learn from you. Maybe you remember how useless you were back when I hired you on? Hell, Maguire, you learned a thing or two from me. You might even take my job someday after I fall over dead. Better learn how to put other people to work."

"What about Claggett, boss? He knows his way around dead people."

"Except he doesn't know anything about the live ones," Stoffleman said.

Maguire started to object. Stoffleman cut him off with a quick wave of his hand. Maguire couldn't imagine taking Stoffleman's job. Riding herd on people like himself struck him as a waste of time. Maguire liked the hustle in the streets. Editors framed the paper from the city room. Staring at the same four walls, day and night and seven days a week, would drive him mad. Stoffleman walked away. Maguire put a match to a Lucky Strike, his favored cigarette brand, and walked back into the city room.

He found Miller's desk neat as a pin. She had gone to cover a story, something involving finger food and napkins no doubt, while he wrote about bloody beheadings. A vague jasmine scent of Chanel No. 5 wafted from a pink sweater hung over her chair. The sweater remained the only element in the entire city room not black, brown, or gray. Maguire knew little about Miller. She covered fundraising announcements and tea parties and social engagements. The Butte she saw, the Butte of money and privilege and sunlight, lived an eternity away from the Butte he saw, the Butte of grit and spit and shadows. The last thing Maguire needed was for this girl from Seattle, a former telephone operator he'd heard, to slow down his pursuit of the Purple Rose Murders. He hoped he didn't misjudge her. Then again, he didn't care. Red attended to the serious business of crime. Stories begging for telling awaited him.

Maguire leaned his lanky frame against the chipped varnished door frame and took a long drag. He hated the habit but it calmed him. He started smoking in Dublin Gulch when the neighborhood boys dared him to take a puff. Pulling on a fag tasted better once he got started. The boys hid their smokes in an abandoned shack where they congregated after school. They kept a glass jar there, too, brimming with a cloudy brown mixture of liquors they pilfered from their parents' cupboards. The brew burned the tongue and invited an aching stomach. A new boy wanting to find acceptance in the social order had to take three deep gulps from the reeking brew every day for a week. He had to inhale five smokes in a row while the other boys watched. He also had to draw blood in a fist fight.

Maguire passed all three tests in the first month he lived on the gulch. The fight came when a bigger boy named Joe O'Malley pushed Maguire to the ground and grabbed his lunch pail one morning outside the school. Joe stood five inches taller than Red Maguire. His oversized head bristled with a hint of red sideburns and chin stubble. A missing front tooth confirmed a lucky hit by somebody who stood up to him. Few did. Joe, at fourteen, already had chunky arms that hung like sides of beef. He walked with the confident swagger of a bully who ran the street. Maguire had seen Joe pound other boys into dust, sometimes as their mothers watched from their front porches, unwilling to interfere. Joe O'Malley, without a doubt, reigned over Dublin Gulch.

Maguire, just a young boy, had hoped his qualifying fight would come with someone other than Joe. He wanted to join the neighborhood gang. Getting his nose mashed and his eyes blackened would leave him weak in the eyes of the other boys. One blow from Joe usually put a boy down. If Joe wanted more, and he usually did, he pulled the boy to his knees to punch him three or four more times in the face. Maguire had seen boys pass out from the beatings Joe inflicted.

That morning outside the school, Joe tossed the lid off Maguire's lunch pail. He reached in with grimy fat fingers to pull out the chicken pot pie that Aggie Walsh had packed. Joe took a big slobbering bite from it. He spit out what he chewed and tossed the rest in the weeds. "Came from somebody's outhouse!" he bellowed with crumbs flaking off lips that Maguire thought resembled a leaky red garden hose. "That old Irish whore dig this up for ya? Get down on her knees, did she now?"

Maguire jumped to his feet. Other boys, sensing a fight, began yelling encouragement. Joe unleashed a fat right fist that caught Red above the ear with the force of a jackhammer. He stumbled and fell. Joe stepped close to jump on him but

Red rolled away and pushed to his feet. He heard voices that sounded far away. Confusion clouded his brain. Joe stood before him, laughing. In that instant, as Joe mocked Red for the benefit of the other boys, Red remembered what his father had taught him about fighting. "Don't try to match punch for punch, son. Fight like you want to put the other kid down. Fight dirty. Go for his balls, his knees, his feet. Kick him, stomp him, hurt him to where he kneels in front of you. Then, boy, go to work on him. Double up your fists and aim for his nose, lips, ears. Let me show you how to make him howl enough that he wants you to stop. That's the only way you'll survive in Dublin Gulch." Sean Maguire hit Red in the face three times to show him how it would feel. He hurt for a week.

Joe made another nasty remark about Aggie. Blinking rage through tears, Red swung out a leg and caught Joe where it hurts with the toe of his boot. The solid kick to Joe's family jewels bent him over and got him screaming. Before he could recover, Red slammed his boot into both of Joe's shins, knocking him to his knees. Joe lifted his face in bewilderment. He held both hands firmly between his legs. Red grabbed Joe by his greasy mop of hair, punched him four times in the nose until he heard it break, then grabbed him by the ears and smacked a knee against his mouth. Joe collapsed face down in a pool of blood and sobbed.

The fight ended Joe O'Malley's rule of Dublin Gulch. Nobody had beaten him in a fight. Nobody had come close. Red Maguire, the new champion, fought all challengers. He grew strong and tall by his sixteenth birthday, his broad shoulders and handsome face earning admiration from both boys and girls. Nobody dared say a bad word about Aggie Walsh after what Red Maguire did to Joe O'Malley. If Aggie ever heard what happened, and chances were good that she did, she never mentioned a word of it to Red. She was a strong woman and to Red, a mother.

Joe dropped out of high school a few years after the fight to run the honey wagon in the Kelley Mine. Lowest of jobs, hauling buckets of piss. Red considered it a fitting job for a bully. In a coincidence of fate, Joe died in the same explosion that killed Sean Maguire. Joe's body came to the surface with a spear-like shard from a timber driven deep into his chest. He reeked of urine.

Maguire thought about Joe O'Malley from time to time. Joe wasn't worth two bits as a friend but Maguire felt bad about his death. How strange that way with Butte's Irish. They would fight one day, stand for each other the next, brag about their kind in the gulch, in Corktown, down Anaconda Road, over in Muckerville. Maguire had a reputation as a scrapper but he didn't think of himself as a pug like Joe. Maguire only beat up other kids when they asked for it. His reputation as a fighter paled with Duke Ferndale, who knew something about boxing. Maguire considered himself just another Butte boy.

Maguire, having smoked an entire cigarette while recalling his glory days in the gulch, snuffed out the butt in an ashtray on Claggett's desk. The elderly obituary reporter took that as a reminder to light one of his own. He rarely looked up from his typewriter, even to put a match to his beloved Old Golds, as he hammered the keys.

The city room had come alive in the disappearing afternoon. Ted Ketchul burst through the door from his labor beat and went to work writing a story. At the far end of the room two of the sports reporters argued over which professional baseball teams would play in the World Series. The New York Giants were a sure thing, one of them insisted, while the other declared the Cleveland Indians would make the finals. Maguire had heard the argument all summer and tired of it. He favored only one team, the Chicago Cubs, in his mind the best team in baseball.

Maguire went to his desk, took off his brown suit jacket, rolled up the sleeves on his white shirt. He lifted the black telephone receiver to his ear and dialed Ferndale. At that moment, Mary Miller danced into the city room, shooting a disinterested glance in Maguire's direction before settling at her desk. Maguire paid her no mind. The ever-hungry *Bugle*, a newspaper of distinction, needed another hot story from crime reporter Red Maguire.

~ 7 ~

New girl on the crime beat

All the big papers in Montana ran wild with the murders. Their stories were mostly rehashed *Associated Press* versions of Red Maguire's original coverage. Papers in Great Falls and Billings and Missoula sent reporters to Butte to pry out new angles. Ferndale ignored their requests for interviews. Reporters from Minneapolis showed up as well. Ferndale turned the same cold shoulder to them. The outside reporters began working the neighborhoods, quoting anybody who voiced an opinion about the murders, squeezing out petty details that got them no closer to the truth. Maguire could see the residents reacted more to details he had reported in his stories than offered new insight into the crimes.

The growing competition got Stoffleman's attention. "Right now those big city guys are running around like blind men chasing a two-legged dog. Don't get too comfortable, Maguire. They're pros. I caution you against underestimating them. Eventually one of them will uncover news that's important to this case if we don't get there first. You and Miller better make sure that doesn't happen."

On Monday morning, Stoffleman motioned Maguire and Mary Miller to his desk. He explained to her that she would cover the Purple Rose Murders. At first Maguire thought she looked scared. Her eyes darted from Stoffleman to Maguire and back again. Both men seemed awkward in her presence, and she in theirs. In contrast to the dreary assortment of black and brown suits and ink-flecked ties surrounding her, she came to work wearing splashy colors. On this day she wore a blue dress, a pearl necklace, and high heels. She swept her hair into a tight bun. She had painted her lips and fingernails red. Maguire observed with some distaste that Miller came dressed for the society pages, not the murder beat, but he knew better than to say so.

Miller spoke up. "What is it that I'm supposed to do, Clyde? Maguire is all over this story. I know nothing about covering crime. Who does my work while I'm helping him with his?"

Stoffleman's face reddened. Maguire had known the editor long enough to recognize a slow burn. Stoffleman hated having his judgment questioned. Being addressed by his first name angered him. He gave Miller a hard stare. "You'll get out there and learn. As for fancy weddings and uptown socials, they wait until your new assignment is finished. Stick with Maguire. He'll show you the ropes."

Having delivered his curt orders, Stoffleman motioned Maguire and Miller away with his fingertips. Stoffleman never told his reporters how to find a story. Disappointing him came at a reporter's own peril.

Miller followed Maguire to the other end of the room. He looked out the window, down three stories to Main Street, busy with traffic on a typical cloudy day. She smiled, seemingly unfazed by Stoffleman's abrupt nature, while he subconsciously felt for the small bundle of love letters he kept in his pocket. He did that whenever a woman looked him in the eye. Mary's baby blues, peering at him so openly, made him nervous. "You know, Maguire, you haven't said two words to me since I came to work here. Are you one of those men who thinks girls have no place in a city room?"

It occurred to Maguire that Miller might be savvier than he first thought. He felt a little ashamed he hadn't paid her much attention. Crime and society had nothing in common. Since his youth Maguire had seen and judged Butte through what cops said and did. He never apologized for his view of the city's underbelly.

Butte, what a rough place. A mining underworld built on fortunes that came from shafts sunk deep where men coughed cruel rock dust from their lungs in small dark spaces. They were men like his father. They were the Kellys and the Townsends, for all their faults, men who found common purpose in back-breaking work. They mined miles of crosscuts off those shafts for copper, silver, gold and zinc. Those riches never would line their pockets. The Company reaped the big profits. The bosses wore expensive suits. They surveyed the Hill from their offices high in the Hennessy Block. No, they didn't dirty their hands like miners. Their wealth came from union-busting tactics. The unions fought for livable wages. They fought for safety. They fought for dignity. Underground, miners died from fires, explosions, cave-ins, falls, and fatal gases known as black damp. Above ground, they coughed their silicosis, known as miner's con, into bloody handkerchiefs. They hobbled along the streets on bent legs. Drug stores advertised running sales on crutches. Too many miners drank away their frustrations, leading to trouble uptown and at home. Butte once had hundreds of bars, sometimes three to a block. Hooch mixed with hardened men led to violence. Few people in Butte understood that better than Duke Ferndale and Red Maguire. For that matter, Lucky Finero.

Maguire looked away as Miller's eyes bore into him. Pretty women made him nervous. Stoffleman knew it and showed no restraint in his ridicule. What a shame, the editor joked, that no respectable Butte women wanted to date a red-haired Irishman. Even a handsome one. Maguire had little experience with women. He hoped to marry once but the woman he loved, Lindy Sue Morgan, broke his heart. Lindy had long legs that looked good in high heels and cinnamon hair she teased into a whirl resembling cotton candy. She worked the betting tables at the Board of Trade. On her days off she hounded Maguire to take her to the movies down the street. She wanted to see all the new releases, even if they arrived in Butte a few months behind their premiere showings. In her estimation none topped *The African Queen*. She told Maguire she wanted to marry Humphrey Bogart. He knew she would hop the next train to Hollywood if she had the jingle. She spent hours browsing the movie magazines at the bookstore. She imagined herself in the arms of every leading man who arrived on the silver screen. Lindy lacked the glamor of the best-looking girls in town, Maguire had to admit, but she wasn't half-bad either. She hated the spray of freckles over her nose that hinted of teenage summers at the lake. Those freckles gave her the illusion of youth, though, a distinction truly valued in ragtag Butte, while her enthusiasm for unfiltered cigarettes won the hearts of men who had nothing else to offer her but a match. Lindy, a hopeless flirt, drank in the attention by the gallon. Maguire recognized how Lindy's appeal to everyone in pants meant she might leave him someday. Pity it came so soon.

Lindy ran off with a clarinet player after a concert at the American Theatre. Maguire wondered where she had gone. Suspecting foul play, he told Ferndale of her sudden disappearance. The detective scratched around for dope. He soon found out what had happened. "People saw her boarding the bus with the band. She and some mug carrying a music case had their arms around each other like nobody's business. Probably breaking your heart by telling you this," Ferndale told Maguire. The detective had a rare sentimental moment. "Ain't no point in moping about her. I say good riddance. Find a good woman who deserves you." The detective put his hand on Maguire's shoulder in a gesture of compassion and walked away.

Maguire then understood. After the first of three nights the band played in Butte, Lindy had shown him an autograph inscribed on a fancy napkin. "To Lindy, with much appreciation, Sal," it read. And printed below it: "Sal Kofferman, the world's greatest clarinet player." It dawned on Maguire that if he hadn't worked late at the *Bugle*, he might have noticed Lindy's growing interest in the band, some Minneapolis outfit coincidentally named "The Love Beats," and that she scurried off to watch the final two performances on the excuse she had nothing better to do on a loveless night in Butte. The band bus headed south to Salt Lake City, the next stop on the tour, while Maguire decided to let her go. He never heard from Lindy again. Once again, his newspaper job trumped his hopeless love life.

Fighting back that memory, Maguire wondered how he should relate to the woman assigned to help him cover Butte's most sensational murder story. In his time, anyway. He leaned toward Miller. "You've been here, what, a few months?" The question sounded more condemning than he had intended.

"Are you interviewing me for a job, Maguire? I distinctly remember Stoffleman hiring me. Since January, thank you for noticing. It's been five months now and counting. You could have at least welcomed me or said good morning occasionally. Are you as socially inept around women as you appear? I sincerely hope not."

"Sorry," Maguire mumbled. Silence, what a poor way to treat a fellow reporter even if she did write pap. "Can I buy you a cup of coffee?"

Mary faked a genuine smile. "That feeble come-on never works on a lady, for the record. But yes, we should talk. A beer would be better. Surprised? Do I need to wear a pair of bib overalls to your favorite drinking hole? What is it, the M & M? The Arcade? Being a block down the street, either one is a destination of convenience, is it not?"

"You look fine," Maguire said, ignoring her sarcasm. "We have much to discuss. The M & M is a good place to talk crime." An hour later, at the bar, they got down to specifics. She lit a Winston, and then another, kissing red lipstick onto the butts with round lips. Her eyes watched him intently as he briefed her on the few details of the murder scenes not already reported in the *Bugle*. She rarely blinked. Maguire thought to himself that she would make a good interrogator. He felt his palms sweat. He cursed himself for feeling awkward around pretty dames. He blamed Ferndale for learning impressions he couldn't shake. To Ferndale, all women were dames or dolls. To Maguire, a woman brought a mystery he never unraveled. He knew his face revealed his lack of confidence. Mary looked at him expectantly. He turned his mind back to the murders. He caught himself before mentioning Ferndale's name. Maguire held back on telling Mary anything about Ferndale as his silent source. She would earn the right to know more. An illuminating story under her byline would be a good start.

"Police really don't know who's behind these killings, Red?" Mary, warming to him. He liked that she called him by his first name.

"Regrettably, no. If they have hard evidence, they're not sharing it with me."

"What of these roses? What is their significance, do you think?"

"I hope a woman who covers garden parties could help me out with that one."

Miller stiffened at his tone. "Ridicule of a girl reporter doesn't wear well on you, Red. I suppose I'm foolish to expect better from anyone in the *Bugle* city room. That said, I think asking about the roses is a fair question, probably the most important question in these murders. It's a practical matter, really, to address that question."

Maguire took a deep swallow of beer. "Sorry, I don't know the answer." He hid his nervous face behind the beer mug. Even in the dim light Mary radiated beauty. Today, everything felt out of place. Miller watched him, her brown eyes never wavering, waiting for some direction to fulfill Stoffleman's cockamamie plan to pair them up. "Maybe it would help to know more about you, Mary."

"Now you're curious? So am I, Red. Is that your real name?"

"It's Kieran, but hardly anybody knows me by that. Kids knew me by the nickname Red in Dublin Gulch. I don't suppose you can figure out why? Nowadays everybody calls me Maguire and leaves it at that."

"You're Irish, obviously. Should this surprise me in Butte? Were you one of those boys who beat up miners and stole their lunch pails as they walked to the mines? I've heard stories."

"Exaggerated, I'm sure. Mostly."

Miller blew smoke in hazy circles. "And now you want to know about me? How I came to this crazy job a million miles from Seattle? What manner of insanity would bring me to Butte? To the craven place we call the *Bugle*?"

"If you'll excuse my embarrassment at not asking you five months ago."

Miller smiled. For the first time, Maguire thought, her smile looked genuine. "As a little girl I got this big idea that I wanted to write. You know how that goes? My mother told me only men wrote the news. She made sure I wore bows and pinafores and shiny black shoes. This doesn't sound like the

Butte you know so well. I'm skeptical that you have any interest in my childhood wardrobe, for that matter, but let me go on. In Seattle we had no mines and smoke and fire and dust. The ocean air brought rain that freshened the city. Not like here in Butte where rain further darkens a drab town. My mother tried to interest me in dolls and dresses. I had different ideas. I wrote poems and kept a diary. When I was older I confronted my mother with my continuing desire to write stories for a newspaper. Mother greeted my obstinance with her bad temper. She handed me the morning *Post-Intelligencer* and defied me to find the name of a single woman reporter. Of course, there were none. I knew Mother as the protective sort. She never tolerated disagreement. She kept me from straying too far from home. She worried something bad would happen to me. She never let me go to the high school prom. I never had a date because I feared her reaction. Surprise you, Red? Yes, I had offers. Boys called me but Mother hung up. When they asked me out in school, I shook my curls and walked away. Mother held my future in her fist. I never resented her. She taught me the importance of principle. She made me safe. I suppose I left the impression of her as a tyrant. Let me explain. I am her only child. She had a plan for me, you see. After high school graduation I went to work as a telephone operator, which is what Mother did, all of us women sitting in a row at the switchboard like birds on a fence. Not like Luverne at the *Bugle*. In a city the size of Seattle the calls never stopped. Chatter on either side of me made it hard to hear over the line. My arms ached after working a shift plugging and unplugging those circuits."

"And your father?" Maguire interrupted.

"I don't know much about him. He left us to fend for ourselves. It's a long story, better left to another time." Miller paused. "Only after Mother died did I work in journalism. I started as a clerk at the *Post-Intelligencer*. After a few years I worked my way into a writing job on the society desk. I have no formal journalism training, as I'm sure you noticed, but I'm told I have the knack of gab. I also can put thoughts into words and words onto paper."

Maguire nodded. "And then you got your big break at the *Butte Bugle* of all places? The publishing voice of labor and crime in the mining city? Guess that's a weak attempt at humor. I've never seen Seattle. I suspect it's a far cry from life here on the Hill."

"In every respect. Pay is miserable in Butte, but who's counting dollars? I wanted to see Montana. Home of the happy and hardy, right? No doubt you are wondering so I'll tell you. I'm thirty-two years old. Never married despite receiving some enticing offers. Mother drilled a heavy dose of suspicion into me. I needed a change that didn't involve matrimony. When I saw the *Bugle* advertising for a society reporter, I thought, 'How bad could it be?' "

Maguire smirked. "A rhetorical question, I'm sure."

"I didn't have a clue. When I came to work at the *Bugle*, Stoffleman walked me to an empty desk. No typewriter, no paper, not even a chair. I said to him, 'Do you expect me to write stories in long hand on the wall?' That's when it became apparent to me, yes, that early in my tenure at his newspaper, that he had no sense of humor."

"You somehow impressed him, Mary. Now you have one of those electrics that clicks instead of clunks. Stoffleman refuses to hand out those typewriters to just anybody. He complains they cost a full thirty dollars more than the regular ones."

"Well, Red, you're more observant than you let on. If you think I have some favor with him you're wrong. Put yourself in my place. Suddenly you're the only man and none of the women working around you take you seriously. I had to fight for dignity in this city room. Claggett leers at me. He thinks I don't see him do it. What a creepy old cuss. Vanzetti and Ketchul, despite being in love with themselves, at least welcomed me. You ignored me. You, the best-looking man in the city room with a face chiseled from granite, failed to acknowledge an attractive woman working right beside you. It made me wonder, Maguire."

"Wonder about what?"

"If you, like the others, saw me as an intrusion. Being the only woman, well, I've frankly wondered how much longer I should stay."

"Forever, if you're anything like your predecessor. Maybe I should tell you about Cass Flanagan. She worked at the *Bugle* longer than Stoffleman at a time when nobody expected to see a woman in the city room. Cass was a crotchety old gossip. She smoked cigars and drank hard liquor at her desk. She swore like a miner when not playing nice with society mavens in pretty dresses. Not the finest writer, either. Cass wrote her stories without commas and periods. Stoffleman made sense of her mangled syntax for the morning paper. Her talent?

Hunting down facts. Relentless in her reporting of Butte's privileged class. I imagine she knew every secret ever told about the daylight crowd who never worked underground. Nobody knew where the bodies were buried in Butte better than Cass Flanagan. I mean that in a metaphorical sense, of course."

Mary smiled again. "Of course. Does crime reporting make you cynical, Red?"

"Something like that. Over the years, I've covered more violence than I can remember. I'm told my stories sometimes scare people out of town."

"Tell me one, Red."

Maguire looked to historical photographs hanging from the high walls of the M & M. One of them showed the notorious uptown bully Caleb Jackson, sneering from beneath a flop hat, a vicious man known on the street as Black Jack. He was the biggest Negro ever seen in Butte. Printing stories of his felonious exploits drained several barrels of ink at the *Bugle*. The reign of terror in Butte bars lasted five years and involved more than two hundred arrests for assault. Victims suffered smashed teeth, broken limbs, and internal bleeding from heavy body blows. When Black Jack began brawling he left no doubt about who would win. "He turned plumb mean after the second or third beer," Maguire began telling Miller. "Everyone in the joint knew it. Black Jack had shoulders and arms like mine timbers. I figured he fought for sport until I reported in the *Bugle* that he had spent time in the state mental hospital at Warm Springs. He thought everybody wanted to kill him. Black Jack, he had an ugly snoot and a temper to match the ugly voices inside his head. When he walked into a bar, picture this, he demanded a beer on the house and sat quiet as a mouse until he heard something said that riled him. It could be anything, family talk, union talk, somebody discussing the weather, you name it. Those evil voices worked Black Jack into a rage. Everyone in the bar saw it coming. Men sitting near Black Jack in the bar, whichever saloon he chose that night, moved to the far side of the room. The bartenders pulled glasses and bottles out of his reach. Everyone in uptown Butte knew that when Black Jack worked himself into a fighting mood, he would throw anything he could lay his hands on, including people."

"Is that man as big as he looks?" Mary asked, her wide eyes locked on the photograph.

"Was," Maguire continued. "It's a relief to everyone who walks these streets that Black Jack is dead. Let me tell you about that in a moment. Soon after Peter Sullivan got run over by that ore car, the cops began telling me tales about Black Jack. A colorful figure all right, but Butte had a lot of them, like Shoestring Annie and the top half of that guy who rolled up and down Broadway on a board with wheels, so I didn't pay much attention at first."

"Shoestring Annie?"

"She sold laces next to the pay office and cussed out miners until they bought from her. Charlie the Cat, Black Jack, the list of characters in this town would unroll halfway down Montana Avenue."

"Charlie the Cat?"

"Some other time, Mary. So, because Black Jack didn't run around killing people, although he came close, I didn't write about his exploits in the *Bugle*."

"Until?" Mary arched her eyebrows.

"Until Black Jack put five miners in the hospital when a fisticuffs broke out in a neighborhood bar. Five. I wrote a story. Then I wrote more stories when he built a reputation for breaking heads. Dangerous enough that when trouble broke out it took four or five coppers to stuff Black Jack into a prowl car to haul him to the slammer. My stories got noticed, all right. Black Jack became Butte's boogeyman. People who never drank in bars thought he would show up in their living rooms and lay waste to their families. We sold papers on the street corners like mad. Stoffleman jumped around like a little kid seeing Santa Claus at Christmas. He wanted me to capture every sorry detail from every fight, dress my stories up with the most drama I could muster, so he could splash them big on the *Bugle* front page. Except."

"Except?" Mary asked, enthralled.

"Except I hadn't taken into account that mean Black Jack wouldn't approve of my portrayals of him. Sooner or later we would cross paths."

"How bad, Red?"

"One night when I walked home to the Logan Hotel after dark, two minutes away, we met on the sidewalk. He stood there waiting for me. Black Jack growled like a bear. A low growl that uncurled my curly hair. Just me all by my lonesome with the brute. He never said a word. Just the growl and then he jumped at me. Worst fight I ever had. Black Jack could lift the front end of a mine truck. Most of the men he hurt so bad tried to wrestle him. I suppose they were holding on for dear life. That's when he took the fists to them. He prefers to club a man's ribs the way a hammer pounds on tin. He threw me against a brick building. The force felt like it came from three blocks yonder. Then he rang my bell with a vicious punch. I almost blacked out. I fought to keep my head because I knew he wanted to grab me to start those body blows. Either that or knock me to the sidewalk and start kicking."

"Red, you're scaring me. How did you get out of it?"

"He gave me an opening when he dropped his hands to grab me. I hit him two or three times in the face, whacked a shoe into his kneecap, and ran. He stood there limping and cursing. He threatened to find me again, of course, but Black Jack had a long dance card. He threatened everybody he attacked. Duke Ferndale gave me a gun, a .38 Special. Not long afterwards, Black Jack died resisting arrest. In the melee, a cop punched him in the throat, crushing his windpipe." Maguire decided not to tell Mary the cop was Ferndale.

"I shouldn't have asked," she said. "Beatings sicken me."

"It's said that when the miners buried Black Jack they sunk his grave a hundred feet deep so he couldn't climb out. Typical Butte tall tale but I drowned it in ink because that's what we do in this city. People worried they didn't bury the rascal deep enough. Then came public reaction. Some of the do-gooders in Butte turned on the *Bugle*. They said my stories had elevated Black Jack to a hero of sorts and spread fear among the law-abiding folk. Letters to the editor kept coming for a month. Stoffleman stuck to his belief that controversy sells newspapers. 'Don't shoot the messenger!' I heard him tell people over the phone."

Mary managed a smile. "I'll remember that one."

"Here's another treasure of wisdom from Stoffleman if you haven't heard it already. 'A newspaper's greatest sin is boredom.' As Black Jack demonstrated, and now the Purple Rose Murders, there's no boredom in Butte."

Mary brushed her hair from eyes to look at Maguire with renewed interest. "Red Maguire the legend. Red Maguire, voice of mystery. No danger of running out of crime stories anytime soon. Given all your bylines in the *Butte Bugle* I must assume you feel comfort at knowing that."

"They say life is cheap in Butte. I've never seen any reason to doubt it."

"Who says that, Red?"

"Pretty much everybody who deals with the bodies. There are two views of Butte and I dwell in the dark one. I don't expect the Chamber of Commerce to invite me over for happy talk."

"Why did you choose this depressing line of work?"

"It's not all work. I fell in love once," he blurted out. Maguire reddened at revealing such a private thought. More so, in telling Mary, someone he hardly knew. Why he had brought up love while talking about Black Jack and a chain of murders, he didn't know, but with Mary he found himself on unfamiliar ground.

"Are you embarrassed, Red? To show something of yourself? Your face tells me you wish you could put the genie back in the bottle. Are you a lonely news reporter like every other lonely news reporter, looking for love in all the wrong places?"

He hung his head. "Never mind, Mary. I don't know why I said that."

"I think I do," she replied.

"Then you know more about love than me."

A cool September breeze swept through the open doors at the M & M. Autumn knocked at Butte's door. Miller reached for her sweater. Maguire, halfway drunk, observed she had sipped hardly any of her only glass of beer. He had little experience drinking with women. Ferndale and other Butte cops, his usual companions, spilled beer as fast as they talked. They drank in great gulps and left puddles on the floor.

"What now, Red? I've never seen the inside of a police department." Mary suddenly seemed all business again.

"No time like the present," Maguire said, welcoming the distraction from his failed romances. He finished his beer in a mighty swallow and stood. He felt unsteady on his feet.

"And the beer, won't they ...?"

"Naw, to these cops a belly full of beer is a badge of honor."

Maguire took Miller over to the jail, walking slower than usual to make it last, while she paraded beside him in her high heels. Mary improved the scenery on the gray street. A few drivers honked. A man in a wheelchair, his legs and one ear missing, whistled approvingly as he rolled past. At the jail, cops stared at her up and down, hardly concealing their interest. How rare for a sober woman in a bright dress, on the right side of the law, to find her way into the police department. Miller looked even more out of place there than she did in the *Bugle* city room.

The sergeant on duty, never taking his eyes off Miller from beneath a gray crew cut, pushed a stack of desk reports across the counter to Maguire. "Make a citizen's arrest, did you, Red?"

"Funny, Bobby. Load of laughs. This is Mary Miller, my colleague at the *Bugle*, who's helping me."

"Somebody oughta," Bobby said, nodding a greeting to Miller. "Check out the overnights. Those micks we got working graveyard tripped over something that might put a bug up your ass."

Maguire thumbed through the pages. He read the usual fare of bar fights, drunk drivers, car accidents and domestic arguments. One resident, in the dead of night, reported dresses stolen off a clothesline. Another summoned police when a man fell on a whiskey bottle. He bled all over the sidewalk from the cuts to his face. Hardly news in Butte. A few pages later, Maguire found the entry Bobby wanted him to see.

Jimmy Regan, patrolling the upper west side near Big Butte, had responded to a complaint about an abandoned sedan sticking halfway out of a ramshackle garage. It blocked an alley. Long and gray, scraped on the passenger side where it hit the garage, suspicious for sure. Regan flashed light on the floorboards. He saw the axe. He saw the blood. The old Irish cop knew every square inch of the Hill. Someone had stashed the hidden car a mile from the Vanzetti murder scene at the Orphan Girl.

Maguire flinched when he read Regan's report. He suspected Ferndale knew about it already. If Maguire hadn't spent the morning wagging tongues with Miller at the M & M, he might already have had the scoop. Surely Ferndale had called his phone at the *Bugle* as soon as he saw Regan's report. Maguire remembered Miller standing behind him, trying to read the cryptic handwriting over his shoulder.

"What is it, Red? Anything of significance?"

"Nothing, apparently," Maguire lied. He had to see Ferndale, in private. Maguire wouldn't pry details out of Ferndale with Miller present. The detective knew better than to give himself away in front of a stranger.

"Do you think this place has a ladies' room?" Miller asked.

Bobby, hating to see her go, pointed down the hall. "On the right, miss. Hopefully nobody puked in there last night. Or had sex." Miller reddened just a bit.

"Ignore him, Mary. It's what passes for humor around here." They both watched her walk down the hall.

"Got a sway, don't she?" Bobby said.

"I wouldn't know," Maguire replied, but noticing all the same. "Ferndale in?"

"Sure as hell. Meeting with the chief. Big confab behind a closed door. Anything I should tell him?"

"That he should call me right away. At the *Bugle*."

Minutes later, Maguire and Miller walked three blocks back to the city room. She stepped around cracks in the sidewalk, keeping her heels on even ground. Maguire struggled with how he would put her to work on this story. She had smarts, he could see that, but what then?

"Red, you found something, didn't you?"

"Something I need to check out on my own. Through my sources. Maybe it's significant, maybe not."

"You're not going to tell me?"

"When I know what's going on, yes."

"Meanwhile I sit at my desk with nothing to do? While Red Maguire, crime reporter, does his valuable work?"

"We know little about the murder of David Fenton. You read my story, right?"

"Should I determine your lack of respect as a lack of faith in me? I read all your stories. Do you read mine?"

Maguire ignored her bait. "So here's where you can help. Find out as much about Fenton as you can. Talk to neighbors, people he sold houses to, anybody who knew him at Rotary or Lions or whatever civic club he belonged to. Reporters and police chase down leads in many of the same ways. Unless people are asked point blank, they usually withhold information about crimes. Reporters sometimes are better than police at asking those questions."

"Except we don't show up at their doors with a badge and gun."

"With no authority and nothing to protect us, Miller."

"Call me Mary. I'm not one of your bar buddies."

"Mary, will you please chase the Fenton story? See what you can shake out for his background?"

"Glad to, Red. And will you please let me know what Ferndale says about that axe found in the abandoned car last night? Intriguing find, don't you think?"

Maguire stopped abruptly outside the *Bugle* offices. "What? You ...?"

"Red, you should never underestimate a girl reporter. In fact, I think you've just now learned I can read."

Minutes later, in the *Bugle* city room, Maguire overheard Miller on the phone chatting up somebody about David Fenton. "Thank you, Mrs. Hill, I'm delighted you liked my story. ... Yes, we do need more stories about the importance of volunteer activities in Butte. ... I agree, yes, you and the other ladies in the Benevolence Club have done so much good for the city. ... I'll get to that story, Mrs. Hill, but I have a temporary new assignment. ... Yes, you've heard of the Purple Rose Murders? ... Horrible. Yes, I know. ... Why do I want to dirty my hands with a story like that? ... We do what our bosses tell us, don't we? ... Yes, I'll let you know when I'm back covering society events. ... Yes, they are important to Butte. ... Yes, Mrs. Hill, but can you help me? I'm wondering if you knew one of the murder victims, David Fenton? ... There is nothing to fear, Mrs. Hill. I'm calling several people today to find out more about him. ... I understand, Mrs. Hill. ... You don't want to be quoted? ... I know, Mrs. Hill. People are scared all over Butte. ... Can you tell me anything about Mr. Fenton without being quoted? ... I mean I won't disclose your name, Mrs. Hill. ... He gave money away? You mean, donated it? ... And had a good reputation, you say? ... You don't see how he could be involved in a crime? ... Terrible murder, I agree. ... Yes, what a tragic death, Mrs. Hill. ... He never got into trouble as far as you know?"

Maguire listened with some satisfaction. Miller would find out fast the difficulty of peeling information about a murder from everyday citizens. Too many people fear retaliation if quoted in the newspaper. Good people often refuse to talk to cops. They're afraid of being stalked by a killer on the loose. Maguire understood their fear. Vanzetti's murder happened close and threatening. Was Maguire next? Regrettably, Miller?

Maguire's telephone rang. Ferndale had news.

~ 8 ~

Ferndale throws punches

"We think it's the same car that tried to run you down," Ferndale said. "Can't prove it. Go up to the impound lot and take a look. We're sending the axe to the crime lab. No conclusive proof it's the weapon used to chop up Vanzetti, but we found fresh blood on the blade. The chief had a look. He agreed it ain't a pretty picture."

Maguire turned away from Miller, still talking on the phone fifteen feet away. He dropped his voice to a near-whisper. "You think the killer drove that old sedan forty miles to Deer Lodge, tried to flatten me, then drove it back to Butte to halfway hide it a few blocks from the Vanzetti murder scene? With a bloody axe conveniently left on the floorboard? It's like the killer is handing us a clue we would trip over." He could hear Ferndale exhaling with some exasperation.

"Too damn easy, ain't it? Jimmy Regan came off shift after finding that car and said he felt like somebody played us for fools. Either that or the killer is dumb as a brick."

"Regan? The same cop standing over Vanzetti's body?"

"If you're thinking we ought to look at Jimmy in this ugly mess, forget it. No more reliable cop in Butte even if he is a mick. He went on break, drinking coffee at Wilma's Cafe, when Vanzetti lost his head. Timing confirmed. No, not Jimmy."

"I figured at this point you consider everybody a suspect."

"Especially you, Maguire. Damn micks. You and Jimmy. Got 'em everywhere in this town. What is it with Butte and the Irish?"

They hung up. Maguire drove over to the city impound lot for a look. The gray sedan stood out in the jungle of cars. The long scrape from the garage ran from the right front fender to halfway across the rear passenger door. He could tell at a glance that the sedan resembled the one that nearly hit him. Survival trumps observation when a car barrels toward a person at high speed. Mud covered the license plates. He scraped it away to reveal the "1" that showed they were issued in Butte. He tried opening the doors. They were locked. He peered through the dirty windows, cupping his eyes from the sun's glare. He saw a dark patch on the floorboard. A blood stain? An item on the back seat caught his eye. The *Bugle,* neatly folded to a story on the front page. Maguire recognized his bylined story about the Fenton murder even through the grime on the windows.

He looked around. He had a feeling of being watched. Years earlier, police had given him a key to the gate, tired of his frequent requests to examine cars implicated in crimes. "Keep your mitts off anything that looks like evidence," Ferndale had warned him. Now, Maguire felt a chill. Call it experience, or intuition, or high mountain air. He looked at the blocky brick buildings surrounding him. Anybody could be watching from dozens of second- and third-story windows.

Many of them opened to abandoned rooms, ghostly quarters once occupied by Butte's working stiffs when a couple hundred mines hoisted tons of ore, every few minutes, around the clock. Maguire had seen the decline in underground mining since he and Sean had moved to Butte in 1923. By the Fifties some of the big mines had ceased their operations when rich veins petered out. Butte didn't seem a city knocked to its knees, not by a long shot, but talk of surface mining had people worried. Shutting underground mines meant fewer jobs. Maguire felt desperation in the air. He had seen it before in labor strikes and Company shutdowns. Crime went up when jobs went away. Maguire, as much as Duke Ferndale, could feel the stares of suspicion up and down the streets. A killer ran loose somewhere in the city.

Maguire remembered being scared a half dozen times in his newspaper career. Two weeks after Black Jack's attack a man took a vicious swing at Maguire with a knife outside the *Bugle* office. Maguire ducked just in time as the cold blade whipped past him and slammed into the stone cornice entryway. The man cried out in pain, cradling his hand, as Maguire seized the fallen knife. "I'll kill you!" the attacker yelled at Maguire before retreating up the street. "Do a better job of it next time!" Maguire yelled after him. Maguire had seen the man in court a day earlier on charges of beating up his neighbor. Maguire's story reported what happened in court, word for word, but the public humiliation of being exposed in the *Bugle* riled the criminal. Too many perps blamed reporters for writing stories about their crimes more than they blamed themselves for committing them. That was newspapering. Maguire wondered whether, unsuspectingly, he had named the Purple Rose Killer in a previous story. Someone convicted of burglary, robbery or another felony, now killing people left and right? Maguire had printed names and crimes of hundreds, no doubt thousands, of assailants and miscreants over the years. Was one of them the killer? Was the killer watching him?

"You're imagining things, Maguire," he whispered as he locked the gate to the impound lot. He tried to reassure himself that he wouldn't wind up like Vanzetti. Surely the gray sedan behind the fence meant nothing but a coincidence. The headlines told it all. Five people dead and little to show for evidence.

Maguire, a good news reporter, sometimes wondered if he was good enough. It was gospel in city rooms that a reporter ranked only as good as tomorrow's story. Editors like Stoffleman had no patience for reporters resting on their laurels. Maguire needed to lead police on the murder investigation. Uncover clues. Expose a possible motive. Isn't that what Ferndale asked him to do? He scoffed at his reputation as a muckraking journalist. "Muck what?" Ferndale had asked him. "Mick is what I thought you were," he said, laughing. Ferndale got a kick out of mocking Maguire's Irish heritage. Ferndale bragged of his Scottish father who settled in Ohio to work the steel mills. Maguire told him that the name Ferndale sounded like a rest home where old people sat on bed pans. He came close to taking a fist to the face from the old detective.

Nobody felt comfortable sassing Duke Ferndale. Even with his boxing glory days behind him, his reputation as a fighter lingered. His legendary fast hands made for big stories told on bar stools. Maguire first saw Ferndale box in an outdoor fight at the Steward Mine. The clattering gallows frame loomed near a ring the union had built. On that summer night, dark and hot, mosquitoes swarmed around the yellow lights and men pressed close for a good look.

Drawn to the excitement, Red Maguire and three other boys from Dublin Gulch slipped through the weeds near the hoist house to evade the burly man taking tickets. They lacked fifty cents apiece to pay for admission at the gate anyway. Red pressed through the crowd of noisy men calling for blood. He reckoned that everyone in Butte knew Duke Ferndale. When Duke wasn't boxing, he roamed the Hill in a prowl car for the police department. On either account, Red had heard, few people messed with Ferndale. The ones who did paid for it. On this hot night, Ferndale would box the final bout, the light heavyweight fight. Even to Maguire's amateur eye, Ferndale's opponent, a mug from Anaconda, weighed considerably more. Ferndale ignored the bearded beast across the ring from him. The Butte cop swung his long arms to loosen his biceps. He turned his narrow eyes to the crowd a time or two with passing interest. The men, mostly rough miners, cheered when their champ acknowledged them. He was, after all, Butte's finest.

Red heard that Ferndale would fight a smelterman, a brawler named Kardanovich, who stoked fires hotter than the deepest regions of Hell. Red wondered whether an ore car had flattened the man's face. To young boys he looked vicious. Even tough Irish boys from the gulch. The man stood a few inches shorter than Ferndale but stouter. He stripped off his shirt to expose a grand belly that draped over his pants like an oversized laundry bag. Both men wore black boxing gloves. Ferndale, unimpressed at the mug staring him down, waited with some nonchalance for the fight to begin. The whistle blew. He stalked into the center of the ring with his gloves up. Kardanovich opened with a violent haymaker that missed Ferndale's head by a mile. Nimbler than he appeared at first, he followed with a smacking body blow that caught Ferndale in the ribs and knocked him backwards. The crowd roared its disapproval. When Kardanovich came again, his gloves bobbing to protect his face, Ferndale flicked a right jab between them. The punch came fast and unforgiving and caught Kardanovich square on the mouth. His head snapped back. His lips sprayed blood. Ferndale kept his potent left punch in reserve as he peppered Kardanovich twice and three times with his right jab. Finally, when Kardanovich lowered his right glove a few inches to block another blow, Ferndale's left shot out like a piston, straight and true.

Maguire read all about it in the *Bugle* the next day. If he hadn't seen it with his own eyes, he wouldn't have believed what came next. Kardanovich crashed to the canvas like he was dead. Being a fighter accustomed to rolling off beer-drenched barroom floors for another exchange of fists, he rolled and belched blood and staggered to his feet. He swung wildly at Ferndale as the mob around the ring yelled mock advice. "Try to hit 'im next time, ya lazy bum!" screamed a shadow-boxing miner standing next to Maguire. The fight got ugly fast. Ferndale, his fists flashing, knocked Kardanovich down three more times. The Anaconda man failed to match Ferndale's speed and finesse. Finally, as two men dragged Kardanovich's prone body away, another man pushed into the ring who had no business being there. This man, a Negro dark as an unlighted stope, stood a head taller than Ferndale and wore bib coveralls and a slouch hat. He clenched and unclenched his fists to reveal great pools of pink skin in his palms. The ring referee, a slender miner, quaked at the man's hulking dark presence and backed away. Ferndale saw the attack a second before the brute unloaded a furious swing. Ferndale ducked the blow and drove an uppercut into the man's kidneys that lifted him to his toes. He nailed the man twice in the face with his right and smacked him with a hard left cross to the jaw. Roaring in pain, his nose running red, the enraged brute charged Ferndale. Red watched as the Negro lifted the smaller Ferndale above his head. Ferndale clawed at the air before the brute threw him.

Someone jostled Red from behind. Suddenly men all around him began cursing and fighting. Some of the Dublin Gulch boys joined in the brawl by punching anybody they could reach. Before a sea of colliding bodies knocked Red to the ground, he caught a glimpse of Ferndale somehow back on his feet, decking the big Negro with a merciless flurry of angry punches. The *Bugle* the next morning put it this way:

Butte boxer KOs lineup of sore Anaconda losers
Smelter boys take licking in fight night brawl
Dozens hurt but biggest injury
was Smelter City pride

The Negro, the *Bugle* reported, worked alongside Kardanovich at the Smelter. After the Negro fell lights out, two more Anaconda men rushed into the ring to meet the same fate from Ferndale's flying fists. Soon he had plenty of help from furious Butte miners. The *Bugle* sports desk reported that Ferndale knocked out two men after the Negro broke two of his ribs. A photograph in the *Bugle* under the headline, "**Boxing cop wins four straight**," showed him thrusting his ugly mug and left fist toward the camera. Maguire never forgot that night. Years later, when he became acquainted with a balding Ferndale, he admitted to the detective that he had witnessed the fight. "Should have slapped the cuffs on you right then and there," Ferndale responded.

"What for?" Maguire said.

"For not climbing into the ring to give me a hand with Black Jack, that's what."

"Me, a punk teenager? I didn't know his name back then, before he moved to Butte, but he scared me plenty."

"He got worse after he started working the mines. They say he had the strength of three horses. Yeah, when stepped into the ring that night I thought a cloud came over the moon. Shoulda seen that man up close. Barely rocked him with my best punch. Want to see?" Ferndale asked, feinting with his left. Maguire never knew when Ferndale kidded. Best not to press the point.

On his walk back to the *Bugle*, Maguire encountered Charlie the Cat. Charlie harbored stray black cats in an upstairs room he occupied in the vacant Butler Block. He hated grays, whites and calicos. He associated black cats with good luck. Heat thousands of feet below daylight at the Belmont mine had cooked Charlie's mind. He wheezed and gasped in the close dark drifts, his clothes soaked with sweat, as he shoveled rock. Sometimes the walls caught fire when miners broke away the rock, exposing sulfide ore to oxygen. In the final two years of his working life, Charlie came to the Belmont cradling his lunch bucket under one arm and a black cat under the other. Shift after shift, he never boarded the chippy hoist without one. When a cat died in the intense heat or got flattened under the wheels of an ore car, Charlie prowled uptown streets at night until he found another. At first his fellow miners objected to cats nosing around their lunch pails. Soon, nobody noticed anymore. Charlie the Cat became yet another Butte legend.

"Charlie, what do you know today?" Maguire inquired, tipping his gray fedora to the shriveled man. Charlie lifted a black cat to show Maguire he was on the job. "Two bits of jingle helps me think better," Charlie muttered. Maguire took note of his appearance. Red nose mapped with purple lines. Bib overalls, soiled and nothing more than rags. Fingers blackened from scratching around garbage cans. Hair, long gone gray, remaining blades of it fluttering in the wind. Right leg bent outward from a mine injury. Black cat, the latest capture, trying to escape Charlie's relentless grip.

Maguire reached into his pocket for a quarter. Charlie reached out and grabbed it. "We got us a problem, Red."

"What's that, Charlie?"

"Them calicos workin' overtime to chase the black ones out of Butte. These days hard to find a black willing to work a shift underground. Scared and running, that's what. Wait! Hear the whistle at the Belmont? Late for work, that's what, chippy hoist loading the day shift. Gotta go, Red, gotta go."

Charlie scurried off, but in the opposite direction from the Belmont. Maguire called after him, "Heard anything about these murders?" but Charlie ignored the question and limped away with his black cat, off on some imaginary quest to mine rock.

Up in the *Bugle* city room, Maguire found Stoffleman smoking a cigar and rubbing his temples. Blue smoke hung around his scarred cheek. "Worst headache I've had since forever, Maguire. Boss called down from the fourth floor. Said he had good news and bad news. You know how publishers run around like their underwear cuts into their manhood. Praised your stories about the murders, then complained about advertisers telling him your stories are bad for business. One car dealer threatened to pull his advertising out of the *Bugle* and another did it. People aren't buying cars because they're afraid the killer is looking for more victims. Figure that. Some damn cause and effect that only a salesman would understand, I guess."

"Hardly an unfounded fear," Maguire said.

"I conceded that to the old man upstairs but I reminded him that covering the news isn't the problem. No point in kicking the messenger. He gets that, but he did make a request."

Maguire squinted. "I think I feel a headache coming on myself, boss."

"Save it, will you? One of the advertisers told him about a rumor of David Fenton being involved in a suspicious business deal many years ago. The old man played it cagey, declined to tell me who made this observation, but said get on it."

Maguire thought of Miller. She might be a society reporter, yes, but she had some salt working the crime beat. He admitted that much. "Miller went to check into Fenton this morning. Did she tell you?" Maguire hadn't seen her since.

"She hurried out of here, said only that she planned to talk to some people," Stoffleman said. "She's not shy about talking up sources, I'll give her that. Maybe she'll come back with some of what the old man wants. As for you, Maguire, I have something more specific in mind." He shuffled some papers on his desk. "A note I made when talking to the old man." He handed it to Maguire.

"Source publisher can't reveal says Vanzetti knew something," it read.

"Get on it, Maguire. If it turns into a story we'll give Vanzetti a shared byline as a parting gift."

~ 9 ~

Flirting with romance

Everyone agreed that Antonio Vanzetti looked reasonably intact in the casket with his head restored to his body. A high collar covered the mortician's stitches. Stoffleman placed a stack of bylined clippings in Vanzetti's pale folded hands as a tribute to the fallen newsman. "Damn fine reporter. He wrote several thousand stories to prove it," Stoffleman whispered to Maguire. "Never had a day of trouble from him when sober. Better than I can say for the rest of you." Stoffleman wiped a tear and shuffled away in his rumpled suit. Maguire noted how the editor danced around Vanzetti's torrid love affair with liquor. Death brings forgiveness.

Maguire and five other men, all reporters and editors from the *Bugle*, carried Vanzetti to his grave in a soaking rain. Bachelor, a respectable man for the most part, come and gone in his fifty-two years without having revealed his personal matters to anyone who worked with him. A small crowd of mourners stood huddled under black umbrellas. Ferndale stood there, too, water shedding off his bald head. Burying a murder victim without knowing his killer amounted to a sorry affair for any cop.

Mary Miller and a few other volunteers stayed in the city room in the Hirbour Block during Vanzetti's funeral in case news broke. Menacing heavy clouds lingered over Butte. The tall windows did little to brighten the darkened room. Nobody had touched Vanzetti's desk. His phone rang twice during his funeral. Not everybody, apparently, knew of his murder. Meanwhile, Miller reviewed notes she had made about David Fenton. A big shot, all right, bigger than she had suspected. He reportedly had a financial empire worth a million dollars. People knew him but mostly by reputation. He kept a low profile. He rarely mixed with the benefactor types Miller encountered again and again in her coverage of Butte's high society. What her sources knew of Fenton came from gossip, she could tell, rather than from knowing him. Miller lit a cigarette and turned to the window. She really ought to stop smoking. Not that any of the men in the city room would notice one way or the other. Rain fell far over the Flats, all the way south to Pipestone Pass. The gloomy day reminded her of Seattle.

Maguire, meanwhile, went home to change into dry clothes. He wondered what Vanzetti had known about the murders. Why didn't Vanzetti tell him? Was Vanzetti planning to scoop Maguire on his own story? That didn't seem like Vanzetti's style. Everyone working in the city room understood that any reporter who landed a hot story, whatever the issue, stuck with it. Vanzetti wasn't the gunslinging type who stole other reporters' stories. What did it mean that Vanzetti had caught "on to something," a vague and practically useless tip? Maguire decided he had better take another look at Vanzetti's final stories about City Hall. Maguire settled into his worn recliner in the room he called home. He clicked on a lamp and began reading. City officials had held meetings to discuss whether land transactions were being properly documented in the public record. Talk of open pit mining on Butte Hill would mean changes to the landscape. The city struggled to keep pace with the fast buying and selling of land. Permits lacked enough detail to reveal problems with water and sewer and disputed ownerships. City leaders accurately recognized the situation as ripe for corruption. Maguire marveled at Vanzetti's skill in exposing lapses in Butte's ability to maintain control.

Maguire pulled Vanzetti's fifth and final story from a stack of *Bugles* on the end table. Unlike the others, this story delved into the checkered history of land transactions in Butte. Mismanagement started long before Vanzetti came on the scene. In an apparent nod to the city's mining heritage, people bought up tracts of land with vague records of buyers and sellers. Vanzetti quoted several sources, including a historian, who told about Butte being built on corruption in property exchanges, dating to the Copper Kings. "Which would surprise no one," Maguire said to himself. When he read further into the story, he lurched out of his chair. There, near the end, Vanzetti had quoted a real estate developer. "People who have money and invest it responsibly shouldn't have to make excuses to the city," the developer said. Not just any developer but David Fenton, interviewed by Vanzetti a day or two before both men were shot and killed. Maguire looked at the story in disbelief. Was it only coincidence both men turned up dead?

Maguire dialed Stoffleman at the *Bugle*. The editor would be back in form, having restored his funeral suit to the closet to await another death. He would be barking orders to reporters from beneath his green eye shade. Stoffleman often said, "The *Bugle* owns this town," meaning it led news coverage. He wouldn't settle for less. Stoffleman's phone rang three times before he picked up. When Maguire explained what he found, Stoffleman whistled. "I should have caught that Fenton reference. I agree, that's significant," Stoffleman said, sounding uncharacteristically apologetic. He quickly recovered to his usual crabby self. "Well, Maguire, what in hell are you doing about it?" Then he hung up. The rain had stopped. Maguire jumped over puddles of muddy water. He turned his Pontiac toward City Hall where Vanzetti had spent most of his days prowling the halls for news. Maguire lacked patience for learning the ways of public policy. Too many men in white shirts sat behind tables for hours on end to debate mundane topics such as sewers and potholes. Maybe he could learn a thing or two by looking at the city's land records. If Vanzetti had found something, the secret he took to his grave might be hiding there.

Later that afternoon, when Maguire returned to the *Bugle*, he found Mary Miller crying in the hallway. She wiped tears with a lipstick-smudged tissue. "Stoffleman jumped all over me, Red. He acted crazy. The way he talked to me felt so, well, damn unprofessional."

"Did he tell you why?"

"He knows I'm looking into Fenton. He thinks I should have a story ready for tomorrow's paper about the guy and his background. I reminded him that it's been two days since he put me on the police beat. Then he really got angry. He told me you found a connection between Fenton and Vanzetti and said if I paid more attention, I would have found it first."

"I'm sorry I didn't tell you right away. Seems to me Stoffleman is more shaken over Vanzetti than he let on. Do you think? How regrettable that he took out his frustration on you."

"It hurts, you know? I didn't ask for this." Miller wiped her tears one more time. The tissue left a red streak on her cheek. Maguire fought the impulse to reach out and smudge it away. He had to admit he found Mary pretty. He felt silly for ignoring her for so long. He wondered if she had a secret boyfriend she wouldn't admit. Since Lindy left town, Maguire had dated women now and then, but he never found anyone much interested in hearing about dead bodies and other morbid details from the crime beat. "Good luck finding a woman who puts up with that crap," Ferndale had told him. Women quickly tired of being married to cops. Newsmen too, Maguire presumed. The newspaper life discouraged love. *Bugle* journalists worked long and often unpredictable hours that, as Stoffleman had warned Maguire years earlier, left no time for a love life. Maguire knew Claggett and a few other *Bugle* reporters over the years paid for sex in the parlor houses down on Mercury Street. Maguire had never gone there except in search of a story. True romance never lasted. Sometimes he thought, vaguely, of the fair-haired girl he lost to the clarinet player. Lindy probably married that mug. No doubt she became a mother. What she once spent on movies now went to diapers and dance lessons. Maybe it worked out for the best. Maguire fit well into the sad collection of loveless men around him. He wondered whether Mary Miller had a real life outside the city room. Somebody should.

They walked to the M & M. Mary managed a smile. "I shouldn't become a regular in this place, Red. People will talk."

Maguire laughed. "You're getting your confidence back. It suits you."

"I'm sorry you found me crying. Stoffleman came at me so hard. What makes him throw dirt at a person like that? Does he hate the people who work for him?"

"If it helps, you're hardly the first. He's not much for playing patty cake. Once you start turning up some news on these murders, he will defend you to the world, you can bet on it. He knows no other way. Did you know he fought against the Krauts in the second big war? Took a break from newspapering in Butte to join the infantry. Forget asking him for details. He's a mystery to the rest of us. Anything outside the city room he considers nobody's business but his own."

"You mean he lost his civility in Europe? Is that it?" Mary's voice suddenly had a harder edge. Whatever weakness Stoffleman had exposed in her disappeared.

They took chairs at a table in the corner. Miller looked around. She leaned her head toward Maguire, keeping her voice low. "Did you find a paper trail on Fenton at City Hall?"

Maguire tilted toward her also, more intimately than he intended, his hand resting on the table near hers. "Land records go way back but they're poorly organized and incomplete. I'm betting some were falsified. I found the Fenton name on a handful of building permits for a housing development he owned on the Flats. Nothing jumped out at me. Standard stuff about lot sizes and streets and utilities and so forth. What isn't clear to me is why Vanzetti quoted Fenton in the context he did. Was it random, you know, needing a quote from any random real estate chump he could find and he settled on Fenton? Or did Vanzetti go to Fenton because he knew something about him the rest of the world didn't?"

Miller looked perplexed. "That's the end of it, then? We'll never know the answer?"

"Undetermined," Maguire said. "I looked through the records in the filing cabinets in the land office. The more recent ones. Tons more are stored in the basement. The clerk said Vanzetti spent some time down there sifting through boxes. I'll go digging tomorrow. What about you?"

Miller ran him through what she had learned about Fenton, mostly anecdotal. Nobody knew how he had come to own so much land.

"You've got some of these sources on the record, by name?" Maguire asked.

"Some on record, others on background. The snooty upper crust citizens in Butte hardly care to get their reputations tarnished with dirty police business. Know what I mean? These are people who trade money for good causes. The word 'murder' scares them and when you multiply times four ..."

"Five, counting the one in Deer Lodge …"

"… most people think if they're quoted in the newspaper they'll walk around with a target on their backs."

"A fear that's stood in time as long as we've had murders," Maguire said.

Mary showed no trace of the tears he had seen moments earlier. She pushed her hair back with long fingers, nails painted red, before touching a match to a new cigarette. She watched Maguire like she wanted to figure him out. Good luck, he thought. Lindy failed at it. Like Maguire's mother, Lindy showed no interest in knowing anything more about him than what she saw on the surface. He knew people thought him aloof and possibly mysterious. Maybe it was better that way. He unveiled the misdeeds of strangers in columns of ink but hid the indecisive and troubled side of himself. Maguire sensed Miller already knew that about him. She observed more of his hesitations than he had realized. Red Maguire had fought his way to manhood in Butte. It had been thirty-one years since he and his father left Chicago. All that time, spent entirely in Butte, taught him that the city wasn't built for vulnerable people. Tough men, working the mines, and their sturdy women. Complainers and whiners, although the city had its share, came and went. In Butte, people survived. In Butte, they hid their secrets deep inside themselves much like miners slipping metaphorically into the inky underground. What irony, Maguire thought.

"Red, I'm wondering."

"About anything in particular?"

"Sarcasm doesn't look good on you, Maguire. In particular ...," she paused for dramatic emphasis, "... why you spent your entire adult life writing about the bad things people do to one another. How can you wake up in the morning to see any good in the world? What's the point?"

Maguire fell silent to ponder Miller's question. Working the crime beat at the *Bugle* paid his modest bills, all right, but he could have asked Stoffleman if he could write sports, or become an editor who rode the desk at night writing headlines, or even go to Helena to cover lawmaking at the State Legislature. Somehow, he plunged into Butte's churning undercurrent of crime and never swam out.

"It suits me, Mary. I don't know why. Once I got started I couldn't stop."

Miller winked at him. "Such superficiality doesn't tell me anything about you. Don't care to share much with the new girl in the city room, is that it? The famous Red Maguire, above idle chat and intent on tomorrow's crime story? You're hurting, Red. I know it and you know it. Hell, I'll bet everyone in this dirty belching town knows it."

Maguire patted the small bundle of letters in his pocket with a big hand stretched over the jacket of his suit. Knowing they were there, faithful to his touch, gave him comfort. If Mary only knew.

"Let's get back to the Purple Rose Murders, shall we?"

"Back to business, Red? Do you ever relent? So, what comes next?"

"Well, Mary Miller, honorary *Bugle* crime reporter, I think we pool our reporting for tomorrow's paper. Do you want to break the news to Stoffleman that we're writing our first joint bylined story?"

"He'll find some reason to be mad about it."

"You can bet Stoffleman will quit chewing on you. Nothing makes his world go around better than printing yet another story on a big case."

"Know what bothers me, Red? That somebody else will die before police solve this case."

"Then we'll work harder at helping them, won't we?"

Mary stared at him. Her direct manner unsettled him. Her dark eyes, deep pools of inquiry in the low light inside the M & M, never blinked. She could persuade anyone to tell her anything. Mary, a woman of persistence, threw out another question.

"What does your newspaper experience tell you about why the killer has eluded capture?"

"Or killers, plural? When we know the answer we'll stop the crime."

"Maybe the police aren't looking hard enough, Red. Ever think of that?"

"It's crossed my mind, but only because I'm a born skeptic. Police have no reason to hold back. No cop wants to come to work thinking a perp owns him. Not the honest ones, anyway."

"You're talking about Harold Ferndale?"

"Duke Ferndale won't turn over for bribes or any other malfeasance, Mary."

"Is he a reliable source of information?"

"So far as I know," Maguire said vaguely, trying to ignore Mary's eyes boring into him. He looked away. "What's your theory, anyhow?"

"Red Maguire, I'm honored you asked. Yes, I have an opinion. I think we're dealing with a clever killer, or two or more of them, is that fair?"

"Fair and probably accurate, Mary. But knowing that takes us no closer to identifying the perp. The cops say they need more clues."

She laughed, coughing smoke. "How often do you hear of murders where the calling card is a purple rose? What more do they need, a billboard in uptown Butte to point the way? A radio show where listeners guess all the clues? Arrows painted on the sidewalks?"

Maguire stood and dropped a fiver on the table. "That might help," he said, feeling foolish.

~ 10 ~

Headlines and bylines

David Fenton, a man of greed, wanted more wealth. He spent little time thinking about the past. Guilt rarely occurred to him. He lived like a rich man, in the pretentious country house behind the trees, such a perfect place to end his life. The interview with Antonio Vanzetti aroused in Fenton a twinge of curiosity about his riches. The killer knew Fenton, a smart and important man, would figure out the murders. He talked about telling that Bugle reporter, Red Maguire, what he knew. Fenton made his greatest mistake when he trusted the killer. Oh, what a fool.

Stoffleman labored over their double-bylined story for an hour, penciling additions to some paragraphs and crossing out sentences in others. When he finished he announced his approval. He even attempted an apology for mistreating Miller. Maguire had observed that behavior from Stoffleman a thousand times. He operated on the edge, his emotions if not his private thoughts wide open for everyone to see, juggling cigarettes and coffee and nightly deadlines so the presses could run on time. "If we weren't the *Bugle* we'd be the *Daily Miracle*," Stoffleman liked to say, usually to impress on reporters the importance of beating the clock.

The story Maguire and Miller wrote did little to advance the Purple Rose Murders case, but the link between Vanzetti and Fenton would get some tongues wagging when the morning papers hit the streets. Maguire had called Chief Morse, asking him to comment, but got another "under investigation" response. Maguire followed the routine to stay in good graces with the chief. Morse rarely said anything newsworthy. *The poor beleaguered chief,* Maguire thought. *If he knows anything, he's not going to tell me.* The rest of the long story told about Vanzetti's history as a news reporter and Fenton's sketchy profile as a businessman. The story made little mention of the men's personal lives. "Sad," Maguire told Stoffleman. "I worked with Antonio Vanzetti my entire adult life. I don't know much more about him than I do about Fenton."

"Get to know people before they die," Stoffleman said bluntly.

Maguire looked at the clock. Mid-evening. Miller straightened her desk. She reached for her purse. Seeing she intended to leave, Maguire hurried over with a compliment. "You did a great job nailing the Fenton profile, Mary. That story moved you on your way to becoming a *Bugle* crime reporter. Take it from me."

Miller smiled. "Thank you, Red. Receiving an apology and a compliment in a single evening is the best any girl could hope for, don't you think?"

"Suppose we could go for a burger and a beer? To figure out our next story, I mean?" Maguire knew he sounded too eager.

"Not tonight, Red, I'm beat. Try again with another offer besides going to the M & M? I know that's where you police guys hang out but there are finer places to dine in Butte. The Board of Trade, for instance, if you're the gambling type."

"Sorry, I meant …."

"And what I mean is that I like your company, so don't apologize. I don't see anything wrong with having a little social time as we puzzle through these murder stories." Miller raised her eyebrows. "Do you?"

Miller sashayed from the city room, her blue dress swishing through the gloom. Maguire watched her go. She would make a nice catch for any man, sure enough. He kicked himself for not inviting her out to a respectable cafe for dinner. Maybe Ferndale could suggest a place. No, on second thought, not Ferndale. To him fine dining meant bar stools and scuffed linoleum floors. Maguire pulled his suit jacket from the back of his chair. He never wrote a story until he took his jacket off and rolled his shirt sleeves up. Stoffleman raised his head from a pile of papers. "Now that you found a link between two bodies in this killing spree, connect the others. Tomorrow, Maguire. No coasting."

Maguire walked down the stairs to the street entrance. He had parked his Pontiac around the corner. Several cars passed through the intersection before he crossed Broadway Street to the small lot down the hill. He had parked near the back, across the alley from a welding shop. Dusk settled over the city. A gentle wind blew from the West. Something fluttered on his windshield. Maguire reached for it. He held his most recent murder story, torn from the *Bugle* front page. Across it, written in crude boxy red letters, were the words, "BACK OFF NOW." He held the scrap of newsprint for a full minute, staring at the scrawled words, knowing he had missed encountering the killer by a few minutes. To the north, across Broadway, yellow light spilling from the *Bugle* city room in the Hirbour Block.

He jerked open his unlocked car. When the dome light came on, his heart jumped. Someone had dropped a purple rose on the front seat. No, not dropped it, but propped it, with the stem anchored on the lower seat and the flower leaning against the upper. Maguire looked around in the disappearing light. He saw three men entering a bar on the other side of Main Street. An old woman shuffled along with two paper sacks pinched in her thick arms. He looked in the other direction, down an alley, where he saw Charlie the Cat.

The old man cradled two black cats as he searched garbage cans for food or treasures. When he saw Maguire he shook his head. "Charlie don't know nothin' except a whole lot of nothin' when his pockets are light on jingle."

"That's right," Maguire said to him. "Jingle helps Charlie remember?"

Maguire handed two bits to the old man. "You saw somebody at my car, Charlie?"

"Somebody leaning over it, maybe. You seen any calicos out causing trouble, Red? Them cats pestering us at the Belmont something terrible."

Maguire pointed to his Pontiac. "Did you see the person leaning over my car? Right before I got here?"

"I seen somebody all right. Don't know who, Red. Somebody from the Belmont maybe. Come to put a calico in that there car."

"A man, Charlie?"

"Sure as shootin' a man. Ain't be said that Charlie don't know the difference."

"How was he dressed, Charlie?"

"Clothes like I wear to work. Overalls, that's it. Dirty blue clothes like all them miners wear. That reminds me, Red. Gotta go. Whistle blows for day shift any minute. Charlie can't decide whether to take Blackie here," nodding to the cat in his left arm, "or Blackie here," nodding to the one in his right.

As Charlie melted away into the twilight, Maguire drove his car the short distance to the *Bugle*, taking care to lock it this time. He hopped the stairs two at a time, surprising Stoffleman when he bounded into the city room. "Hot scoop?" the editor inquired, but only mildly interested. He looked deeply involved in preparing the morning paper. Four editors worked around him. Their cigarette smoke circled in a lazy ring above them. Maguire knew better than to trifle with Stoffleman once the editor switched his mind from gathering news to printing it. Stoffleman marched through the night with a soldier's precision. "When I put my stamp on the morning paper, that means beginning to end," Stoffleman told Maguire once. "Pay close attention if you want my job someday."

Maguire went to his desk where he flipped through the telephone directory. He almost dropped it twice in his haste. Finally, he found the number. He almost hung up after four rings but then she answered. "Hello?" came her voice, full of hesitation. Maguire knew why. Being listed in the city telephone directory left her open to crank callers.

"Mary, it's Red. Are you all right? Something's happened."

"What, Red? Are you hurt? Yes, I just got home after stopping at the grocery store for eggs and milk. I'm fine, really, but you?"

Keeping his voice to a whisper, Maguire told her about the torn *Bugle* clipping and the rose. He felt in a mood to confess his true feelings. Even over the phone, he could picture her attentive brown eyes, probing. "For the first time, Mary, I admit to being scared. Sounds silly, doesn't it? Me, Red Maguire, telling you that?"

"Don't apologize, Red. Given your line of work I suspect you've heard threats more than once in your life. Even Black Jack couldn't take you down."

He took a breath. "Sure enough, but I have no desire to become murder victim number six, Mary."

"You don't strike me as a man who scares easily, Red. You think the killer is trying to get your attention?"

"If he intended that strategy, it worked," Maguire said.

"Did you tell Stoffleman? Maybe he knows what to do."

"He'll put me to work delivering papers. Work is his way of dealing with matters like this. I'll head home. Sorry to have bothered you. I wanted to make sure you were safe."

"Now you've got me worried. Come to my place, Red." Mary gave her address. She lived on Butte's west side. "Hurry!"

Maguire hung up and dialed Ferndale at his office number. The detective picked up on the first ring. "You got nothing better to do than bug a cop who can't crack a case, Maguire?"

He listened as Maguire explained his discovery in the parking lot. "It don't surprise me that you got somebody gunning for you, whoever that bastard is," Ferndale said. "Could be the killer, could be somebody playing games. I'll send a black and white over that way to ask around about someone messing with your car. Chances are, nobody paid attention except Charlie the Cat, but like you said he ain't one for detail. I don't have to tell you to watch your back."

Maguire stopped to talk with Stoffleman but the busy editor waved him away as he and his deputy editor, Don Morgan, argued over placement of stories on the front page. The ritual took place nightly in the city room. Morgan, a big Scot, laughed more than he complained. He had accumulated a fair measure of mileage, much like Stoffleman, but time had dealt him a fairer hand. Morgan wore the only beard in the city room. The red showed no sign of gray. As he argued with Stoffleman, his voice booming, he let his opinions be known. "You want to lead with the purple roses again, Clyde? You ride this horse any longer and the readers will shoot it themselves."

Then came Stoffleman: "What have you got that's more important, Don? That mine union controversy lights a few fires, agreed, but is it the story that will sell our paper on street corners in the morning? And that wire story hashing over President Eisenhower's growing worry about communism in southeast Asia? He floated his domino theory a dozen times since he gave his news conference last spring. Who heard of Indochina in 1954 anyway? Go local, Don. Go with what sells."

Back and forth they went. Maguire looked around. Calvin Claggett slept at his desk, his face squarely planted on top of his typewriter, his arms resting on either side of it. Maguire had seen the obituary reporter slumbering like that too many times to presume he suddenly fell dead. Maguire ambled down the wooden stairs to Main Street. Lights blazed in a clothing store and a jewelry shop up the block. People pounded the sidewalks, enjoying the cool summer air that arrived after dark, their laughter mingling with the roar and clatter from mining hoists higher up the Hill. Maguire climbed into his Pontiac. He felt strange going to Mary Miller's house. He hardly knew her. How typical of his flimsy attractions to women. Sure, he had a thing for her, hard to admit. Sure, Ferndale would describe Mary as "a real doll, bets she looks as good in the morning as she did at bar closing the night before." Ferndale got right to the point.

Maguire thought about the story he and Mary had written. The killer would see her byline next to Maguire's when the *Bugle* hit the streets at dawn. She would be in danger soon. Killers read the papers. Maguire knew this after two decades of crime reporting. Any killer who escaped the first time came to love reading descriptions of his slayings in print. Rarely did a criminal get away with one killing, much less two or more. Now Butte had a madman who murdered five people. Maguire pictured a shadowy face leering over the *Bugle*. He saw the sickly smile, the flecks of drool, the habitual tugging on an ear. The killer pulled the hammer back on the deadly gun while reading every sentence in Maguire's stories. There it would go, flicked into firing position with a click and eased off, repeated absentmindedly as the killer pored over the story. Somewhere in Butte. Somewhere in the night. Somewhere in close proximity to his next victim.

The Purple Rose Killer relished making people crazy with fear. He read Maguire's stories before making his next move. The killings had become a game. A killer who toyed with people, playing on their fright, worried Maguire more than someone who erupted in a drunken rage to commit sudden murder. The Purple Rose Killer held the cards now, Maguire knew, calculating the perfect opportunity for his next crime. These thoughts ran through Maguire's mind as he pressed his foot to the gas pedal. The Pontiac clipped through neighborhoods of chipped brick and old wood to the West side. Patches of brown and yellow shone through window shades. Behind one of them, somewhere, the killer waited. Maguire, the cold-eyed crime reporter, felt oddly protective of Mary. He felt ashamed for having ignored her for so long. He so rarely felt any lure to women in his life. Suddenly he and Mary were bound by a powerful common purpose — to stay alive.

~ 11 ~

Memories of Lily

Maguire's mother once surprised him in her rare sober moment. His longing for her touch, for her recognition of being a mother, filled this early Chicago memory. She smelled vaguely of lilac perfume. On the morning of his ninth birthday, Lily told him she had planned a family outing, another rare occurrence in Maguire's memory. They would be going to Wrigley Field to see the Cubs play the Brooklyn Robins. "This is a special day, Kieran, so move right along, will you? I wish you a happy birthday, me son." She handed him a new blue Cubs baseball cap. Maguire pulled it forward on his head and inspected his appearance in the mirror. He rummaged through the closet to find his leather mitt, beaten sandy brown by dust and gravel on the corner lot where the neighborhood boys played. Every boy with a new ball cap needed an old mitt.

His father and mother laughed all the way to the ballpark. His father parked their rusting pickup. His mother took his hand as they walked through the ocean of cars to Wrigley Field. Windshields gleamed under the midday sun. Tall grandstands loomed over them. Men with red aprons waved pennants on sticks, barking for buyers, as spectators surged through the broad doors. Kieran's father bought a pennant and handed it to him. "Chicago Cubs, 1907-08 World Series," read the red letters on a field of blue. They found their seats near the third base line. Kieran's favorite players, famous people he knew only from the sports pages, trotted onto the field. The crowd roared. He sat between his parents, each with an arm around him, for the moment oddly at peace with one another. Kieran looked at his mother. She brushed a curl of red hair from her snapping blue eyes. How pretty, his mother. He loved her. He had never imagined anything so wonderful as this day.

A couple of innings passed. Kieran's favorite pitcher, Sheriff Blake, breathed fire from the mound. Intent on watching every detail of the game, as the Cubs led by two runs in the third inning, Kieran missed his mother's growing disinterest. Finally, she said something to his father before standing and pushing through the crowded seats. Kieran glanced at his father. Sean watched Lily disappear into the throng. He had that angry knowing look Kieran had seen so many times before.

When the game ended, the Cubs sadly surrendering 12-9 to the Robins, Lily hadn't come back. Kieran felt anxious. He clutched his mitt and new pennant much like he wanted to hug his mother. His father led him to the exits. They waded through a swirl of people past the beer concession. His father, too late, tried to turn him away. Maguire saw his mother, obviously drunk, groping a sailor in his dress whites. The man hovered over her as if he expected something in return. Maguire's father, his fists clenched, swore and stepped toward the sailor. Then he stopped, seeming to remember Kieran, and steered him toward the parking lot. They drove home in silence, just the two of them, that last image of Lily heavy on their minds. The pickup rumbled past dark warehouses and stretches of row houses. Finally, his father spoke. "Your mother, when she wanted to celebrate your birthday at the ballpark, I thought here's a fine day for our boy. Bought the tickets herself, she did. Good thing she did for you. I hoped today might be different than all the times before. I'm so sorry, Kieran. You deserve better." The boy sensed his father's deep hurt. Kieran went to bed, thinking of his mother, the mother he hardly knew, wanting her sober and loving his father. Hours later, after sunset, Lily came home. He heard the motor. He lifted the window shade to see her step from a red coupe at the curb. It roared off, honking. Minutes later he heard his parents shouting. His father bellowed the word "birthday" once or twice. His mother screamed something in a slurred voice. Kieran couldn't make out what she said.

His last memory of Lily left him sad and hurting. Suitcase in hand, clutching an odd assortment of kitchen items under her arm, she lurched away from the house with a belly full of hooch to the waiting arms of the sailor from the ballpark. He looked half her age. She never said goodbye. Kieran waved as she slid onto the front seat beside the sailor and never looked back. Two months passed without a word from her. "Your mother is gone from our lives," his father said simply. After the divorce, Sean loaded the pickup and ordered Kieran to climb aboard. The boy left Chicago without saying goodbye to his friends. As the endless neighborhoods and suburbs and eventually empty plains rolled past the windows, Sean explained they were heading for a city in Montana named Butte. He would find work there, he said. Kieran cried all the way to Minnesota, his fingers locked on his Cubs pennant, his best and worst memory left behind at Wrigley Field. Over the years the pain faded. He never shied from admitting his broken heart. Nothing he learned about himself as an adult lessened his fear of abandonment. Maybe that's what made him a good crime reporter. He understood flawed people. He was one of them.

Mary waited at the door as Maguire arrived. He thought about showing her the purple rose, its petals wilting, but decided not to make matters worse. She looked worried under the porch light. Maguire stepped into Mary's living room. Clean but sparsely furnished. As if reading his mind, she said, "You know how it is surviving on a *Bugle* salary." She motioned to a maroon couch. He fell back against the cushions as she poured coffee in the kitchen. She hadn't pulled her shades. Maguire thought suddenly that the killer might watch them through the dark windows. He kicked himself for thinking that way. Fear never made a man stronger. In Dublin Gulch, no boy got the best of him, not once. Boys thinking they could intimidate the new arrival from Chicago misjudged his anger and hurt. His fight with Joe O'Malley came soon after his father rented a little house. The bully had a shock of dirty brown hair that hung in his eyes and a snarl that curled his lips. "Never back down," his father said, "or all them boys will peg you as a loser and come at you again and again." When Kieran unleashed his fury against Joe he earned respect. Soon

Kieran grew bigger and stronger. He fought at the first hint of a threat. No boy in the gulch dared taunt him. Maguire, as a man, knew the real reason he fought and won as a boy. To shed anger over losing his mother. He soon learned, when he started covering crime, to recognize the truth behind the violent tendencies of his youth. For that matter, the truth behind the violence of other people, the perps and victims he named in his *Bugle* news stories.

Mary stood beside him. "I said, coffee, Red? You are seriously lost in thought. I asked you twice." Maguire nodded his appreciation and reached for the cup. Mary settled beside him. "I worried about you and, frankly, me," she said. "We have no idea what goes on out there, do we? Someone makes the news, we report it ..."

"... and we voluntarily and publicly surrender our identities in front page bylines," Maguire said, completing her thought.

"I can't imagine you being afraid, Red. You've seen too much."

"Not my style, not since I was a kid. I've had enough close scrapes as a news reporter to respect fear, but afraid, no. I won't be intimidated into backing away from covering this story. Having five people dead is bad enough. I doubt we've seen the end of it."

"Wasn't what happened tonight a threat on your life?"

"It appears so." Maguire blushed. "I apologize for burdening you with this mess and rushing over here. It's just, well, I'm worried for you."

"I know, Red. I'm worried about you as well. As much as tonight troubled you, your first thought was protecting me. How comforting, Red. I wondered for a long time when you would notice." Mary set her coffee cup on the end table and slid closer to him. He watched her eyes, searching, probing his.

"I shouldn't be here, Mary. I'm not built to run from threats. You and me, we work together. This is so ... I shouldn't —"

Mary touched her lips to his. Maguire felt a mix of confusion and joy. She broke the kiss to press against him. He felt her fingers in his hair. "Tell me again where you got all these red curls? I've wondered."

"It's the Irish stereotype, Mary. My father, full blood Irish, had the same."

"And your mother?"

Maguire winced. "She had red hair, too, last that I remember."

"Do you have a secret, Red?

"Like everybody, I suppose."

"The other day at the M & M, you started to tell me something that mattered deeply to you. Then you pulled back. You wear mystery like a suit of armor. Does anybody truly know Red Maguire?"

He fidgeted. "Not so much, I suppose."

"Do you keep a diary, Red? Not that I'm asking to read it if you do. I see you patting the pocket of your suit jacket like you've got something there you don't want to lose."

"No diary, Mary, just some old letters."

She eased away and locked on his eyes and waited. Suddenly Maguire found himself telling her about his mother's bitter parting so long ago. Ridiculously poor timing to reveal so much of himself. He regretted sharing his past with an essential stranger. He had so much to say but, feeling embarrassed, cut his story short.

"You never found her?"

"Not the one time I tried."

"I'm so sorry. How sad to lose a parent like that." Mary leaned her head into the crook of his neck. "You don't make it easy for a woman, you know. Oh, those so many times I tried to draw your attention in the city room. I figured it would be easy, me being the only woman, the only person not dressed like an undertaker in that room full of dour men. You didn't even look my way. So I confess. You shook my confidence. You're a handsome man, Red, much more attractive than your lack of social confidence would suggest. I had hoped you would ask me on a date to a place with some class. Or at least acknowledged my existence."

"What about Vanzetti?"

"What about him?"

"I mean, here's this guy with the movie star good looks of Marlon Brando. I thought maybe you two had eyes for each other. Only recently did I learn why not."

Mary laughed. "Feeling inadequate, are we? Then you heard Antonio liked men? That he kept his personal life secret for good reason? Think about it, Red. Did you ever hear him talking about anything other than work? What do you think his drinking binges were all about?"

"How did you …?"

"Call it women's intuition. I never knew for sure. I can tell you with certainty that he never showed more interest in me than in you."

Maguire's eyes opened wide. "Now there's a thought that will keep me awake at night."

"Forget that one. Here's a new one," Mary said, yanking the chain on the lamp. The room went dark. Maguire felt Mary reaching for him. Her fingers passed lightly over his face. Her lips, wet and soft, touched his neck and ears. "Oh, Red," Mary whispered. Her inquiring lips came to his. He felt them searching, caressing, exploring his deepest desires. Her womanly warmth flooded over him in ways he never knew with Lindy. He reached out to Mary, encircling her with his arms, pressing her close. He felt an unfamiliar sincerity. Perhaps he had never thought of marriage because he hadn't known this feeling.

"Sweet darling," Maguire heard himself say.

~ 12 ~

Rhonda

The next morning, Stoffleman demanded to see the purple rose left in Maguire's Pontiac. The old editor held the rose, its petals browning around the edges, examining it from end to end. "I don't know what I'm expecting to see," he said. Maguire and Miller waited on either side of him. When Stoffleman finished turning the rose over and over, his way of thinking through a difficult problem, he handed it back. "Damn nice of you not to get knocked off last night, Maguire. Did you report this to police?"

"I told them, yes."

"With that accomplished, let's focus our efforts on the one thing we can control, which is tomorrow's paper. I want another story that addresses the threat against you last night. We don't know if the note and flower came from the killer or some looney admirer of the killer, but in any case we need people to know what happened. That's not all. Maguire, tear into those land records today. Miller, you ask around about connections between those dead miners and Fenton and Vanzetti. Nobody is saying these murders are random, and the recurring purple roses pretty much prove they're not, so let's look for a common denominator. And Miller?" Stoffleman held up the *Bugle* front page with the double-bylined story.

"Yes, boss?"

"If anyone threatens you after seeing your name on this story, don't wait until tomorrow morning to tell me about it. Got it?" Stoffleman walked away before Maguire could object.

"He's a hard case, isn't he, Red? You tried to tell him."

"This is nothing," Maguire said. "The real show begins if we get scooped by a competitor on a big story. If that happens, run for the street."

"Have you ever been scooped? On a big story?"

Maguire led Mary toward the windows where Stoffleman couldn't hear them. "Once, soon after I started at the *Bugle*. I covered an accident at the Anselmo. Two workers died when the chippy hoist that lowered them underground jerked unexpectedly. They were thrown headfirst into the metal above the cage. I know now that the Company suits ignore safety problems that kill workers. Back then, I let the Company waltz me around on that story because I didn't know better. The suits up the street denied anybody died and said I would have to wait until the next morning for the rest of the story. With some experience I would have known the Company's familiar stalling tactics. The Company paper hit the streets that morning with a squeaky-clean tall tale it ran through the laundry. Stoffleman hit the roof. He ranted and raved about how he'd taken a chance on an Irish punk from the gulch. How I failed him. How I dishonored the *Bugle*. How I might apply for a mucking job half a mile underground at the Anselmo given the Company's safety assurances at the mine. How I should know the Company suits laughed about how they played me for a fool. My ears burned for a month. The old cuss doesn't tolerate losing. Nor should he. The *Bugle* lacks the resources of the Company press. We survive by beating them. I believe in that now as much as he does."

Mary smiled knowingly and walked back to her desk. Maguire watched her sashay away. He went to his own desk where he saw a sheet of typing paper, folded. He flipped it open to see carefully crafted cursive in blue ink. "Thanks for being there for me last night. … In so many ways … Mary." Below her handwriting she left a bright red lipstick kiss. He blushed and tucked it into his shirt pocket. He looked over at her. She winked.

Sleepy from the night's activities, Maguire resigned himself to a visit to the coffee pot. When Stoffleman arrived in the *Bugle* city room every morning he brewed a black concoction resembling coffee that he expected everyone to drink. The editor tapped the seemingly bottomless urn through the day into the night when the presses ran. How he slept after that caffeine consumption, or whether he slept, aroused occasional idle curiosity at the *Bugle*. Stoffleman, more reliable than the clock, his fierce presence expected and never questioned.

An inscription on Maguire's cracked green mug read, "I'm Butte Irish." He poured Stoffleman's bitter coffee from the urn and took three sips before his tongue told him to stop. He splashed the rest of the cruel brew into the waste basket when his telephone rang.

"Maguire? See me in ten." Lucky Finero hung up. Maguire pictured Lucky's scowl over the telephone line.

When Maguire climbed the stairs on East Galena Street, he found Finero's office door open. The bounty hunter, leaning against a dirty gray wall in the dim room and clutching several official-looking papers in his meaty hands, got right down to business. "Got a prospect for you in those Purple Rose Murders, Maguire. You'll owe me."

"I figured I might," Maguire said.

"One of the fools who kissed off a court appearance is an ex-con named Fenton. Name ring a bell? Two-bit hood is what he is. Lives up in Centerville. This boy runs around looking for trouble. I dealt with him a few times. Despite having a permanent address nowadays he's a slippery one. Seems to know when I come for him. Mind you I ain't admitting that I can't nail a slimy bail skipper like him."

"What makes you think —?"

Finero held up a hand to stop Maguire. "I'm getting to that. Keep your pants on, will you? Well, if you can. I hear that's a problem lately." He laughed like a Saturday night drunk at the M & M.

Maguire reached into his pocket to feel the note from Mary. "Is there anyone in Butte who doesn't know my private business?"

"Maybe Charlie the Cat. You and me, we know everything about this town, remember? You want the goods on this boy or not? Now listen close as I ain't inclined to repeat myself. So I come across this warrant for Clifford Fenton's arrest. Same last name as the dead guy. Our man in Centerville is a confirmed troublemaker. Known for packing heat. Simpleton, easily manipulated. No functioning brain that anybody's been able to tell. Adds up to something, don't it? Now if I go nab his sorry ass I make some jingle. Or, I play nice guy and give you this warrant and you take it over to your washed-up boxer buddy at the cop shop to see what he makes of it." Finero held out the warrant. He pulled it back when Maguire reached for it.

"Put in a good word for me with Ferndale or we ain't got a deal. He ain't had time for me since I got sent over to the joint for making that bail jumper pretty a few years back."

"What did you do that for, anyway?

"Cosmetic surgery, Maguire. He looked better without them big ugly ears."

When Maguire returned to the street, he tucked the warrant inside his suit. Ferndale could wait. First, Maguire had business at City Hall. He went inside, asked for the key to the storage room, and went downstairs to the basement. He found dozens of boxes of land records, marked by decade, and began reading. He felt sleepy. He should have forced down more of Stoffleman's coffee. Mary had kept him awake most of the night. Even with his eyes wide open, in the midst of the musty cardboard boxes, he saw her hair silhouetted above him in the moonlight from her bedroom window. "Red, what are you doing to me?" she had cried out. He tried to push Mary from his mind. He might miss an important clue to the murders. The basement's solitude, and his memories of her, made it difficult to concentrate. The clerk from upstairs appeared momentarily. He carried a stack of documents to stash them in the paper graveyard known as the city archives. Maguire waved at the man, a chunky fellow named Homer, before turning back to the tedious task of reading files. He had no idea Butte had compiled such a checkered history of property transactions. What secrets they must contain. Vanzetti knew something that got him killed.

Back at the *Bugle*, Mary Miller opened a phone directory. She had exhausted most of her regular news sources in her previous story about David Fenton. People who obeyed the law didn't much care to soil their reputations by commenting on murders. Miller shook her head at the odd role Stoffleman had assigned her. He persisted in pushing her into the Purple Rose coverage. Did he intend compliment or punishment? She thought of Maguire. What a handsome man. Passionate lover, too. Mary knew his reputation. People all over Butte talked about Red Maguire's stories. They knew him as a local celebrity in a city full of characters. He wrote prolifically. He also got his facts straight. Deeply sourced, a blue-ribbon reporter, a bulldog who bit on a story and never shook it loose. She suspected he had an insider at the police department. Somebody much like Maguire. She had a lot to learn. She would stick close to Maguire. He would lead her to the facts of the case. She thought of him, carrying her love note in his pocket, and of the night they spent together. How suddenly he had come into her life. How long he had taken to get around to it.

Miller began a new round of phone calls, acting on Maguire's advice that she call the homes of the two slain miners, Kelly and Townsend, to see if anybody answered. This old reporting trick, he told her, gambled on reaching talkative friends and relatives at the residence of the deceased. They tended to gather there on occasion as if it would bring them closer to a loved one. Feeling some anxiety, she dialed Mike Kelly's number. She let it ring nine times before hanging up. Then she tried the number listed for Rodney Townsend. After the third ring, a trembling woman's voice came on the line. "Whoever this is, please. Rodney can't pay his bills. He's dead. Please stop calling."

Expecting the woman would hang up, Miller broke in. "I'm not a bill collector, ma'am. Sorry to bother you. Will you talk with me? I'm Mary Miller, a reporter for the *Bugle*. I'm so sorry for your loss. Can you tell me about Rodney?"

"What good will that do? Somebody killed him three weeks ago. Don't you read your own paper?"

"We're trying to solve the case. You want to help, don't you?"

"Ain't that what police are for?"

"Yes, and that's also what the *Bugle* is for," Miller said.

"Guy named Maguire from the *Bugle* come around after Rodney died right after I come up from Alabama. I slammed the door in his face. I don't want to tell no stories about Rodney. You ever lost a loved one? My mother, this done broke her."

"You are Rodney's sister?"

"Yeah, that's me, Rhonda. Rodney's twin sister. I'm cleaning out his apartment on Platinum Street." Rhonda sounded defeated. "Why would somebody do this here criminal act to my brother? He ain't done nobody no harm."

"Can I come talk with you?"

"Makes no difference to me I guess. I'm not slamming no more doors. You sound like a nice lady. Rodney went to Butte High, you know? Played football for the Bulldogs. Big enough that they put him at right tackle. Won all-conference his senior year. I'm holding his game jersey. Number 72, do you remember? After Rodney graduated he went digging rock. Had the arms and shoulders for it. I told him he might get hurt working in them mines with all them accidents. He don't listen. He survives down in them tunnels but somebody goes and kills my brother above ground. That make sense to you? Tell me why someone would do this to Rodney? I ain't got another brother or sister and now he's gone too."

Miller spent the afternoon with Rhonda as they looked through Rodney's possessions. Rhonda, inclined toward spitting brown juice through corroded teeth into a waste basket, mumbled past her mouthful of chew. Once Rhonda got to talking she didn't stop. She told Miller about her father being sent to prison. "The thing is, my brother, he ain't know the full story," she began, brushing strands of brownish-blonde hair away from her fat cheeks. "He never cared to know what Daddy did to deserve being sent over to Deer Lodge. Me, I wanted to know everything. Daddy weren't no saint. He slapped Momma around until Rodney got big enough to stop him. Sometimes when I was little Daddy come into my bedroom at night and touched me in private places. Him going to prison made me safe. People always thought Rodney knew what Daddy did to that man that night in the bar. Rodney never asked. I kept after Momma till I heard it all."

Maguire, by late afternoon, decided to give up his search. He had inspected hundreds of documents. He wondered if Vanzetti had plowed this deep into Butte's past. Maguire reached for one more handful. He shuffled through the papers quickly, nearly missing the two words he had been searching for all afternoon. Suddenly, the name "David Fenton" jumped at him from a 1930 land transaction. A man named Harry Anthony deeded Fenton 1,200 acres of land on the Flats. The document made no mention of a purchase price. Details seemed ridiculously brief. Maguire sorted through other documents in the box. No other mention of the transaction. Who was Harry Anthony? Why had he deeded the land to Fenton, a mere boy at the time? Despite the mystery, Fenton had enriched himself, selling housing plots worth far more than the original price of the land. But why?

Maguire thought of the bench warrant in his pocket for another man named Fenton. He hurried upstairs and across the street to Ferndale's office. "Hell, I got pretty much nothing," the detective said when he saw Maguire. "Can't even find the ham sandwich I brought for lunch and it's nearly time for dinner."

Ferndale seemed unimpressed at hearing what Maguire had found at City Hall. "Can't see where you're going with that, Maguire. Fact is, those murder scenes were clean. We dusted for prints. Weren't nothing there worth chasing. Killer wore gloves. No witnesses, no murder weapon on the scene, no bullet casings. Nothing but a straight shot to the heart of every victim and those damn roses left behind. I lose sleep over this case, Maguire. Shut off *Dragnet* last night because Joe

Friday solves murders in half an hour while the chief threatens five times a day to take my badge. People watch that show and ask me why I take so long to break this case. Our killer ain't some street hack, I'm sure of it."

"Which makes the case for looking into how the victims might be connected?" Maguire said.

"I'll leave that up to you and your woman friend at the *Bugle*. What's her name again?"

"Mary Miller."

"Does she know you and I compare notes off the record?"

"No, and she won't."

"Been here too long to get booted without my pension. Not that it won't happen anyway to a dumb police dick who can't break a murder case."

"Understood."

"Now that I've told you what you can't write up, give me something I can take to the bank, will you? How come your *Bugle* byline says Red Maguire anyway? Don't you have a real first name?"

"You've asked me that a thousand times, Duke. You ever heard anybody call me Kieran? Anybody call you Harold with a straight face?"

"Damn mick. You and the rest of the Irish ruined this town, I swear. Should have built a high fence around Dublin Gulch and Corktown to keep you in."

Maguire ignored Ferndale's familiar dig. "I have something else that might interest you." He handed Ferndale the warrant. The old cop looked it over. He blinked when he saw the name. Ferndale closed his office door and leaned on his desk. A framed photograph on the wall behind him showed Duke clubbing some punch-drunk sap in an amateur bout at the YMCA. Maguire had seen it a couple hundred times but never tired of appreciating how the photographer caught Duke's blurred left hand the instant it struck his opponent's unprotected jaw. Maguire knew the rest of the story. The man, knocked cold, took a belly flop to the canvas. It took him a week to wake up.

Ferndale took another look at the warrant.

"Figured you'd come across this sooner or later. Yeah, Clifford Fenton's a suspect and a good one. Been watching him for a week. Ex-con, no kills on his record, but he's got the particulars that get a dick like me thinking he's capable of capping people when he works up a head of steam. You can take that to print. Only thing is, don't name this version of Fenton or he'll run on us. Chief signed off on me spilling to you. Between you and me, he's tired of Helena riding our asses on this investigation. Every day, he tells me, some bureaucrat jacked about all the crime in Butte calls him with advice about how to run our shop. As if those state morons know where to find any credible evidence anyway."

"As if it's something new," Maguire said. "Butte's always had a crime problem because she's a crazy lady who likes to fight. Keeps you and me in rent jingle anyhow." Maguire pulled out his Lucky Strikes. He offered one to Ferndale who waved it off.

"Tell me, Duke. How did you settle on Fenton? More than his name?"

"Can't say much more, Maguire. Strange character, that man, like about half of everybody walking around in this town. Our boys watched him for weeks. What aroused your suspicion?"

Maguire told Ferndale about Lucky Finero. "He wants to kiss and make up with you, Duke. Says you don't appreciate him like you should."

Ferndale shrugged. "The only good thing about that ugly cuss is that he stays out of my way. He ain't wrong about this suspect, though."

"When were you going to tell me about Clifford Fenton?"

"Just did, Maguire. Tomorrow's paper ain't come out yet, has it?"

"What's the rest of the story, Duke? Since when do you hold back on me?"

"Can't tell you on chief's orders. I blab and I ain't got a job."

"Hasn't stopped you before."

"Chief ain't kidding this time either."

Maguire hustled back to the *Bugle* to knock out the first paragraphs of the story. When Mary Miller arrived in the city room they exchanged a knowing smile and a brief touch of hands. Stoffleman would flip if he knew the loving that went on between them. Searching for a killer electrified the editor. So did the prospect of sending Maguire to work in a hot coffin-like tunnel to the noise of jackhammers and dynamite explosions.

"Got anything to add to tomorrow's story?" Maguire asked her, realizing his voice sounded more accommodating than he intended. He showed her the top of it:

"Butte police have a suspect in a series of murders haunting the Mining City since the first one occurred in June. No arrests were made, but police confirmed Tuesday that a Butte man is under investigation. It's believed someone known as the 'Purple Rose Killer' committed the four Butte murders and a fifth in Deer Lodge. The flowers, rare in Montana, decorated the bodies."

Mary patted Maguire in appreciation. "That will wake people up in the morning. The whole city will fall under suspicion. Going to share his name with me? I suspect you know."

"Not yet," Maguire lied. "Got anything to add?"

She told him about her visit with Rhonda Townsend. Rhonda at first freely volunteered information about her family like a Catholic at confession. Suddenly, she refused to answer questions about her father.

"You pressed her, Mary? Is she hiding something?"

"The answers are yes and maybe, Red. She's a mess, all right, crying and confused like you would expect of a twin sister cleaning out her dead brother's apartment. I think she knows more than she's saying. She also has a peculiar personality. I wouldn't put anything past her."

"You figure her for a suspect? That she would kill her own brother?"

"I think the cops should be looking at her. Maybe she didn't kill her brother. Maybe she did. Maybe she killed the others. There's something about her I don't trust. I sensed a deep and dark hurt. Call it my woman's intuition."

Maguire nodded. "You saw something in Rhonda that maybe I wouldn't. What is it? Blood under her nails, eyes that evade yours, itchy body language, something she said that hints at a killer's secret?"

"Jumpy, Red. Agitated. Full of anger and disbelief, on edge, vengeful. Rhonda had all of that but I confess I don't know how to recognize a killer's look."

Maguire smiled. He knew the dilemma. Familiar territory for him. "Real killers usually don't look mad and violent. That's the thing I learned from all these years on the crime beat. You think killers are big and mean, breathing fire, until you see them in court. A few of them resemble that, yes. Most aren't. We look around at ourselves and wonder who did it. Truth is, killers can lead two lives. One is what they want people to believe. The other is who they really are. Each murder brings new mystery."

"Red, who knows for sure what happens on these streets after dark?"

"Now you're talking like a crime reporter. From me that's a compliment, you know."

"You flatter me, Red," she whispered, running her fingers lightly over his hand. Maguire shot a quick glance toward Stoffleman. The editor, preoccupied under his green eye shade, missed seeing Mary's amorous gesture.

Maguire typed the story while Miller suggested changes. He folded in details he uncovered about the David Fenton land transaction. She contributed a colorful description of

Rodney Townsend and his sister. Rodney, by Rhonda's account, worked around the mines since being old enough to zip his pants. He grew big enough, as Butte boys do, but by Rhonda's account he rarely caused anyone trouble. Rodney stored his treasures from childhood in a dresser drawer, the one below his socks and underwear. There was a rabbit's foot. A leather pouch of marbles. A stack of dog-eared Captain Marvel comics. Beneath a box of toy Civil War soldiers, Rhonda discovered a faded black and white photograph of a husky young man, his sleeves rolled above his elbows, a hat cocked sideways on his head. "Is that your father, Rhonda?" Mary asked.

"I ain't never seen this picture," Rhonda said. She gripped it, trance-like, with both hands. "That's how I remember the old man before he went to prison. Ain't too many good memories of him. He called me Sissy, did I tell you that? It weren't no name I liked. He whispered it when he come into my bedroom. He came out of the joint an old man. His hair gray, thinner. Prison carved deep lines in his face. He died soon after they set him loose. The mines took him like they do half the men in this town. Cough and spit and die."

Mary took the photo from Rhonda and looked closer at his face. His eyes gave him away. Something suggested disturbance, even malevolence, a fierce evil lurking behind a seeming veil of stupidity. "Did your father get the punishment he deserved?"

Rhonda, her eyes cloudy with tears, turned away. "Does anybody?"

~ 13 ~

A dead man's tip

The killer read every story Maguire wrote about the murders. Maguire proved himself a wily investigator, better than the cops. The killer knew his stories by heart. He got most of it right, yet, he had reported so little about why those five people died. If only he understood how deep the pain cut. But how would he know that unless he solved the crime? Five people dead, yes, but what was the real story? The killer wanted the truth to come out. All of it, all the details. Maguire had promise, yes, but he moved too slow. It soon would be time to leave Butte. The killer had one rose left. Maguire and the cops tied themselves in knots over trying to figure out the purple roses. It pained the killer to watch them struggle with the meaning of it. The killer unfolded the most recent Bugle, the one that uncovered evidence of Fenton's land gift. Maguire had so much more work to do before he got to the heart of the Purple Rose story. The killer smiled at that. Now the cops had a suspect. How did they plan to catch him?

That very morning, Rhonda Townsend stopped at her brother's apartment. She loaded a few boxes of his possessions she planned to keep. The people at St. Vincent de Paul would take the rest. They would toss Rodney's clothes on top of the emptied wardrobes of other dead people. Soon a stranger would wear his shirts and pants without caring of their origin. Rhonda's ailing mother sat at her window staring at the street in hopes of seeing Rodney walk to the door. Thinking about him, as she did relentlessly, made the old mother cry. She wrung her tears into embroidered pink hankies she ironed after every wash. She never spoke of Rhonda's father. She hid her private knowing of the many times he had his way with Rhonda.

In the morning light, Rhonda regretted she had revealed so much to that nosy *Bugle* reporter, Mary Miller. The woman came across as nice enough, even comforting, but she asked too many questions. Her father paid a stiff price for the beating of that shoe salesman so many years ago. She had no business sharing family secrets with a stranger. Rhonda hadn't seen the *Bugle* that morning. She didn't read newspapers. It didn't occur to her that she would be named in a story being read all over Butte. The city felt dreary and sad. Thunderheads rolling over the mountain threatened rain. Last box in hand, Rhonda hurried to her car, a 1942 Chevy sedan that sagged and chugged. After saying goodbye to her mother, a parting both would dread, Rhonda would make the long drive back to Alabama. She wedged the small box into the trunk beside the others and slammed the lid. She left her father's photograph behind.

Soon, Rhonda Townsend headed south off Butte Hill toward Pipestone Pass. She drove five miles before pulling the Chevy into a field of sagebrush on the Flats. Rhonda, no brighter than her fallen twin, occasionally had a clear thought.

"My business here ain't done," she said aloud, finding comfort in her epiphany. She whipped the steering wheel around and headed back in a roar of dust.

As Rhonda drove toward uptown Butte, Red Maguire and Mary Miller huddled over breakfast at Martha's Cafe on Front Street. They had made love until dawn when the paper boy tossed the *Bugle* against her door with a thud. Maguire felt mildly worried. Suddenly he thought more about Mary than about the five murders they were trying to expose. Sitting in a booth, under flickering fluorescent lights, he felt drawn to her like no woman he had known. Those few women, including the fickle Lindy, surely burdening Sal the clarinet player in ways he never imagined. Maguire didn't want to admit he barely knew Mary. She showed real interest in his life. Mary, he decided, matched him. They were self-made people from broken homes. They needed each other. He leaned over the table to kiss her. She placed her hand on his cheek and returned his kiss passionately. Maguire looked around but none of the other seven people in the cafe paid attention. He dreaded having to write yet another story about the murders. He wanted to run away with Mary. During the night he had spoken of his desire to take her to a place of sunshine in Florida or California. Maguire's long career at the *Bugle*, the sum of his drab life in Butte, suddenly seemed much less urgent. He imagined Mary dressed in a pink swimsuit. She would wear it well. An image of her long bare legs, stretched out in the sand on a beach glistening with sea water, crossed his mind. Suddenly he wanted to put the *Bugle* behind him. He and Mary would work together, more closely together than anyone imagined, until the cops found the killer. Maybe Maguire and Mary would solve the crime before Ferndale figured it out. Perhaps she would inspire him to work harder, work faster, before taking her away from Butte's grimy landscape. Stoffleman would show no mercy until Maguire wrote the final story. His eyes locked on Mary. He hoped he could solve the Purple Rose Murders before he lost his enthusiasm for the job.

After breakfast, Maguire spent the day digging deeper into land records at City Hall. He found no further mention of David Fenton or his benefactor, Harry Anthony. Vanzetti had reported the disarray of property transactions with dead-on accuracy. Still, he must have known more. Merely quoting Fenton in a story wouldn't get Vanzetti killed. He knew more, much more. His death mirrored the others except for his beheading. Was the killer sending a message? Maguire sat on the stack of cardboard boxes. What would Vanzetti leave behind? Suddenly, Maguire remembered. He raced back to the *Bugle*. Stoffleman saw him burst into the city room, gasping for air.

"Somebody chasing you, Maguire? You see ghosts?"

"Vanzetti, boss," Maguire said as he caught his breath. "He left something behind." Stoffleman watched, curious, as Maguire went to Vanzetti's desk and pulled open a wooden drawer. Vanzetti had kept his notebooks stacked and labeled. "Here they are, boss. Vanzetti's notes from his City Hall investigation."

"Don't plan on getting a kiss for finding something Vanzetti didn't include in his stories," Stoffleman said. "If you prove me wrong, I'll give you a day off sometime." The editor laughed and turned back to his work.

Maguire thumbed through the notebooks until he found it. Under the heading, "Fenton interview," Vanzetti had filled four pages with blue ink. He had circled the name "Harry Anthony" and written beneath it, "Uncle to Fenton. Land given as gift. Fenton never knew why, happened when a boy. Inherited land worth at least $50,000 when transferred to Fenton." Maguire blinked and read the reference again. He turned the page. He found the last mention of Anthony in Vanzetti's orderly handwriting. "Anthony reputed as persistent notorious Butte wheeler/dealer. Many scrapes with law. Died years ago. Fenton won't talk current land value, says nobody's business, admits sudden wealth result of uncle's generosity."

Maguire slipped the notebook into his coat pocket. He would use Vanzetti's notes in a future story. First, he had to find out more about Anthony.

"Do dead men tell tales?" Stoffleman barked from across the city room.

"Enough to lead me in a new direction," Maguire told him.

Miller, meanwhile, went to see the widow Maud Kelly, old and crippled from arthritis. They sat at a small table in a small kitchen in a small clapboard miner house high on the Hill. A silver tin pail caught rain dripping through the stained ceiling. Maud's pinched face squinted at Mary. "You are the young one, aren't you now?" Maud said with a lilt of an Irish accent. "Me parents brought me from the old country. Me Mike, we named our son after him you know, he and I come from New

York with our baby boy before the big war. Nothing but misery here in Butte. Me Mike took to the drink with them other Irish men in Corktown, two sheets to the wind they were. He come home from shift at the Mountain Con long enough to eat dinner, complained about what I fixed, then set off to them pubs and gambling houses half the night. I begged him to save his wages for food and rent but when it come to paying bills he was thick as a plank, that one. If'n you get me meaning."

"Why did he go to prison?" Mary asked.

"Them men fighting in the Helsinki weren't his fault. Mike weren't no fighter. That other man, Townsend, lout sure enough. What a bad one. He done most of the hitting and kicking on that man who gave them trouble. He weren't supposed to die."

"What man, Maud?"

"Name of Addleston. He started the fight in the Helsinki. All his fault. You know?"

Mary stared at Maud. "Tell me more, please."

"Some man wearing a fancy suit and big rings on his fingers come over to the Mountain Con when Mike and that lout Townsend come off shift, says he knows somebody the Company hired to bust the union. Me Mike, father of the chapel, he don't like people messing with the union."

"What's that mean, Maud, father of the chapel? I don't —."

"Boss in the union. That Townsend bloke, him too, but the kind who never shut his gob. Had a mouth on him. Always looking for trouble. Sharp as a beach ball, that one. Me Mike and Townsend, they headed right off to the Helsinki to find the union buster. Couple of hotheads they were that night."

"And then they killed him."

"Oh no, missy, not like that. Never intended to kill that man. Me Mike, he tried to tell the judge. We come to Butte for a better life. Here, let me show you." Maud eased away from the table and hobbled into her living room. She returned with a framed portrait. "This is us, before the troubles began. Me Mike, good man when off the drink. And me son. Oh, me son. Only the three of us, you know. We tried for more children but ain't nothing come of it."

The man standing beside a younger Maud Kelly had a thin gaunt grin. Tall and slender, so much different in appearance from Townsend, built like a fireplug.

Mary patted Maud's folded hands. "And your son, why would someone kill him?"

"Methinks to punish his father," Maud said, her voice trailing off.

That evening, Maguire and Miller fashioned another story from bits and pieces of news they had collected that day. They took too long to wrap it up, fawning over details of the story as secret lovers, enjoying the collaboration. Stoffleman reprimanded them from the far end of the city room. "You're not birthing a baby over there. Let go of the goddam story, will you? I need to look at it before the presses roll, and they're rolling in twenty minutes."

Maguire felt sheepish. Never had he missed a deadline. He rarely agreed to writing a story with anyone else. Mary wasn't anybody else. He fell in love with her after ignoring her for months as she worked a dozen feet away. Now this. Two reporters writing a story together usually meant bickering. Each of them had a different view of how the story should shape up. Such debates were common in city rooms. They took place every day as reporters and editors argued over what constituted news and where to put emphasis. Maguire knew he spent too much time bringing Mary into the story, just as he had spent too much time bringing her into his life. Maguire kicked himself. He should be tougher. He didn't write murder stories to make Mary Miller look good. No, Red Maguire caught killers.

"Not bad considering you took all night to write it!" Stoffleman yelled through the hubbub of editors scrambling to deadline. His eyes landed on Maguire longer than usual. "Maguire, a minute," Stoffleman called to him.

Mary glanced at Maguire, sending a silent goodbye. As she departed the city room, Stoffleman led Maguire across the hallway into the dingy meeting place, especially dark because it had no windows. He flipped on a yellow overhead light. The room smelled of cigarette smoke and old varnished wood. Fifty years earlier, in that very room, men in spats and bowties argued over the news. Stoffleman lifted his glasses to rub his eyes. The vicious scar across his cheek looked redder than usual. "Dawdling isn't your style, Maguire. You have more street sense than any reporter in my long experience at the *Bugle*. While you're chewing on that, tell me, what gives?"

Maguire leaned against the table. "It's my first time writing a story with someone else. I'm trying to do right by both of us, boss."

"I can see that. Let me give it to you straight. Miller's got some hint of newspaper talent but so far it's limited to backgrounding people. You, Maguire, you're the newshound in this shop. Don't compromise your skills to make her look good. I didn't pair you with a society reporter so you could hold tea parties and fold napkins. I put her on this story to help you, not to make you equal partners. She's not as good as you, Red. Not by a mile. You go harder and let her work harder to keep up." Maguire opened his mouth to speak but Stoffleman shook his head. "Give me the work of the best damn crime reporter in Montana. Bust this story wide open, will you? Miller can't do it. Appears the cops can't either." Maguire nodded agreement. Stoffleman turned to leave the room. He stopped, shooting Maguire another knowing glance. "It's clear to me and everyone else working here that you and Miller have something going on. Whatever it is, keep it out of the city room or I'll kick her back to covering garden parties and you'll join her. This is no time for tiddlywinks." Then he turned and went back to work.

Maguire sat alone in the room, staring at photographs of reporters and editors tacked on the walls. Antonio Vanzetti smiled from a portrait taken in his early *Bugle* years. Beside him, a similarly distant photograph showed a young and cocky Red Maguire with a brown fedora atop his head and a lanky smoldering cigarette hanging from his lips. Maguire remembered that day. Named Sullivan's permanent successor. Suddenly a real *Bugle* reporter. He knew so little about journalism except what the other reporters and Stoffleman taught him. He had no idea how to cover news those first several months on the job. The grit of writing about desperate and dead people quickly dulled his romantic notions about the business. At first, Maguire came back to the city room with his notebook full of facts and no idea what to do with them. Stoffleman, more patient than he let on, revised Maguire's early attempts at writing news from top to bottom. Watching the editor hack away left him discouraged. Soon he found sources who would tip him off to news. After he gained Ferndale's trust the more sensational stories came in droves. They were stories that defined Red Maguire. He got better at writing, too. The cache of crime stories he wrote over the years confirmed his worth.

So Stoffleman noticed Maguire's affection for Mary Miller. Nothing escaped the old editor's attention. What an ever-observing compendium of knowledge. Maguire thought momentarily of blaming Stoffleman for pairing him with Miller. He knew better. Nobody carried things too far except Red and Mary. He had spent all of his adult life being married to the job. Now he thought, foolishly he knew, about being married to Mary. He imagined winding up like Stoffleman and Duke Ferndale and Lucky Finero, old and cranky, wondering who would remember them other than bitter ex-girlfriends angling for their bank accounts.

Maguire switched off the lights. He headed outside to his Pontiac. For the first time in three nights he drove to his own residence. His room on the second floor of the Logan Hotel remained familiarly dark and quiet except for occasional shouting by the feuding couple down the hall. They beat each other up for foreplay. Maguire hardly noticed anymore. He felt a twinge of regret. Mary would be disappointed he hadn't come to her. He reached into the fridge for a brown bottle of beer. Butte Lager. He popped the cap off and took a deep swallow. The blinking neon sign outside his window flashed orange streaks on the wall. Maguire wondered whether all crime reporters suffered a destiny of dying alone.

The very moment Maguire nodded off, Rhonda Townsend paced in her brother's apartment five blocks away, wide awake and angry. Her finger twitched expectedly on a loaded handgun. By now she had found the story those meddlesome *Bugle* reporters had written. Rhonda hated seeing her name in print. That Mary Miller, sweet and syrupy, had used her family tragedy to sell newspapers. How dare she interfere in Rhonda's private affairs? Rhonda hadn't been away from Butte so long that she forgot how wronged people took care of business. She caressed the cold trigger with her forefinger. Rodney had taught her how to fire a gun. Her father gone, now her brother, who next? "Someone's gotta pay," she muttered to herself.

Sleeping soundly, Maguire jerked awake when his telephone jangled. He turned on the lamp beside his bed to see the alarm clock. Half past two in the morning. Bar closing, when drunks made phone calls. When he picked up the heavy black receiver a man's thick voice came on the line. "You think we don't notice when you splash names all over the front page of that *Bugle* rag, Maguire? You been hanging around Butte long enough to know how things work here so watch your back. Leave them miners alone. Keep this up and you can expect your sorry ass kicked from hell to Walkerville. You got a death wish, Maguire? We know where you live. That broken-down hotel ain't built strong enough to keep us out." Click.

Maguire rolled back on his pillow. He lost track of how many threatening phone calls he had received over the years. In 1952, somebody shot through his window. The bullet hole remained in the wall above his bed. The slug nearly hit the old man shaving next door. He had shrugged when Maguire apologized for the trouble. "Damn near parted my hair but hell, this is Butte, boy. Fired off a few rounds myself back in the day. Get yourself a piece and shoot back." Maguire had no experience with guns. Ferndale laughed at that and slipped him the .38. Maguire disliked carrying it around in his pocket, even with the safety switched on. He kept it wedged under his mattress where he could reach it quickly if somebody broke down his door during the night.

Two hours later, the phone rang again. "Hello, I'm trying to sleep," he said, hoping to head off another anonymous caller.

Instead, he heard Mary, her voice filled with fear. "Red? Where are you? Someone prowled outside my house a few minutes ago, tapping on the windows, scaring me to death. Maybe it's Rhonda. I have an awful feeling about her. Come over, will you? Please hurry."

Maguire reached under the mattress until he found the revolver's cool metal. No matter that he never fired the gun. The killer intruded on personal love. Maguire would do anything to save Mary.

~ 14 ~

In dark of night

Ferndale rode in a prowl car that night with Jimmy Regan in Centerville. They drove the high streets of Butte to a stretch of miners' houses huddled close enough that a thin man couldn't squeeze between them. Moonlight washed over their shabby brown walls. "See anybody, Cap?" Regan asked. He swept the black and white's spotlight over the tiny yards, some orderly, some tall with weeds.

Ferndale pointed to a battered Ford sedan. "Shine it over there, Jimmy."

The light fell on a man slumped behind the wheel. Regan eased the prowl car backwards a few feet, away from a possible line of fire. "Careful, Cap. He might be faking it." Stepping out of the car, Regan pulled his service weapon and trained it on the window where the man's head rested. Ferndale crept to the Ford, his gun drawn, until he reached the door handle. He swung the door open and stepped back. The body fell onto the street. An empty liquor bottle clattered and rolled away. In the spotlight, the man looked about thirty years of age, slender and balding. Ferndale saw a bloody hole in the fringe of brown hair. Regan came with a flashlight. They looked in the front and back seats and on the floorboards. "No purple rose," Ferndale said, surprised at his disappointment. A porch light switched on behind them. A woman in a tattered robe, alarmed at the scene, crept outside. "Clifford? I heard a shot. What's your trouble, where's my Clifford?" When she saw her husband's body she let loose with a loud and otherworldly scream the dead Clifford surely heard.

As Ferndale investigated yet another murder, Maguire raced toward Mary's house. He blew three stop signs. Somebody lurked out there, the killer or someone else, who wanted them dead. He hoped he made it in time. He had rushed outside without calling Ferndale. A crime reporter, not thinking of cops? His loaded revolver rested on the seat beside him. Yellow light from streetlamps flashed off the barrel as he drove.

Maguire found Mary's house aglow. He pocketed the gun and ran to the front door but found it locked. He pressed his face to the front window. A table lamp, its bulb lighted and its shade knocked askew, laid on the floor. He ran to the back of house, tripping over a tangle of bushes, leery of attack. He found the back door ajar. Maguire pushed it open. Kitchen chair tipped over next to a broken coffee cup. Sheets and blankets jumbled on the bed. Magazines scattered on the living room floor. Closet door standing open. Clothes pulled off the hangers. Maguire dreaded he might find Mary's body stuffed underneath, but nothing. He went back outside for another look. The bright moon left inky shadows behind Mary's house. Maguire drew his gun.

A few dozen blocks away, in the heart of the mining district, Ferndale thumbed through the dead man's wallet. He found four dollars in silver coins and a paper fiver, a membership card for the carpenters' union, and an expired driver's license. He confirmed the man's name as Clifford Fenton, Ferndale's prime suspect in the Purple Rose Murders. The cousin to the dead real estate agent David Fenton now became a shooting victim himself. Someone had fired at his head through an open window. The slug entered his skull above the left ear at close range and departed through his right temple at a downward angle before slamming into the dashboard. Ferndale suspected Clifford died from the same caliber weapon that killed the other five. Ferndale had watched Fenton for weeks. He had learned Clifford worked for his rich cousin building houses. A common carpenter, by some reports not a reliable one, who worked on a framing crew. Clifford Fenton kept an erratic schedule. He came and went from construction scenes unpredictably. Ferndale suspected Clifford Fenton fell into some deep trouble in Butte, the kind that got his cousin killed, but why? Ferndale had many eyes on the streets, informants he had come to trust after his three decades at the police department. Now he questioned his judgment. Was he watching the wrong suspect?

Five minutes after Ferndale returned to his office, Maguire burst in. "Duke, it's Mary Miller, my colleague," Maguire informed him. "I think she's been kidnapped."

Maguire related what he knew of her call and disappearance. Ferndale sized it up. "Instead of calling us, she called you?"

"There's more to it," Maguire admitted. He told Ferndale about their love trysts. Ferndale, a crafty old cop, probably knew most of it anyway.

Ferndale rubbed his eyes. Like Maguire, he had hardly slept. "I never figured you for a fool. Was she worth it?"

"I thought so," Maguire said quietly. He slid his fedora backwards and ran his fingers through a crown of red hair. This new turn of events left him puzzled.

Ferndale shouted out to Mallory, a sergeant supervising the night shift. "Get our graveyard creepers searching for one Mary Miller, will you? Maguire will give you a description." He closed his office door. "This doesn't go anyplace but between you and me right now. Tonight we found another body, that Clifford Fenton, the guy we thought might be the killer. I planned to tail him because I thought he might be up to something. We got there too late. One shot to the head, dead as a doornail, but no purple rose so go figure."

Ferndale laid out the details of the murder. "Except for being my prime suspect in these murders, I'd say somebody done the cops a favor. He weren't in line for Butte's good citizenship award. Less jingle for Lucky Finero, I gotta figure, who burned the midnight oil chasing him down."

"Or tired of doing it," Maguire said.

Maguire told Ferndale about the threatening phone call he had received at the Logan. The old detective and the veteran police reporter hashed over the night's strange occurrences until dawn. The sun rose over the Continental Divide when a bleary-eyed Red Maguire walked into the *Bugle* city room. The cops had failed to find any trace of Mary. If only he had gone to her house in the first place. What happened to her? Who threatened him on the phone?

He found the city room at that hour strangely empty. Stoffleman would be dressing for work. Maguire pictured him at his kitchen table scowling at the fresh edition of the *Bugle* he had helped put to bed only hours earlier. Nothing pleased Stoffleman except the prospect of compiling yet another daily newspaper, better than the last. Maguire lingered at Mary's desk. Butts of filtered Winstons colored with red lipstick filled her ashtray. Otherwise, unlike heaped desks elsewhere in the city room, hers had only her typewriter atop it. Mary kept her desk like she kept her house. The few things she owned looked in order. Maguire shuddered at the thought of her never coming back alive. He remembered the taste of her sweet lips and the feeling of her hair, the color of honey. Where had she gone? Hurt, or worse? He pulled open a few drawers, looking for clues. Nothing seemed unusual. He fished a stack of notebooks from the bottom drawer and leafed through them. She lacked Antonio Vanzetti's thorough reporting. It appeared she had used all of her scant notes in the news stories she and Maguire had written. Maguire found one fuzzy quotation. "He don't scare easy," she had written and underlined. Maguire stared at those four words for a moment. "Probably someone's quote about one of the dead guys," he said to himself. That very moment, Stoffleman appeared in the city room, wearing the same black suit and wrinkled white shirt from the previous day.

"I'm surmising, Maguire, that something went haywire overnight. You look like hell, sonny. You are here way earlier than I've ever seen you on the job and don't take that as a compliment. You're also sitting at the wrong desk."

Maguire yawned. "You're a quick study, boss."

"Better be a story in it for tomorrow or you'll be mucking rock on the Hill before the next deadline. Come tell me all about it while I fuel up the coffee pot." So Maguire did while Stoffleman listened without interruption.

Over at the police department, Ferndale fell asleep puzzling over Miller's disappearance. Clifford Fenton's murder caught him off guard. He had planned a stakeout to see where the man would go next. The tip Ferndale received, which he considered reliable information, said Fenton would leave his house in the middle of the night. For what, Ferndale didn't know. If only he and Jimmy Regan had arrived sooner. A foolish fender bender involving two fighting drunks got in their way. If the night remained a mystery, the morning brought pandemonium. The chief decided to call another news conference. The coroner wanted details about the murder to write a report that would please the mayor. Everyone had a theory about the killer. Ferndale finally took his phone off the hook, closed his office door, and lowered his head to his desk. The Purple Rose Murder case, the toughest he had handled in all his years on the force, drained him. He needed to solve it soon or it might be his last. He fell asleep in seconds.

Butte bolted wide awake. Soon word of the latest murder filtered through the neighborhoods. Residents gathered outside their houses to guess who might be next. A radio crew went door to door in Centerville seeking to interview someone who saw or heard the murder. Most of their knocks went unanswered. A few people offered comments but knew nothing about the murder. At the house belonging to Clifford Fenton, Maguire knocked to seek a quote from Clifford's tearful wife for his next story. Clutching her housecoat to her throat with a reddened fist, she slammed the door in his face.

Ferndale woke with a start when Chief Morse, riled, burst into his office. "Damn it, Ferndale, I'm not paying you to take naps. Bad enough already, then comes this murder this morning. Blew the lid off this town. Our uniforms are scrambling all over this worried city on reports of killers on the loose. Everybody thinks the killer lives next door. We've got perps walking down the street, drinking in bars, carrying mail, selling purses, living next door, working the midnight shift, hell, even hiding under laundry baskets. Somebody at the library thinks the killer is down there checking out books. Hell, the mayor just kicked my ass to the moon and back. He wants answers and wants them yesterday."

Ferndale sat up, rubbing his aching neck. "We talked about all this an hour ago, chief. If you want my hide, you can have it right now."

Morse looked wary. "Yeah? Then what happens?"

"I walk and you'll never catch the real killer," Ferndale said. He eased back in his squeaking chair, trying to focus his mind on the crisis at hand. "Give me twenty-four hours, chief. If we don't nail the killer by then you can take my badge."

Read all about it!

In the mountains between Butte and Deer Lodge, far away from people, a pair of hands snipped the final purple rose. The woods were dark and quiet. Soon blankets of cold air would settle over the flimsy greenhouse. The killer smiled at the eventful summer. The plan worked to perfection except for killing Vanzetti. How ugly, his beheading. Linda Danvers wasn't part of the plan either. She meddled. Dispatching her proved easy in Deer Lodge where the streets rolled up after dark. In Butte, Ferndale at least knew how to catch sloppy killers. Premeditated crimes strained his knowledge. He lacked sophistication to see the big picture. Only that newspaper reporter, Maguire, had the smarts to figure out the killer's motive. Maguire lost his concentration when he fell head over heels in love with Mary Miller. He might get back to the murder story. Or, he might not. His pathetic need for love made him hopelessly distracted. Time had run out. This last purple rose, now snipped, awaited the final victim. What a pity Clifford Fenton died without a rose to adorn his pathetic soul. Despite the hurried decision to shoot him, the aim was true. Fenton, a reckless man, nearly gave away the story. What a drunken simpleton. The last rose would go to the only man who had earned the killer's respect. Red Maguire had hoped to break the big story. Give him credit for trying. What a shame he had to go.

Back in the *Bugle* city room, Maguire struggled after a crazy night, trying to ignore his last memory of a smiling Mary Miller. He slammed down four cups of Stoffleman's bitter coffee to stay awake. The editor wanted to publish an *Extra* edition to report the overnight news. Unfortunately for the *Bugle*, the presses had printed the morning paper, handing the local radio stations rare exclusive reporting on a big story. Stoffleman ran upstairs to persuade the old man to start the printing press in mid-afternoon. Minutes later, Stoffleman emerged from upstairs as if shot from a rifle. "You've got two hours to write a big-ass story, Maguire. Throw everything into it including the kitchen sink. The old man says if he's springing for an Extra that it better read like one or he'll be looking for a new editor and a new crime reporter, and that's a direct quote."

Maguire rolled a sheet of paper into his typewriter and hammered an opening on the keys. The *Bugle* needed him now, more than ever, to write the biggest crime story of his career:

"The Purple Rose Murders took a sharp and disturbing turn early today when an unknown assailant shot a prime police suspect dead and a Bugle news reporter went missing. Police said the investigation entered a dangerous new phase as they believe the unknown killer might be involved in each of those incidents."

He kept typing, stopping briefly to phone Ferndale to confirm a fact or two. Stoffleman hurried to his desk to grab the latest pages from his typewriter. Even as Maguire wrote the latter portions of his story, most of it from memory, editors kept a flow of copy going to the composing room where men at clattering Linotype machines set the story in hot lead for the printing press. Stoffleman shouted orders. He found a photo of Mary Miller, taken the day she started working at the *Bugle*. He also included photos of the five other victims. Ferndale told some clerk in his filing room to send over a mug shot of Clifford Fenton. By the time Maguire finished his story it filled the front page and an additional full page. Stoffleman added a few pages of national news to fill the other pages. The advertising staff produced a full-page appeal from the Butte Betterment Society calling for law and order. "That ought to please the old man," Stoffleman said when Maguire handed over the final sheet of his typewritten story. "Lock up the final pieces, boys!" he yelled to editors furiously working on the story. "Press rolls in thirty!"

Outside the *Bugle*, two dozen boys and three girls waited to swarm uptown Butte's street corners with the special editions. Soon they would bark out the big headlines to fancy spenders under the bright lights at the Board of Trade down on Park Street. They would flash front pages along the bar stools and booths at the M & M where cigar smoke hung blue and heavy. Their cries of "Extra! Read about the latest in the Purple Rose Murders!" would be heard outside rooming houses, beauty parlors, auto dealers, clothing stores, leather shops, banks and everywhere else where people gathered.

Maguire dialed Ferndale for the third time in an hour. "Hope your story won't make us look like damned fools," Ferndale said. "Just because we are."

Maguire rubbed sleep from his eyes. "I repeated what you told me about the killer having skills with a gun, shooting people without being seen, leaving no evidence and all that. Maybe a witness will come forward. Given all the publicity of the murders, somebody must know the identity of the perp. Do you think so, Duke?"

"We can only hope, Maguire. Say, something you ought to know. We traced that call to your room at the Logan this morning. I had a hunch it came from Clifford Fenton. We don't know for sure because the call came from a pay phone."

"Fenton? Why?"

"Still holding onto this damn theory of mine that he hustled these killings somehow. If I'm right, I'll buy you a tall glass of Butte Lager one of these days."

"That would be a first."

"What a joker. Watch your sorry ass, Maguire. I don't want to hear that you're stretched out in an alley smelling like a purple rose."

Maguire fought the impulse to sleep. He joined Stoffleman downstairs to watch the mighty press, its cylinders thumping, unlimber a slow stream of newspapers onto conveyor belts. The press idled in slow gear while men scurried over the machinery to adjust page plates. The foreman, satisfied, punched an ink-smeared red button. The press roared, issuing a river of headlines that read:

Mystery deepens with overnight murder
Bugle reporter goes missing,
cops consider kidnapping

Stoffleman pulled two dozen fresh papers rolling off the press and handed them to Maguire. "Take these to your buddies over at the cop shop," he shouted over the cacophony. "I'll take the rest upstairs to the old man. Your story should keep us employed for another day or two."

As Stoffleman headed upstairs, Maguire walked to police headquarters. Maguire dropped four papers on Ferndale's desk and plunked the others on the front counter. Cops snatched them up before he reached the door. Already, on the street, newsboys clamored for buyers as people rushed them with jingle in hand. Just like the old days in Butte, Maguire thought. It might be 1954 but hot news sells newspapers the way it always did. He walked back to the *Bugle*, exhausted and with no purpose in mind. Stoffleman greeted him when he entered the city room.

"No point in sleeping away the afternoon, Maguire. We need a fresh story for tomorrow's paper and you're the hottest ticket in town."

"I'm beyond beat, boss. Worried about Mary, too."

Stoffleman's fiery mood showed no mercy. "I hear you on both counts, Maguire. But you snoozing in the middle of the day won't help find her, now will it? I'm thinking another story will. We can't let this one walk away from us. Or would you rather read about it in the Company press when they get around to it?"

"You know how to turn the screws, boss."

Stoffleman smiled. He accepted Maguire's observation as a compliment. Now he turned to uncharacteristic flattery. "So what does Montana's finest crime reporter do now?"

"Guess I had better figure that out. Got to find news." His mind felt heavy with fatigue.

"One word of warning, Maguire. Resist your temptation to run off on a personal manhunt for Mary Miller. Leave that to Ferndale. Love and crime don't mix." Maguire, looking guilty, nodded his assent. Stoffleman read him like a book. "And Maguire? Try not to get yourself shot like a damn fool. I'm running short of reporters, sure enough."

Maguire, shivering in a cool wind, walked to his Pontiac. A squall blew over the mountain, bringing even more rain, another dark day. Summer had taken a fast train out of Butte. Bleak days reminded him of Lily. He shook his momentary sadness and drove up the Hill toward Walkerville, high enough to look down at the city and its imposing gallows frames that lowered miners into the hungry earth. Maguire turned into a muddy field scarred from digging and dumping. Below him, big ore-hauling trucks crawled over the torn landscape. Even farther away, cars hurried along the streets in the powdery mist, their reds and blues looking strangely out of place in the gray city. Maguire parked the Pontiac, its nose pointing down. He inhaled several deep breaths of thin air to clear his head. He had written about so many angles to the Purple Rose Murders, all those parts, but parts of what? Maguire knew he somehow missed the big picture.

He took one more look at the panorama before him, pulled a notebook and pen from his suit jacket, and began writing names. Mike Kelly and Rodney Townsend and their fathers. Linda Danvers, David Fenton, Antonio Vanzetti, Clifford Fenton. What an odd collection of people who had nothing in common. Maguire listed other names he and Mary Miller had reported in the *Bugle*. Rhonda Townsend, Maud Kelly, Harvey Addleston. Harry Anthony and several other people who were quoted in stories but had little to say. Maguire stared at the list. Of all the names, he knew the least about Addleston and Anthony. They were murky figures from the past. They were linked somehow. Addleston died after being stomped by Kelly and Townsend, the fathers of slain sons. Anthony had given away an impressive tract of land to his young nephew, David Fenton, cousin to Clifford Fenton. Did Addleston and Anthony know each other? How did Danvers and Vanzetti fit into the picture? Mary had suspicions of Rhonda Townsend. Rhonda seemed so genuinely sad over her brother's murder. Maguire knew better than to rule her out as a suspect. Clever killers, like magicians, covered their tracks with misdirection and sleight of hand. Rhonda's apparent grief might be hiding something more disturbing.

Maguire put the notebook back in his pocket and looked around. Once again, he sensed somebody watching. The nearest houses stood a hundred yards away. A peek in the rearview mirror showed his arched red eyebrows, tired drooping eyes, an empty field behind him. Maguire started the motor. Yet another victim would die soon. Not Mary, he hoped. He thought of her bound and scared as the killer held a gun to her head. Or worse. Shaking the thought, Maguire locked the doors of his car before starting back down Butte Hill toward the *Bugle*.

~ 16 ~

Aggie and Red

Over at the Forever More Funeral Home, an elderly
undertaker read the *Bugle Extra* with more than passing
interest. He had embalmed the young miners Kelly and
Townsend, shooting victims of the Purple Rose Killer, and the
Bugle reporter, Vanzetti. Fatal shots pierced the hearts of Kelly
and Townsend. Preparing them for viewing at their funerals
had amounted to nothing more than a minor job as body
repairs go. Small entrance wounds in each man, hardly bigger
than a dime, allowed easy concealment in the casket. The
bullet fired at Kelly exited his body below his left shoulder
blade. Townsend's bullet lodged inside his stocky body. No
matter. He died anyway. The old undertaker, Arnie Petrovich,
folded his slender arthritic body onto a wooden chair in the
embalming room. As he read he paid no notice to a corpse
stretched out beside him. The ancient woman, her blank eyes
staring at the ceiling, died four days short of her century
birthday. Arnie embalmed many of Butte's oldest residents.
Even gone silent they kept him company in the dark
basement. Sometimes he sang to them. He ate a sack lunch
while he worked.

Arnie marveled at Red Maguire's knack for finding himself in the middle of sensational crimes. Maguire's story in the *Bugle Extra* read like the Dick Van Loan stories Arnie read in *Phantom Detective* magazine until it folded in 1953. Maguire wrote from personal observation unlike his competitors who quoted "official sources" who never revealed all the facts in their banal statements. Arnie Petrovich felt some kinship with Red Maguire and Duke Ferndale because they all witnessed ugly violations of the human body. Antonio Vanzetti came to the Forever More in two pieces. Reattaching his head, a gruesome ordeal, required stitching all the way around the neck. Arnie had seen worse damage but he couldn't remember when. Why would a killer do such a thing? As Arnie read the *Bugle* story, his marbled eyes straining to focus on the tiny print, he stopped at a name. He remembered that man. He had embalmed Harvey Addleston. The man's beaten remains required every skill the undertaker learned in mortuary school. Those violent miners mashed Addleston's face into a red pulp. They caved his rib cage with hard kicks from their heavy boots. But something else troubled Arnie. Something that nagged at him. Something he couldn't quite recall. He went into a storage room where he kept records of past funerals. He pulled open a drawer marked "1929-30" where, after ten minutes of searching, he found the Addleston notes. There he saw it, that odd request, a queer gesture of family sentimentality. He shuddered at the mental image. The undertaker went to the phone. With trembling fingers he dialed Red Maguire at the *Bugle*. Luverne, the switchboard operator, took a message.

That very moment in Deer Lodge, several concerned citizens arrived at the jail to voice a complaint with Police Chief Sam Williams. Many people had come to know him during his employment as the city compliance officer. He took after the town's unleashed and barking dogs like a man possessed. His resume included four bites, two punches to the face from dog owners, three snarling dogs shot in commission of duty, but a tripling of fines from tickets he issued. Meanwhile, the old police chief retired after thirty years on the job. Three of the five City Council members, awash in sudden income from guilty dog owners, stated their desire to promote Sam Williams. They saw him as a pillar of law and order in Deer Lodge. A town of fewer than four thousand residents needed a police chief who withstood local politics. His record on writing parking tickets wowed them. They commended his diligence in enforcing the town's lawn sprinkling ordinance. In the end Williams became the new chief by unanimous vote. The City Council failed to consider that Williams, in his four years of wearing a badge, had never investigated a murder.

Copies of the *Butte Extra* that had arrived in town worried residents that more murders might come their way. The chief reclined in a creaking wooden office chair, his feet propped on his desk, when six men from the Rotary Club and two bankers in respectable suits spoiled his nap. One of them handed him a copy of the *Extra*, pointing to the photo of Linda Danvers.

"Every resident in our little town is in danger, Sam," said one of the visitors. "It's getting worse over in Butte. What are you doing to protect us from this killer? What's Deer Lodge got to do with these murders anyway?"

The men watched as the chief lowered his boots from the desk and pushed back the mustache that drooped over his lips. Their stricken expressions revealed they doubted he had done much at all.

"Gentlemen, I understand why you're riled up —."

"Riled up!" exclaimed another. "Concerned for public safety is a better way of putting it, Sam. Do you at least have a suspect? Somebody of interest? Anybody?"

Williams raised his hands, fingers extended, in a stopping motion. "Whoa, men. Take a breath. You know how it goes over in Butte. Haul murder victims to the morgue by the busload is what they do. Here in Deer Lodge we keep a tight lid on the criminal element. When's the last time a barking dog disturbed your beauty sleep?"

Rolf Barkley, the Rotary president, tried a diplomatic approach. "Come now, Chief, we're not here to complain about dogs. It's the two-legged variety that has us concerned. What's to say the killer won't strike down one of our citizens out for an evening stroll, or walking home from church after Sunday services, or leaving the grocery store carrying a sack full of canned goods after dark? We need assurances that our town is safe, Sam. Here, look at this," Barkley said, holding the *Bugle* in front of Williams, "this reporter Red Maguire describes a serial killer who enjoys the thrill of the chase. Maguire says right here on the front page that the killer knows nobody can stop him."

Williams motioned again with his hands. "You say you believe everything you read, Rolf? How would this newsie Maguire know anything about crime anyhow?"

A man shouted from a cell toward the back of the jail about wanting lunch. "Shut up, Zimmerman, damn it!" the chief shouted back to him. To the men standing before him he confided, "Case of drunk and disorderly, again. Third time this month."

The chief straightened his holster. He meant the gesture to show the town men of his authority. "Nobody wants murders in our town. Me and the boys, we're out there looking. Only three of us on the city payroll, nights and weekends too, as you know. You want to know about murders? Not much to report, I'm afraid. Hardly anybody knew Linda Danvers. She didn't live here long enough for that. I can't get anything out of that idiot daughter of hers. Maybe Linda brought along some trouble when she moved to Deer Lodge. We couldn't find any sign of it."

"Sam, what about those roses?" one of the men said.

"I talked to the chief in Butte. Other than the purple rose left on her body, there's not a shred of evidence to connect Linda's murder with the others. But that strange rose —."

One of the men interrupted. "She's been out snapping pictures of every tree and plant from here to Butte. I don't know what nature photographers do but she did plenty of it. Maybe she bumped into the killer when she went out with her camera. Seems to me flowers and nature photographers have something in common."

"No reason to think it," the chief said.

"Shot behind the laundromat," said another man. "My wife had dropped her nickels in the machine not ten minutes earlier to dry the kids' school clothes."

"What for, Marty?" asked yet another.

"With that fire smoke blowing off Mount Powell she didn't want to use the clothesline."

The chief looked exasperated. "Take it home, boys. We'll catch this guy. Soon, I'm sure."

"We hope so, Sam," said one of the bankers. "You need to know people in this town are scared enough that there's talk of forming an armed posse to patrol the streets. I keep my rifle within easy reach. I'm not holding back if the killer threatens my family."

"I've heard the talk, Elmer. Last thing this town needs is a band of vigilantes running around waving guns."

"Then catch the killer, Sam. Soon. Some of my neighbors have itchy trigger fingers. The killer isn't getting any younger."

The chief watched the men leave the jail. He pulled a peanut butter sandwich from his desk and took a deep bite. His mouth full, he shouted to the drunk locked up in a cell down the hall, "They have no idea!"

In uptown Butte at the M & M, Ferndale inhaled his first beer, one of those no-names but straight from the tap and cold. He hoped Maguire would drop in. The way things were going, Maguire soon might be Ferndale's only friend. Ferndale struggled with what to do next. He propped his scuffed black shoe on the rung of the chair next to him. Two men playing darts across the room shouted their glee whenever they hit close to the bullseye. Ferndale wished he could make the Purple Rose Murders go away. Instead, the awful problem hung like an anchor around his neck, still unsolved.

Ferndale had promised to find the killer within twenty-four hours. He had half a dozen dead bodies and a missing woman. Nothing added up. He took a deep gulp from his second beer. The fatigue he felt earlier had evaporated, strangely, but his anxiety grew. Ferndale knew the feeling well. Everybody expected cops to solve murder cases overnight. He knew better. Being a detective meant weeks and months of searching for leads. Sometimes, they came easy. Sometimes, not at all. Even so, one murder rarely led to another. Ferndale's greatest worry as a cop? Failing to solve a crime in time to stop a succession of others. He had seen the pattern with burglaries and robberies. They came in bunches, like a series of violent storms roaring over the mountains, each more daring than the others. Now Butte limped along with something much worse. Ferndale cursed himself for not catching the killer after the Kelly and Townsend murders. He should have known where to look. All those years of experience, wasted? He hated being a tired and cranky old cop.

A few years earlier, during an argument with the chief over wages, Ferndale demanded to see his personnel file. He found it stuffed with commendations and a few memorable disciplinary actions. Ferndale regretted his suspension back in '42 for fighting on the job. In those days Ferndale boxed with gloves in the local clubs and bare fists in the streets. His bosses took note of his scarred hands and bruised face and warned him to keep his punches in the ring. Despite his occasional personal shortcomings, Ferndale stood clear of scandal. Not everybody in uniform respected an honest cop. He tread on some toes, made some enemies, crushed some bad actors. Ferndale despised cops on the take. In his long career in Butte he had known plenty of them. When Ferndale investigated a robbery behind Mercury Street, in the place once known as Venus Alley, he discovered a cop on duty committed the crime. Ferndale presented eyewitness evidence to the chief. The dirty cop, fired within the hour, resisted arrest when Ferndale tried to cuff him. He swung at Ferndale's head with the cuffs dangling from his right wrist. Ferndale leaned away and countered with a smashing blow to the man's jaw. That should have finished it. Ferndale lost his temper and punched the dirty cop several more times. The man fell unconscious to the floor. "Went beyond police protocol to inflict bodily harm," his disciplinary letter from Chief Morse read.

Ferndale had taken his share of licks over the years. He hated being played for a fool. In his book, everything had pointed to Clifford Fenton as the Purple Rose Killer. He needed to catch him in the act. Criminals like Fenton sent out signals like radar. A bar robbery earlier that summer in Elk Park, a few miles up the highway from Butte, caught Ferndale's attention. Two nervous men arrived minutes before closing time. The owner noticed one of them watching the door. When he told the men to leave, hoping his suspicions would leave with them, the one lurking at the bar struck him in the head with a gun butt. The bandits tore strips from the dress worn by the bar owner's wife, exposing her white matronly underpants, to gag them. They bound her with an electric cord and the husband with a strip of horsehair and threw them to the floor behind the bar. The crooks stole fifty dollars from the cash register. They shut off the lights when they left.

Fenton, on parole for shooting a man in the leg in a dispute over unpaid rent, resembled a description the bar owner gave to police. That's when he fell into Lucky Finero's bail-jumping arena. Like many parolees from the state prison in Deer Lodge, Fenton left the joint aboard a Greyhound bus, taking a short ride to Butte where he roomed in a shack on East Park Avenue with a few other parolees. Some months later, after pocketing some jingle, he married his current wife and moved to Centerville. Ferndale knew Fenton as an unremarkable drunk, a no-account type of man, much different in reputation from his cousin David Fenton. Why one bothered to associate with the other remained a mystery. Maybe family blood, maybe stupidity, maybe something else more sinister. Ferndale bet his badge on the latter.

As Ferndale soaked his regrets in beer, all five black and whites prowling Butte's streets searched for Mary Miller. Every woman wearing a colorful dress got a close look. Ferndale suspected he would find her dead. He knew that Maguire, wise to the ways of the streets, feared the same. First Vanzetti, now Miller, probably Maguire next. *Bugle* reporters falling like dominos. No leap of imagination required. Ferndale never thought of telling Maguire to leave town until the cops found the killer. Maguire had a job to do. The crime reporter wasn't the type to wither and hide because of death threats. Big enough to stand his ground in a fight but a bullet from behind, in the dark, ignored the rules.

Up in Dublin Gulch, where wood smoke hung heavy on the street, Maguire parked his car in front of Aggie Walsh's rooming house. Machinery roared on all sides as rumbling giant steel cables lifted tons of ore from deep below the surface. Maguire found the commotion strangely comforting. Aggie lived in a flat on the second floor. He knocked on her door. "Red, me boy!" Aggie cried, lifting him to his toes in a mighty bear hug. She stood a head shorter than Maguire but had the strength of a miner accustomed to shoveling ore. She wore a full-length yellow apron over her blue dress. An enticing aroma of fresh-baked cinnamon bread filled her flat. Aggie and Maguire settled at the kitchen table. After they exchanged small talk, dosed with a slice of that bread and a deep mug of whiskey-laced joe that put Stoffleman's muddy brew to shame, Maguire got down to business.

"I fell in love, Aggie."

"With an Irish girl, I hope? After all these years?"

"Not sure. Her name is Miller. I suppose Irish if she's not Scottish."

"Don't make me pull this out of you, Red. You remind me of your father sometimes. Man of few words when expressing any personal desires. I know you are capable of description because I read it every morning in the *Bugle*. Now get on with it." Aggie leaned forward on her chair. Feeble daylight filtered through a dust-coated window beyond her. Aggie earned a meager income washing and cooking for families in the gulch. Every month, when the *Bugle* paid Maguire his salary, he arrived at Aggie's door to hand her a new twenty-spot. He had done that since his first month of employment. He paid for her *Bugle* subscription, too. Maguire wondered if he did enough for her. He wouldn't trade Aggie's motherly presence for gold.

"She's a reporter at the *Bugle*, Aggie. Mary Miller. You've seen her byline." Aggie nodded but didn't interrupt. "I know it's quick. I finally paid attention to her a few days ago when we started working together on this Purple Rose murder story. Then it came to me that she had been right for me all along if I had cared to look. Now she's missing. Kidnapped. Maybe she's dead. That consequence crossed my mind. What bothers me is that I fell in love with somebody I hardly know. What if time has run out for me? For her? I waited too long and now Mary's gone."

Aggie nudged the plate of warm bread toward him. He reached for another thick slice and buttered it. "Indeed, what a predicament, Red. Let's hope they find that poor girl alive and healthy. That's my hope for her. Put her kidnapping aside for a moment." Aggie twirled a pencil she had stashed in her loose bun of reddish-gray hair. She studied Maguire over the top of her glasses, which had slid down her nose, and reached for his hand. Here it comes, Maguire thought.

"Red, me boy, on this other matter of you falling in love, I wonder sometimes. Remember a few years ago when I tried to interest you in Sarah Cavanaugh? Over on Placer Street? I had my reasons for trying to make a match. Not even that she is Irish, or that her husband died violently like your father, these dangerous mines be damned. You need a good woman by your side. Sarah needed a good man. Someone like you, Red. How long have I known you? Well, long enough to know your torn heart. Now Sarah's married to a wife beater. Did you know that? No woman bargains for a violent man who throws her around like a rag doll. Goes by the nickname Boot Lace because he walks around with untied shoes. He's an ugly sort. Go straighten him out, Red, like you did to Joe O'Malley and the rest of those boys. Do it for Sarah. Now, about this other woman who won your heart. Here you are, mooning over a woman who's a stranger to you. I doubt you bargained for that either. Who can fully explain the ways of love? No, when me parents came from Ireland, they left behind loving brothers and sisters they never saw again. I never understood how they could do that." Aggie shook her head and let go of Red's hand.

"Why didn't you ever marry, Aggie?"

"Because I lost the only man I ever truly loved in a mine accident, Red. I suppose I should tell you that your father proposed to me a week before he died. We wanted to tell you after you returned from that trip to Chicago to find your mother, bless her wayward soul. How sad how things turned out for you and me, all of it."

Maguire felt his eyes go wet. "You're my mother, Aggie. That's what I learned when I went searching for Lily. Never there for me then or ever. You always were."

Aggie reached into the pocket of her apron for a tissue. "Did you come up here to make an old woman cry?"

"You're far from old, Aggie. What, fifty-five years tops?"

"Red Maguire, you know damn well I'm fifty-nine. If I make sixty you bring the candles and the Butte Fire Department and we'll throw a big party here in the gulch before the pit swallows it up. Now, you came here for advice about that missing girl so that's what I'm giving you. You are a searcher, Red, and not just for Lily. Any woman in Butte would crave your attention. Look at you, tall and handsome, Irish to the core. You turn heads on the street. Did you know that, Red? All those pretty Butte women wait for you, hope you will notice, but you leave them disappointed. You shop but you don't buy. Instead of making the first move with a girl you let life pass you by. Everything to you is work. Late nights at the *Bugle*. Weekends at the *Bugle*. You and those cops, wringing every last gory detail from every last crime, that's all you see of Butte. I watch you pat the pocket in your suit and I know why. You've done it three times in the half hour we've sat here at my table. You do it without knowing it, like other people brush back their hair. Those letters in your pocket bring you comfort. No, I don't want to know what they say. None of my business, me son. I see your broken heart. That's what you're reaching for. That's what you're trying to fix. Maybe this Mary Miller will mend it or maybe not. I know this, Red. No woman wants to marry a newspaper crime reporter. She wants the man. Show more of yourself, the man you really are, you'll find love. Listen close, me son. When you find true love, Red Maguire, you'll never want to let go. Let's pray the love you find is a good Irish girl. Now shoo, I've got bread to bake."

Maguire drove down the hill to the *Bugle*. He figured to find Ferndale down the street at the M & M drinking away his woes. Maguire fought the temptation to join him and went upstairs to the city room. Beside his phone he found a pink message slip from Luverne at the switchboard. Call Arnie at Forever More, it said. Maguire dialed the number. He had known Arnie Petrovich for most of the time he had worked at the *Bugle*. In more ways than one, Arnie knew where Butte's bodies were buried. He resembled the obituary reporter Calvin Claggett in that respect. Some men lived with one foot in the grave.

Arnie picked up on the first ring. "How's she go, Maguire? Say, I have something that will interest you."

"No more dead people, I hope."

"I'm neck-deep in them, as you know. Tell Claggett to get over here tonight to help me embalm the latest arrivals. I need his help painting faces, too. Everyone wants Aunt Sadie looking adorable for the last goodbye. But here it is. You mentioned Addleston in today's *Bugle*. I had to look back on the man."

"So?"

"So I handled his funeral back in '30. His wife made a special request, an unusual one. We don't get asked for many favors outside our standard funeral services."

"Arnie, what request?"

"She wanted purple roses placed on his casket."

~ 17 ~

Embalmer has a clue

Red Maguire opened a notebook and scribbled furiously. He asked Arnie for every detail, however insignificant, he could recall from Addleston's funeral. "I wrote down here, for my personal records, that his wife would provide the flowers. He grew them himself."

"He grew the roses?" Maguire shouted over the phone. Stoffleman, at his desk, reared his frazzled gray head at the prospect of another big story.

"Terribly unusual, I thought at the time. Yes, I wrote it down right here. She wanted the roses presented just so. Fussy woman as I recall. She wanted them laid on the casket once we closed the lid."

Maguire whistled as he pictured the scene. By this time Stoffleman stood beside his desk straining to hear the other end of the conversation.

"But that's not all, Maguire. My notes show she wanted a single purple rose, on a long stem, placed on the chest of the deceased. She brought a fresh one to the funeral home the morning of the funeral."

Maguire whistled. "A fresh rose? On his chest like these murder victims? Where did she get it?"

"Red, I doubt I knew that twenty-four years ago."

"The wife, Arnie, what do you remember about her?"

"Very little. I can't recall whether she showed emotion. According to my notes she paid for the funeral and burial in cash. I never saw her around Butte after that. Not that I get out much with the living, mind you."

"What about family members? Did she have children?"

"One, I think, but I can't recall whether boy or girl. Sorry I can't remember more. Say, Maguire? You know that I have an eighty-fourth birthday coming next month? Stop by the Forever More for a slice of chocolate cake."

"Hell, Arnie, for this I'll buy you a bakery."

After they hung up Stoffleman's face brightened under his eyeshade. "Now you've really got something, Maguire. Maybe I can make you into a genuine crime reporter yet. Find out more and you've got tomorrow's front-page topper." The editor smirked and walked away.

Maguire thought of Ferndale. He hustled down to the M & M where he found the old detective half asleep at a table in the corner. A cigarette wedged between his fingers burned dangerously close to his scarred knuckles.

"Drinking on duty, Duke? Can't you get fired for that?"

"Since when?"

"In that case, I'll have one myself."

"Can't hurt," Ferndale said. His eyelids sagged more than usual. "Say, watch out for Mayor Tinklenberg. He's blowing wind like he's got something important to say."

Maguire lifted his glass for a deep gulp. "More than usual is what I hear. It got around how he put the screws to the chief. He's got a head of steam for sure. The mayor barged into the *Bugle* a few days ago with a beef about a headline. Stoffleman took the heat for a moment and then burst out laughing like a hyena. It was the ears."

"Them ears. Tell me again how the mayor keeps on his feet in a strong wind?"

"Sails on a ship, Duke. So Stoffleman failed to hold it in as did most of the people in the city room. Oddest pair of ears I can recollect in Butte and that's saying something. Look around at the specimens walking among us."

Ferndale snorted beer. "Funny, Maguire," he said, wiping foam from his upper lip. "What's got me worried is that his eyesight ain't too bad. You can bet the mayor's loaded for bear and taking aim at my sorry hide. So's the chief. Right now I don't even know how to grow a purple rose."

Maguire flopped his fedora onto the table and brushed ruddy fingers over his square jaw.

"We've got a break if you want to chase it down." Maguire told him about Addleston's funeral. Ferndale raised his head. The news invigorated the old cop. "We've got to find the wife. Her name again?"

"Martha. If you recall, Duke, we looked around but couldn't find her."

"That's right. Company tore down her house. Probably left town after the old boy got knocked off. Lots of hard feelings hang around when somebody dies from a beating. Seen it way too many times."

"Was justice served?"

"Never is, Maguire."

"Found anything new so far?"

"I reckon you're asking about your girlfriend Mary Miller. We're trying, but nothing. The way she disappeared squares with every other crime in this case. Done clean, no evidence left behind, nothing to go on. We dusted her house for prints. Just hers and yours. Found them all over the damn bedroom and especially on the headboard. Boys in blue got a kick out of that. Our friend Maguire, pouring the pork to the doll from the *Bugle*. Should I consider you a suspect, Maguire?"

"You're bluffing, Duke. No way you've got my prints on file. Or Miller's. I just got, well, a little exposed. I barely knew her."

"Looks to me like you knew her plenty."

"Well, there's that."

"We'll find her, hopefully alive."

"Should I admit to you I'm tired of dealing with this mess?"

"Preaching to the choir, Maguire."

"What happened to that waitress named Myrtle?"

"Now you're asking about my love life. Fair is fair?"

"Something like that."

"She told me to take my orders someplace else."

"At least you had a few wives. Shirley came last?"

"Third and final. Another woman who told me to take it someplace else. Story of a cop's life. Crying in our beer don't make things better."

"We're a sad pair, Duke."

"At least you were getting some."

"Buy you another beer?"

"Can't hurt, Maguire. One more cold one before I head over to the Forever More to hear the sorry tale about Addleston's funeral straight from Arnie. I need to file a report before the chief reads your story in the *Bugle* and asks again why I'm on the city payroll. Little embarrassing choking on your dust all the time. I remember you as a punk kid from Dublin Gulch who didn't know shit. Still don't, maybe. What happened?"

"I grew up, I guess."

"Don't josh me," Ferndale said, taking a swallow of his third beer.

"There's something bothering me, Duke. How did Harvey Addleston and Harry Anthony know each other? I can't put it together."

"Open to speculation. A two-bit shyster, Anthony. Ran some rackets uptown back about the time I got my badge. Gambling, some petty theft, romanced with whores on Mercury Street now and then. Nothing going on with him that you couldn't say about most underworld operators in those days in Butte. City ran wide open, three shifts in the mines, thirst ran deep. You know the story."

"I paid little attention beyond the boundaries of my neighborhood. What I remember is kids fighting for turf."

"Same with small-bore criminals like Anthony. He cornered vice uptown. Grifter from way back. Never heard of him putting anybody down with his fists. He talked other people into doing it for him. Addleston, now, he weren't like Anthony. No sir. Distinguished man, wire eyeglasses, church man, never seen without a proper haircut. Sold shoes in a respectable store on Broadway. Place smelled of new leather.

Old Myrtle, my wife at the time, she wanted me looking fancy on the job. Sent me to Addleston's to buy a pair of black Oxfords with them wax laces. I told her cops don't wear dress shoes but that damn Myrtle ordered me around like a rented mule. Packed sauerkraut in my lunch, did I tell you that? Wore those new shoes for a week until I ruined them in the mud carrying a stiff that dripped blood all over them. Being a cop, it ain't for dandies."

"You never told me that. About Addleston selling shoes, I mean."

"Just came to me, Maguire. How Anthony snookered Addleston into going to the Helsinki that night, who knows? Buttoned-up type of medium height, no more, wanders into a working-class bar in Finntown. Probably wore a suit with cuff links. No taste for hooch. Man never downed a beer. Imagine that in Butte."

"You never told me that either."

"I'm sixty-three. Give me a break."

"I'm still wondering. How do these men know each other?"

"Beats me. Digging out ancient history is your job, not mine." Ferndale dropped his empty glass on the bar and stood to leave. "You'll be the first to know if we find your sweetheart. Nothing much to go on, as usual."

"I'm worried, Duke. When she called me from her house last night, she sounded desperate. I can't get it out of my mind," Maguire said.

Ferndale stopped. "From her house? No, that ain't it. We traced her call to a pay phone in uptown Butte. Same phone your threatening caller used. Lady working the city switchboard remembered plugging to your number."

Maguire set down his beer mug.

"I don't understand. Why ...?"

"Kidnapper might have told her what to say to throw you off."

"That's another key detail you almost forgot to pass along."

"Catch me on a day when I get a good night's sleep. You might hear different."

Maguire shifted on the bar stool. "Can we afford to shut our eyes to this case?"

Ferndale slapped Maguire's shoulder. "You and I, we've been around the block enough times to admit to each other we should expect the worst. Find out more about Addleston and Anthony, will you? Unless we nail the killer soon I'll be waiting at the mailbox for my pension checks. Presuming they give me any. These purple roses, they ain't making me happy."

~ 18 ~

Secrets from the tenderloin

The killer carefully wrapped the final rose in a wet Bugle Extra. Maguire's latest story barely mentioned Harvey Addleston. How disappointing that Harvey's murder, the original one, lacked the publicity it deserved. Drying leaves from quaking aspens showered over the mountain cabin. The foolish Danvers woman had blundered into this private place. Her first mistake. Her note said she came exploring with her camera up the road, nothing but an old logging trail, eleven miles from Deer Lodge. "Saw your quaint cabin," Danvers had written. "I stopped to say hello but since I found nobody home I went on my merry way in search of wildlife to photograph. Lovely little greenhouse, by the way. Gorgeous purple roses!" Then came the woman's second mistake. The note included her full name and address. How neighborly of Linda, the killer thought. Linda would have to die quick before she blabbed about the roses. The killer watched the Danvers residence that evening as nightfall approached. A woman in a red headscarf carried a laundry basket to her car. She drove a few blocks to the main street of this no-account town. The killer had no patience for distractions. Danvers went inside a bright but empty laundromat. The killer saw the back door open and waited in the alley. Luring Danvers outside took less than a minute. The killer called to her from the alley. Danvers didn't suspect a thing. She had a pleasant open face and trusting eyes.

Foolish woman. The killer held up a pillow. Danvers looked perplexed, but only for a second, when the pillow muffled the shot. The bullet pierced her heart. She landed on her back, dead. The killer awarded her a purple rose. An honorary distinction.

Full of beer, Maguire returned to the *Bugle* city room. He felt dizzy and distracted. The afternoon had evaporated in a blur. He watched Stoffleman pull a blackened chicken leg out of a greasy brown paper bag. Maguire looked out the tall windows to Butte's outer reaches. The hazy mountains beyond the Flats hid so much. Mary, held captive somewhere, dead or alive. He slumped in his chair and nodded off. How long he slept, he didn't know, but he awoke when Stoffleman rapped his knuckles on Maguire's desk. "Wake up, sleeping beauty, you have a story to write."

"You're unrelenting, boss." Maguire blinked hard at the interruption. His short slumber included hot kisses with Mary. He struggled to hang onto the sensation.

"We're only as good as what we do tomorrow, Maguire," the editor said, repeating one of his cherished admonitions.

Maguire straightened, grudgingly let go of his dream, and rolled a sheet of paper into his typewriter:

"Purple roses decorated the casket of a Butte man who died after being beaten 24 years ago by two miners whose sons were slain in a wave of murders this summer."

"Whew," Maguire said to himself. "This parade of victims is getting complicated. So is this story."

"Police said that the victim beaten in 1930, Harvey Addleston, might hold the secret to this summer's wave of murders. Purple roses decorated the bodies of four men shot dead in Butte and a woman shot dead in Deer Lodge. Police said the death of a fifth Butte man slain by gunshot might be related to the others, but it's not known why the killer deprived him of a purple rose."

Stoffleman came across the room to show Maguire the headline for the *Bugle*'s front page. "Early Butte death linked to Purple Rose Murders," it read. The editor ran his hand over the flaming scar on his cheek. "I suppose it's occurred to you, Maguire, that when this story hits the streets those big shot reporters from out of town will chase the Addleston angle like a pack of mad dogs."

Maguire nodded. "Unless I get it first, boss, which I fully intend to do." Hearing what he wanted to know, Stoffleman nodded and walked away.

As Maguire typed, trying to squeeze news from his sleepwalking mind, Ferndale headed home for a long nap. The old cop ate a cold hotdog from the refrigerator and a stale donut from the kitchen counter before stumbling to the couch. Exhaustion clouded his mind. His service revolver, encased in its shoulder holster, jabbed him in the ribs. Someday he would take it off for good. He would spend his days fishing for trout on the Big Hole River, watching clouds go by, forgetting the awful things people did to one another. Someday. His mind tumbled over a waterfall into a deep pool where it sank, ever deeper, to a place black and quiet.

Ferndale, in his relentless fatigue, failed to detect the intruder. His brick house, like others on that block, looked narrow from the front but longer on the side in "shotgun style" construction with four rooms added end on end toward the back. Ferndale slept in the front room. Fading light fell across him on the couch. He began snoring. Night fell.

Maguire finished his long story. He embellished it with details gleaned from his conversations with Ferndale. He also threw in a statement from Chief Morse along the lines that police committed all available resources to the investigation. Maguire knew what that meant. The entire job fell into Ferndale's hands as the bosses in the front office ran in circles. Stoffleman grimaced at the clock, noting the late hour, when Maguire handed over the final pages of his story. The editor commenced to marking them up with his blue pencil. He crossed out words and added others. "I'll make your story sing," Stoffleman said, waving his pencil like a maestro flourished a baton. He had his corny moments.

Maguire's head hurt. Drinking beer with Ferndale only made him sluggish. After Stoffleman asked a few questions to clarify what Maguire had written, the crime reporter left the city room, watching apprehensively in the dark stairway leading to the street. He drove to his home at the Logan. The blankets on his bed were flung aside, just as he had left them when his phone rang early that morning. He read his notebook at the table. He thumbed through the pages until he found the names Addleston and Anthony. These men were connected somehow. If he found the answer he might solve the murders. In the morning, he promised himself, he would hurry to the courthouse to look for files on these men. Maguire felt a momentary pang of defeat. If no link existed between them, what then? And what if the killer came for him? He locked his door. The deadbolt clunked into place. He pulled his window shades to shut out light from the neon marquee. For the first time in years he wondered if he would live until morning.

Maguire fixed a small dinner of fish sticks and fried potatoes. When he finished the last of it, he dialed Ferndale at the police department. No answer. The detective must be home sleeping off the afternoon beer drinking. Maguire dropped the telephone back in its cradle. He didn't know why he wanted to talk to Ferndale. Something about the night felt strange and tense. Maguire switched on his television to the year-old KXLF station. *Dragnet* appeared on the black and white screen. He remembered Ferndale's scorn for Joe Friday. In every episode the TV cop interrogated a witness with his methodical "just the facts, ma'am," drill. Great, Maguire thought. Friday makes crime-fighting look easy. If only the Purple Rose Murders could be solved between commercials.

Maguire shut off the set. Only an occasional car passing on the street below interrupted the still night. He settled into a chair near the window and pulled the shade aside. A man stood at the corner, under a lamppost, his cigarette glowing. Maguire felt a momentary jolt of trouble until the man swayed down the sidewalk and into a bar. Maguire thought of his mother. She had disappeared, with that drunken sailor, to a place where she forgot being a mother. She had rid herself of Kieran Maguire. She had bleached him from her life. Maguire, as a boy, knew a few other kids whose mothers had abandoned them. Like him, they pretended they didn't care. They hid their hurt by fighting and stealing and roaming the streets long into the night. Maguire sat now in a drab room he called home, a grown man missing his mother, longing for a chunk of his childhood ripped from him and never replaced. It bothered Maguire to die without his mother.

Fleeting thoughts of warning Ferndale crossed his mind. About what exactly, he didn't know. Maguire had reported crime news for so long he sensed trouble before it happened. The unfolding calamity contrasted with those cut-and-dried cases shown on television. Crimes happened to actual people like Addleston, Kelly, Townsend, Danvers, Vanzetti and the Fenton cousins. They bled for real. Murder tore their lives to pieces. It left their families consigned to suffer storms of grief that never dissipated. Murders were bad, tragic, never easily solved even by somebody as savvy as Ferndale. Despite his every attempt to stay awake, to puzzle through his next *Bugle* story, Maguire slid into a slumber.

As Maguire nodded off, his .38 now under his pillow for easy reach, Ferndale drifted deeper on his couch. He dreamed happy thoughts at first. The dream took him back to being a young man, a new cop, prowling the streets of Butte in a black and white. He saw his pretty wife, his first, smiling and happy. Frances loved to bake banana cream pies. He felt some rare euphoria in his dream. He marveled at a life full of promise. Soon his dreams turned ugly as they always did. Images of shot bodies appeared. Ferndale flinched in his sleep. He saw Kelly and Townsend dead on the ground. Vanzetti's severed head, with its eyes frozen wide open, talked to him. The head loomed large, its face full of secrets, its tongue wagging with a description of the killer. Ferndale heard himself screaming. As he stirred, wiping the nightmare from his brain, he heard a sudden metal click. Precise and deadly, a gun cocking.

Across town, Maguire awoke with a start. His mind swam with a compendium of facts, of Butte history, of sources quoted in the many thousands of bylined stories he had written for the *Bugle*. Somehow, in his slumber, he had connected Harry Anthony's name with a source on Mercury Street. Ferndale, in his portrayal of Anthony as a small-time criminal, had mentioned his association with prostitution. Maggie O'Keefe, Maguire suspected, would know something about Harry Anthony. Maguire quoted Maggie several times over the years, sometimes because of crimes committed in Butte's red-light district and often because she knew by experience and reputation anybody who made jingle in vice.

Maguire drove to the Windsor Hotel in the dark. He remembered the place as Irish World, the name so often mentioned when he lived in Dublin Gulch. Red light glowed from windows in the Windsor's three stories. After nightfall, the Windsor opened for business. Maguire knocked on the front door. A house matron swung it open after looking him over from a peephole. He stepped into the front parlor. Four women wearing hardly anything at all lounged in overstuffed chairs. Some of them walked toward him in their lingerie, beckoning, looking ghostly in the soft light. Maguire peered through the gloom. "Is Maggie about?" he said to the nearest one.

"It depends, honey. I'm Iris. I love a man with thick red hair. It also happens I'm available right now. Do you like what you see?" She pulled open a satin housecoat to reveal a skimpy white bra and panties barely concealing her womanly features.

"I'm not here for that, welcoming as you are," he told her.

"What a disappointment. At least you're a charmer," Iris said, studying Maguire from head to toe. "Hold on, honey, I'll get her."

Maguire waited as other women in the parlor flirted with him. One blew in his ear. Minutes later, Maggie O'Keefe emerged from somewhere in the back of the house. Maguire knew her history. Like him, she had come to Butte from Chicago. Like him, she bragged of her Irish heritage. She got her start prostituting in the Dumas brothel down the block. Now she ran the house at the Windsor. She made it clear to anyone who asked that she no longer sold her services. Maggie kept a full house of prostitutes who did. She wore a fashionable red dress that would pass for sophistication on a public sidewalk. When she saw Maguire she brushed strands of gray hair from simmering brown eyes that locked on him. Maggie's stare reminded Maguire of the nun at St. Mary's Elementary School who taught him mathematics. The same eyes, the same studied examination. Those eyes, boring into him, seeking the story beyond his expression. Like Mary, those probing eyes.

"My friend Red Maguire, *Bugle* reporter, did you come to write a story about the positive benefits of paid sex in Butte?" Maggie flashed a white smile. Despite her advancing age she had an alluring come-on presence about her.

"Hello, Maggie. You'll recall that I've printed more than a few good words about you and the Windsor over the years."

She nodded. "And I see from your serious expression that you've come to collect what I don't sell. Follow me, if you please." They walked through a hallway past several closed doors. Maggie seated herself behind a large wooden desk with shapes of angels carved into it. She motioned Maguire to a chair.

"I thought of you tonight, Maggie."

"Did you now? I should be flattered given I have a couple decades and maybe then some on you."

"It's about the Purple Rose Murders."

"Oh, that disturbing crime wave police can't solve? Being an astute observer, you no doubt noticed we have a quiet house tonight. Business is slow lately because of that killer on the loose. People are scared to go outside after dark. Know what that does to a parlor house? Ask me anything, Maguire, but don't quote me by name. I don't need the trouble."

"No quotes, Maggie. What do you remember about a street operator named Harry Anthony?"

"Came across him, did you? What a bugger, that one. They called him Harry the Ham. Slick as snot that man was. He came around the Dumas wearing his expensive fedoras and double-breasted suits, wanting us to believe he had a Chicago connection. The mob, you know, but I never saw Harry as

215

anything more than a two-bit hustler. He threw big tips to the girls, got laid now and again, bragged about cutting rich money deals uptown. You know the type."

"You've heard the name Harvey Addleston?"

"I've read your stories. I knew that name would bring you here."

"Then you know something."

"It's not easy running a house these days, Maguire. Priests and civic do-gooders want us gone. The mayor sends health inspectors in here every few months to scare the girls. Cops come around wanting sex off the books. People won't admit the truth. If Butte didn't need us, didn't feed on us, we wouldn't be here."

"You could have called me, Maggie. You held back."

"It's your job to ask questions, Maguire. It's in my best interest to keep secrets."

"So I'm asking. How did Addleston and Anthony know each other?"

Maggie opened her office door, inspected an empty hallway, then closed it. "Here's what I heard all those years ago. Print what you want of it but none of this came from me." She stood by the window, looking out, as Maguire pulled out his notebook.

"You probably know about Addleston's shoe store on Broadway Street. Respectable place, Addleston and his employees dressed to the nines, catered to the suit and tie crowd mostly. We never got his business down here in the cribs. Hardly the type to mix with working girls. Dull man I heard, known for a personality the color of shoe leather. I didn't pay any mind until one night at the Dumas when Harry the Ham arrived stinking drunk. He wanted me and only me. I couldn't stand being with that man, but it's jingle, you know? The drunken fool fell flat on his face trying to take his pants off. He laid on the bed bragging about how he took a dumb shoe salesman for his life savings. I asked him how much. He said fifty grand and change. Big money in a working man's town. Harry had a bottle of the hard stuff with him. The more he drank the more he flapped his tongue. He told me he talked Addleston into investing in a partnership to build a big-ass hotel in Meaderville. We're talking what, a couple of miles from uptown? It made no sense, any of it, with this city already choking on hotels and rooming houses and the Anaconda Company wanting to dig a big damn open-air pit up there. Addleston bought the story. A man talked into making fast jingle will believe anything, I suppose. The scam had Addleston doubling his investment. Harry the Ham drew up phony papers. He never intended to build a hotel, you know. A devil, that man, a shyster right out of the Dick Tracy comic strips. Harry persuaded Addleston to hand over his life savings in cash if you can believe it."

Maguire paused his furious notetaking. "How did he manage to do that?"

"Harry had a gift of gab that could talk chrome off a trailer hitch," Maggie said, returning to the chair behind her desk. "He also liked to brag when he had a pocket stuffed full of jingle. I imagine he stole most of it. Shyster all right, that Harry, but no different from a hundred other men like him profiting from uptown vice in those days. Maybe better than most."

"So much for Butte being a mile high, a mile deep and everyone on the level, huh, Maggie?

"They got the first two measurements right, anyway. Nobody is on the level in this town. From where I sit, everyone has an angle, hustling these streets night and day for a buck."

"What about the cops?"

"What about them? Half of them were on the take themselves even back then. You know what I pay the cops to stay open? Running a parlor house in this town never came easy. Now it's worse."

"What happened next?"

"I only know what I heard. Not from Harry the Ham. He took a liking to one of the sporting girls who roomed in the Copper Block. He never came back to see me at the Dumas but word gets around Butte. I heard Addleston found out he had been tricked. One of the Croats down in Dogtown bought a pair of shoes in Addleston's store the very day he heard Harry drunk and bragging in a bar about what he pulled on Addleston. That man Addleston, no dummy. His fatal flaw? He trusted people. You know how that goes in a town like this. Addleston made threats to Harry that he would go to police. Harry asked Addleston to meet at the Helsinki bar to talk things over. He never went, as you probably know, because that coward Harry tricked dimwits into doing his bidding for him. Instead he hired one of his crook friends to stir up a couple of miners on the idea that Addleston cooked up a plot to bust their union. Harry always dreamed up one mess to cover another. Far-fetched tale, that union-busting, but that's why they called him Harry the Ham, you know. He sold foolishness like nobody's business. Those miners were supposed to rough up Addleston, put a scare into him he wouldn't forget, but they went too far. They were a couple of simple joes, dumb as sticks, gullible to the core. As you've reported, Addleston died from the beating he took."

"And those miners were Kelly and Townsend?"

"So I've heard. When Ferndale rounded them up they couldn't even name the man who sent them to the bar that night. They weren't the brightest ones."

"And the jingle, Maggie?"

"Harry panicked after Addleston died. He bought land with Addleston's life savings, deeded it to a relative of his. Laundering hot money, you know. I don't know much about that sort of thing. I doubt people who ran this city back in those days had the vaguest idea. Nobody paid attention to a land purchase in Butte unless it involved mining property. Land exchanges went on day and night."

"He gave it to David Fenton."

"Yes, some boy in the family he hardly knew."

"Harry the Ham thought he would double back when the heat was off and take the land back from the boy?"

"We'll never know. Harry had a heart attack while on top of his best girl at the Victoria. He died getting screwed."

"Poetic justice, Maggie?"

"Call it what you want, Maguire. I read your stories. You're not as flowery as your predecessor Sullivan, who loved to implicate my girls in every metaphor he wrote, but you get the facts straight."

"I owe you, Maggie."

"It's never good to owe a madam, unless of course she's Irish. Now tell me what you make of all this, *Bugle* crime reporter."

"Someone who wants revenge for Harvey Addleston's death is the killer, Maggie. Find out who and these murders will stop. Do you think I've got it figured right?"

"If I thought you ever missed the point I wouldn't confide in you, my scribe friend. Now, come back some night when you have other intentions in mind. I might even come out of retirement." Maggie winked. She came from behind her desk, leaned over, and kissed Maguire on the lips before leading him through the red glow to the parlor. A man wearing a ragged undershirt, his suspenders hanging loose from his shoulders and his pants yawning open, paced near the stairs, ranting that the girls cheated him. "Now, Mickey," Maggie cooed to him. "I've told you before, if you want more than a nickel's worth you've got to last longer than two strokes."

Female laughter rippled through the room. Maguire regretted that he had to miss the scene that would follow. He left the Windsor and hurried to the *Bugle*. He had a scoop.

~ 19 ~

Scoop of a lifetime

Stoffleman show no surprise when Maguire burst into the city room out of breath. The erstwhile editor, winding down yet another fifteen-hour shift, straightened. "You've got something," he merely said.

"I've got the motive, boss, from an off-the-record source." Maguire gave Stoffleman a quick rundown of what he heard from Maggie O'Keefe. The editor glanced at the clock. "You're cutting it close. Almost midnight. Fifteen minutes to top your story with scoop. Press starts in twenty."

Maguire went to his desk and tapped out a first paragraph:

"New evidence has emerged that the killer in the Purple Rose Murders is retaliating for the murder of a Butte businessman more than two decades ago over a phony land deal."

Maguire's successive paragraphs laid out the scenario. He also wrote the obligatory "police have not confirmed" disclaimer. He owed that much to Ferndale. Maguire tapped out the news with urgency. He was, after all, a veteran crime reporter who knew his business. When he finished, Stoffleman and two other editors at the other end of the city room scrambled to change the *Bugle*'s front page from its earlier version.

The new headline read:

Motive revealed in Purple Rose Murders
Killer angered over fake hotel investment
Bugle source confirms
shyster arranged beating

Compositors downstairs raced to set new type. After a five-minute delay, the building quaked as the press roared into action. Stoffleman disappeared for a few minutes, returning with a handful of newspapers straight off the press that smelled of wet ink. Maguire looked over his story. The skillful Stoffleman had blended Maguire's frantic writing into a smooth narrative. The story broke new ground. Now, who pulled the trigger? Rhonda Townsend? Or a man, a hired gun, a triggerman? No woman would shoot like that. The Purple Rose Murders were hard-boiled executions. Some skilled thug employed to avenge Addleston's death. He should call Ferndale to hash over details. Maguire looked at his watch. Dead of night. Let the old detective sleep.

Deep in his nightmare, Ferndale didn't hear the assailant creeping through his dark house. An instant before the intruder pulled the trigger, Ferndale shifted on the couch, sensing danger. He flinched from a powerful blow to his left shoulder. Instinctively, he reached for his gun. Something wet and warm dripped onto his hand. He felt the familiar grip, thumbed the hammer back, heard the explosion that filled his house. Someone ran. Shoes pounded on the wooden floor. Then silence. Ferndale listened to make sure his assailant left the house. He tried to stand to call for help. As his body went numb his mind tumbled with confusion. Gun still in hand, he felt himself falling, this time not from a waterfall but from a cliff.

Maguire expected his telephone to ring during the night but it didn't. He awoke on his bed still dressed in his rumpled suit. The clock said half past eight in the morning. He raised the window shade. Outside, across the street, a shopkeeper pushed a broom over broken glass. A delivery driver unloaded boxes from a truck. Children walked to school. Maguire dialed Ferndale's number at the police department. No answer. He browned some toast and slathered it with strawberry jam. As he gulped down his breakfast he again read the *Bugle* story he had written only hours earlier. Who would grieve enough about what happened to Harvey Addleston to exact revenge on people who didn't kill him? To draw attention to the summer's murders with the same purple flowers that decorated his casket at his funeral several years earlier?

Maguire splashed water on his face and changed his suit. He had a closet full of white shirts, none of them ironed. His mother, ever the hopeless drunk, relentlessly ironed his clothes in those strange days back in Chicago. He remembered that oddity most about her but never understood why. Even as a grown man he hated the sight of an unfolded ironing board. Maguire reached for his revolver. He slid the .38 into the side pocket of his suit coat. It felt bulky through the thin fabric.

After he shaved he again dialed Ferndale's number. Again, no answer. "I'll try the chief," he said aloud to himself. The young Irishman had taken to talking to himself as lonely men do. Morse picked up on the first ring. "That damn Ferndale!" the chief ranted. "We have murders around every corner and our detective can't get out of bed. I'll have his badge! Go roll him out of the sheets, will you? Tell him we have work to do."

Maguire knew who did the grunt work. Ferndale deserved better than the heat coming from the chief and the mayor. Maguire had a feeling something had gone terribly wrong. Ferndale never missed work. Maguire looked in the mirror, saw an exhausted man with puffy eyes staring back at him, and decided to go find Ferndale.

Several blocks away that morning, the killer read Maguire's story in the Bugle with some satisfaction. People all over Butte, and beyond, would read his story. Finally, Maguire wandered into the heart of the matter. Still too slow, too late. What an obvious clue, those purple roses, screaming for attention. People should have remembered. Ferndale, despite being a wise cop, distracted from the story. Maguire depended on him too much. Shooting Ferndale wasn't murder but a mercy killing. The old man had lived long past his prime anyway. He put up a fight as the killer knew he would. Firing wildly into the dark didn't help him a bit. He missed by a mile. What a shame he too died without receiving a purple rose. The one purple rose that remained soon would brown and wilt. With Ferndale dead, Maguire would come looking for Mary Miller, his next logical move.

Maguire parked in front of Ferndale's house on Zarelda Street, high on the Hill in the neighborhood known as Big Butte. He saw Ferndale's car parked in the alley. Silence greeted his urgent knocks at the front door. Maguire peered in the window. He saw Ferndale, collapsed and bloodied, ten feet from him through the glass. Maguire smashed in the locked door with two hard kicks. Ferndale sprawled half off the faded green couch. His skin ghastly gray, his eyes closed, his face frozen with pain, his right fist gripping his gun like he never wanted to let it go. Maguire had seen more murder scenes than anyone in Butte except for Ferndale. Victims turned white as their bodies drained blood. Their expressions told the story of their tragic final moments. Maguire kept his emotional distance when viewing slain bodies. A *Bugle* reporter, after all, a disinterested observer committed to impartial telling of the news. Vanzetti's gruesome murder shook him. Seeing Ferndale shot up hit him even harder. Ferndale had died in a tragic caricature of his life as a cop. Maguire turned away from the gray rumpled body and cried. Tears ran down his ruddy Irish cheeks.

Suddenly Maguire heard a raspy whisper. "Stop blubbering and get me to a goddam hospital, will you?" He turned. Ferndale, a dead man with breath, stared at him with sunken eyes. "Maguire, remember to check a pulse, will you? Damn mick anyway. Here, take my weapon before it goes off and finishes me. Ain't no pension in suicide. Careful, the hammer's pulled back."

Maguire uncocked the gun and placed it on the floor. "I thought you had taken a ride to the other side, Duke. What the hell?"

"A journey over to the afterlife crossed my mind a time or two during the night. I forgot how a gunshot wound hurt so bad. Worse than the hardest punch I ever took. Had one foot in the grave as this bullet bled me out. Useless trying to call for help. Every time I woke up, I passed out."

Maguire grabbed Ferndale's telephone on the wall. "Chief Morse? No, listen, this is Maguire and nobody's sleeping in. Cop down. Ferndale's been shot. We need an ambulance at his house. Affirmative, his house. Fast. He's hurt bad. Send black and whites. Maybe the shooter is still around. Yes, I have a gun if it comes to that before your men get here."

In the minutes before they heard the sirens, Maguire pressed towels against Ferndale's shoulder. The old detective looked back at the younger man with weak and pleading eyes. His fingers shook as he reached for the lapel of Maguire's suit. "Not much blood left in me, Red. Hell, it's bad. I figured I'd be dead by lunch. One old detective out of the way. Ought to please the mayor, that glad-handing bastard."

"You already missed breakfast. Don't make a habit of skipping meals."

"Maguire, listen close. Get this purple rose mystery solved, will you? The killer stood right here, right in this room, plugging me in my own house. Couldn't see him in the dark. I got a round off. Check around for blood, will you? His, not mine." Maguire searched until he found a bullet hole in the wall. He saw no evidence Ferndale shot his assailant. He looked around in the other rooms.

"The back door to your house is standing open, Duke."

"So damn tired last night I forgot to lock it, I guess. Never use the front one. So tired now."

Ferndale closed his eyes as screaming sirens arrived. The ambulance driver and half of Butte's cops charged into the room as Maguire knelt over his friend. "Find the killer," Ferndale whispered.

Thirty minutes later, when Maguire walked into the *Bugle* city room, everyone had heard. Claggett asked for details, showing disappointment he wouldn't be writing Ferndale's colorful obituary after all. Stoffleman, never comfortable with sentiment, stated his desire that Ferndale would survive the ride to the hospital. When he saw the worry in Maguire's face he shifted to another topic. "The old man called me upstairs to compliment your reporting, Red. News racks and counter copies sold out first thing. Advertisers are clamoring to buy space in the paper because they know everybody is reading it. We're running circles around the Company rag is what he wants you to know," Stoffleman said.

Maguire sank into his creaking chair and looked around. Vanzetti's desk sat empty now, its contents swept away into a box shipped to some distant relative. Mary's desk remained hauntingly quiet. She had last been there, what two or three days ago? Maguire had lost track of time. Yesterday seemed like last week. He had stared out the window, remembering the vacation he hoped to take with her to Florida, numbly studying the mountains to the south. Only a fool would leap to a fantasy like that while people were being shot dead. Maguire leaned against the windowsill and crossed his arms. Thirty-eight years old, a strong young man still, wanting less of the bad and more of the good. In writing about murder he drafted the last chapter of a person's life story. Dead bodies left no dispute. Murder blackened reputations, ruined bank accounts and forever destroyed happiness. Families never recovered.

Ted Ketchul came into the city room. He had ten years on Maguire and a trusting, earnest face that worked to his advantage when covering news about miners and their unions. Butte thrived on unions. Like Maguire's crime stories, Ketchul's labor stories were exclusive to the *Bugle*. The Company suits up the street chased only news that favored the bigwigs.

"Red, word at Local 333 is that Ferndale took an ugly fall. Confirmed?"

"True, Ted, but the old cuss kicked up a fuss when he got hauled off in the meat wagon anyway. He tried to tell the driver to stop uptown for beer." As Maguire told Ketchul about finding Ferndale shot, Chief Morse walked into the city room. He motioned Stoffleman over to Maguire's desk.

"Thought you boys would want to know where Ferndale stands," he said. "They took him into surgery and pulled a slug out of his shoulder. We think it's a .44 caliber. Doc says it made a mess of some bone and muscle but missed his heart by several inches. The gunman shot high. Higher than intended, I think, firing a round in a dark room. If Ferndale hadn't shot back, who knows? Doc says the ornery old dink will live. I don't know if this comes as good news or bad news depending on your point of view." The chief attempted a smile. "Don't expect him back behind the badge anytime soon."

Maguire shook the chief's hand. "That's a relief on all counts."

"Figured I should tell you right away, Maguire. You saved Ferndale and I'm indebted." The chief nodded and left.

Stoffleman gave Maguire one of those crooked looks. "I hate to say it ..."

"I know, boss. You want a story for tomorrow's paper."

"You're catching on, Maguire. And you, Ketchul, what news do you have out of that union meeting this morning?"

Maguire lifted the receiver on his telephone. He put his index finger in the "O" slot to turn the rotary dial. "Luverne, city 4285 please. Not now, Luverne. Yes, it warms my heart that you call me honey. Do you look good in pink? Ravenous, Luverne. I know you leave work at five. Later, Luverne? I'm in a hurry."

A moment later Lucky Finero picked up. "Maguire? You ain't shot yet?"

"The day's young, Lucky."

"You need a private eye? I could take a break from wrangling deadbeats. Fifty bucks up front to find the broad. Fifty more afterwards."

Maguire knocked himself in the head with the telephone receiver. "I know you've got connections, Lucky, but if the cops can't find her —."

"Those dicks in blue ain't Lucky Finero."

"You've heard some whispers then?"

"About the broad? What's her name again, Maguire?"

"Mary Miller, did you forget? You know everything, right?"

"Heard nothin' but I ain't exactly gone lookin' now have I? That's Ferndale's job ain't it? Right now he's doing a piss-poor job of it, blowin' kisses at nurses while the rest of us work. So, anyway. Kick me fifty and I'll get on her trail."

"Makes perfect sense, Lucky, but Duke Ferndale would club me senseless after his head clears from that whiff of ether they gave him in the operating room."

"Suit yourself, Maguire. I ain't seeing any progress in catching your chickadee from the dicks wearing the badge. Now Ferndale goes and gets himself shot up and where does that leave ya?"

Lucky had a point. "Tell you what," Maguire said. "If the cops can't find Mary by tomorrow, you're hired. If you hunt for Mary I presume you'll run across the killer. I want the story, right then. Not the next day. On scene. That's the deal."

"Lovestruck, ain't ya?"

"Not that I'll admit publicly but there's no use denying it to you, Lucky."

"Well, you ain't dead yet, hard as you've tried. What I hear is that every saloon on the Hill is running bets on where the next purple rose turns up. Most of the jingle falls on one name. Guess who, Red Maguire? Them boys figure they have a winner. Hell, I placed five on you myself."

"No kidding, Lucky? I might do the same."

When Maguire hung up he looked down the long room to where Stoffleman worked. Involving Lucky Finero in police business would infuriate the boss. Maguire walked over to Ketchul. "Ted, a minute?"

"A minute, Maguire. I've got a story to crank before Stoffleman blows a gasket."

Maguire knelt before Ketchul. "I'm thinking of hiring a private eye to find Mary," he whispered. "Will it put me in the middle of the story? What's your take? I won't go to Stoffleman unless I'm sure."

A rare smile crossed Ketchul's granite face. "I'll fight the temptation to tell you this is a great idea and send you over to tell him," he whispered back. "Get hold of yourself, Maguire. A news reporter in the middle of the biggest story of a lifetime better not fork over jingle to someone to change the outcome. If the boss wants somebody tailing Miller he'll ask the old man upstairs. Your byline is a bigger club than a private eye anyway."

"I thought as much, Ted."

"You would have told me the same thing if the tables were turned. Maguire? We all know you have eyes for Miller. Don't do anything stupid."

Maguire's telephone rang as he returned to his desk.

"It's you!" he uttered. Mary's voice came hurried, scared. "Oh, Red, please. She said she would kill me. You've got to help."

"She? My god, it's Rhonda Townsend after all. Where are you?"

"She's got a gun on me. She wants you to have the final piece of the story." Mary's voice echoed on the line. "She's taking me to a warehouse off Platinum Street. Look for my green car parked in the alley. That will be the one. Be quick, Red. And listen close to what I'm saying now. Don't tell the cops. Come alone. If you bring help, she will kill me. She's not kidding." Click.

Maguire stood and hurried from the city room. He avoided Stoffleman's questioning gaze. Saving Mary meant going alone. His heart raced as he drove south off the Hill. He tried to picture the scenario. Rhonda shot Ferndale. Now she held Mary at gunpoint. Rhonda, smarter than she sounded in the *Bugle* story and crazier too, kidnapped Mary to force Maguire into her trap. Maguire tried to figure out Rhonda's motive but his mind lingered on Mary. Minutes later he arrived at a row of warehouses. Some were in use, others boarded and dilapidated, all of them hulking and dark. He turned into the alley to see Mary's green car, a two-door sedan, parked near a rear door to an abandoned building. "Butte Machine and Tool," said a weather-blistered blue sign hanging askew above the door. The Pontiac slid to a stop. Maguire checked his revolver. It had four bullets. He hoped he didn't need five. He cursed at his lack of preparation for a shootout. In all the years he had owned the gun, using the .38 remained a distant notion, much like romance in his life. Ferndale, never an optimist in his line of work, warned him against trusting anyone. "Just when you think you don't need the piece it will save your life," he told Maguire.

The door to the warehouse hung on rusty hinges that protested like a loud drunk at closing time when he pulled it open. He stepped into the darkness. The building reeked of a cave, wet and cool, mingled with odors of spilled motor oil, rusting metal and rot. He edged into the gloom, shuffling forward, until he bumped his leg into something with a hard edge. A concrete step. He stood quietly and listened. Pigeons fluttered in broken windows two stories above him. Wind blowing through the door he had swung open pushed empty cardboard boxes across the floor. He hesitated, listening.

Then came Mary's pleading voice, above him, echoing in the empty building. "Red, up here, hurry. Follow the stairs."

Maguire felt for his gun. Walking into a trap didn't scare him. His beloved Mary, held hostage, would die if he didn't confront Rhonda Townsend. He climbed the stairs, dreading at what awaited him. He pictured Rhonda holding the barrel of her gun to Mary's pretty head. If Maguire made one slip, one quick move, Rhonda would blow a hole in the woman he loved. How cold-hearted. Criminals were full of secrets and deceptions. He knew that all too well.

At the top he saw a wooden door to an office. The room had windows opening to the warehouse floor. Once a foreman's office, he thought. Someone who looked down on the workers to keep them from goofing off. Maguire turned the rusted doorknob. He stepped into a dark room. He heard rustling. A light switched on. Mary stood solemnly before him, alone. He hardly recognized her. She wore boots, black pants, and a heavy blue jacket. A black watch cap, pulled over her honey hair, gave her the unsettling appearance of a bank robber. Her face looked plain, even ordinary, without lipstick and makeup.

Confused, Maguire looked around the room. Empty except for broken furniture and a box of machine parts. A typewriter rested on top of a small scuffed desk. Next to it he saw a wet newspaper folded around something. Mary watched him from under a light bulb hanging from the ceiling. One hand held a cigarette. She hid the other in a side pocket of her jacket. "Red Maguire, dogged police reporter, always the first to arrive on a scene where people die. Thanks for coming, Red. I wondered whether you were up to it considering the pace of your news coverage the past few days."

"This doesn't look right, Mary. Where's Rhonda Townsend?"

"Mary Miller sent her away, Red."

"Meaning what? Is there another Mary Miller?"

"You know only one Mary Miller, Red."

"Why are you talking about yourself in the third person, Mary? What's going on here?"

"You might ask Rhonda, Red, but she's not up to taking questions anymore. That girl couldn't make sense of anything at all, could she?"

"You killed her?"

"I thought about making it easy for her, I really did, but she took care of her final exit all by herself. You see, Rhonda needed a little guidance, a little coaxing. Once she understood that a shot to the temple hurt no more than a millisecond, as if I would know, she knew what to do next. Rhonda was a simple one just like her old man. Angry but stupid. I helped her understand she was the only person needing her bullet."

Maguire looked doubtful. "Mary Miller wouldn't do such a thing."

She took a deep puff, exhaling the smoke in an arc. "That's because I'm not Mary Miller. Where did you get that name?"

"Sure you are, Mary. What are you talking about? You're a *Bugle* reporter."

"I think you're mistaken."

"We made love."

"You hardly knew me, Red Maguire. Remember the first day we started working together? You barely knew my name. You foolishly confused me with Mary Miller."

"Then who ...?"

"This was my worry, Red. This is what kept me awake at night. I set the entire story before you. Still you failed to see it. Your frivolous fling with Mary Miller spoiled the plot. You lost your concentration. Now we've run out of time."

Shaking from surprise and confusion, Maguire leaned his broad frame against the wall. He patted the bundle of love notes, Mary's included, in his pocket. He stared at the woman standing before him.

"You lost me, Mary. Why are you dressed like that?"

"I'm Nancy Addleston, you fool. If only you had looked deeper, seen me for more than your kitten in bed, you might have guessed." Her voice suddenly had a hard edge to it. "You were getting close to knowing, as I hoped you would, but it became evident you're a man prone to distraction. You failed to recognize Mary Miller as an illusion, come and gone like an overnight chinook in this ugly city full of holes. It was Nancy Addleston I wanted you to find and remember. You didn't live up to your reputation. Montana's best crime reporter, is that what Stoffleman said? What a laugh."

"So you're Harvey's daughter. His only child," Maguire said.

She laughed. "Pity that fact didn't dawn on you earlier, Maguire. You could have taken it to print. You came so close. I wanted the full story told. I couldn't tell it myself, could I? How my father, framed and killed, became a nobody? How a shyster the police ignored left my mother and me destitute? Do you know that every year on my birthday he gave me something purple? My favorite color. 'Here, little rose,' he would say to me. Nobody cared when he died. This town turned its back on us. I struggled to understand why someone would kill my father. Pined over his absence, our sad house, his hat hanging by the front door. Think of me as a little girl only eight years old. When those weak-minded miners killed Daddy, they killed me. I lived a hellish life. Nobody survives a murder."

"Including people you deprived of their loved ones like the Townsend mother and Maud Kelly and the crazy Danvers girl? By killing their loved ones, people who had nothing to do with your father's murder, you sentenced them to lives of misery. Did you take them into account?"

"Nice try, Maguire, but misplaced compassion. This is my story."

"What about Rhonda? What role did you assign her in this sordid affair?"

"Only a fool would believe she should get credit for cleaning up this town."

"She had a gun."

"The very one she used to put a bullet in her brain."

Maguire spit on the floor in disgust. "You let me believe she killed the others."

"I only hinted at the possibility if you remember. Your imagination filled in the blanks. It's a shame your abundant talent for story-telling didn't include a true appreciation for facts."

"I'm armed, Mary. ... Nancy."

"I see that, Maguire. You are astute enough to know that I'm gripping the death weapon under this jacket. That's right, the gun that killed the others. No doubt you hope your gun will save you from mine. I'm betting you've never fired it. To the contrary, I never miss, as you have reported in your monotonous stories in the *Bugle*."

"The police know I'm here."

"I doubt that. Your love contortions over Mary Miller wouldn't permit you to put her life in danger."

"Ferndale knows I'm here."

"You can't expect a dead man to rescue you."

"Then you know someone shot him?"

"I was the first to know. I killed him."

"Ferndale had nothing to do with your father's murder."

"He bungled the case, Maguire. Yes, he caught those idiot murderers Kelly and Townsend, I'll give him that. Ferndale never had the sense to figure out the big picture. Not then, not ever. The dicks back then blundered even the recovery of my father's money. They didn't believe my mother when she told them a criminal stole it."

"So, you killed Ferndale because of it?"

"Whatever glory days that old wreck of a boxer might have had as a cop were long gone. I killed an old man wasting away in misery."

"What if I told you Ferndale survived your attempt to kill him?"

"Impossible. I told you, I never miss."

"If you're blaming everybody else, why not blame your father for losing his life savings?"

Nancy gestured to a dusty chair in the corner. "Sit, Maguire. I want to tell you my father's story. Don't even think of attacking me. I shoot with deadly precision." Keeping her hand in her pocket, she leaned against the old desk.

"It goes like this. A young girl loses her beloved father because thugs and outcasts pounce on his kind nature. He was naive, yes. The outcome shows that. But do you know he gave free shoes to people who couldn't even afford a meal? That he contributed generously to the Red Cross? That he collected donations from churches in Butte to feed unemployed miners? My father never turned his back on anybody in need. He never got the recognition he deserved. We lived simply but he had savings inherited from my grandfather, a banker in Minneapolis. I never knew how much until I read your story this morning."

"You didn't know about Harry Anthony?"

"I know all about Harry the Ham. When I was young I didn't know the truth. Later my mother played it out for me. I knew enough to understand Anthony took everything from my father, including his dignity, because of selfish greed. It's a sad thing, isn't it, stealing another man's money for personal enjoyment? Calling it jingle seems so trivial, Maguire. Not pocket change. Our future. My father saved and compounded it in a bank for our family's future. This shyster Anthony spent it on whores and bad liquor. He killed my father over that money, and for what?"

"You wanted revenge, but Harry died long before you could inflict it on him. All the others suffered for his sins. Am I close?"

"Collateral damage, Maguire. I suppose you want details?" She told him how the purple roses decorated her father's casket. The only pretty thing she remembered from that day. His remains resembled a wax statue she had seen in the five and dime, his misshapen face coated with white powder and his fingers wilted like drying weeds. Only the flowers brought some life to his death.

"I loved you, Mary."

"Quit sniveling. Forget that other woman. I'm Nancy. Stay on track, will you?"

"And if I reach for my gun?"

"You won't get your hand halfway there. I will shoot you dead where you sit."

"Just like you shot the others?"

"Those punks Kelly and Townsend were easy. Their fathers killed mine in the most violent heartless manner. Vermin born of vermin. I denied them time to beg. Danvers got in the way. Cute all right but unlucky. David Fenton fell for my flirting.

When I came to his house that morning you found him dead, he showed no alarm at all. I wore my best dress. The blue one."

"My God, you played him like you did me."

"What fools, both of you. You nearly caught me standing over his body. When I drove away you passed me on the highway."

"Why Vanzetti? He was one of us."

"He thought of Mary Miller as his friend. Sadly for Antonio, his investigation into land fraud took him ever closer to finding out about Harry Anthony's connection with my father. Not Antonio's story, but yours, Maguire. He cried when he saw my gun."

"You chopped off his head."

"How indecent of Clifford."

"Clifford Fenton?"

"Does it surprise you that I had an accomplice? He watched his cousin grow fat and rich off my father's money. He never understood why I recruited him. A man like Clifford never does. Clifford wanted David's money. That's what motivated Clifford. A simple man, prone to suggestion. Clifford made some use of himself by performing menial tasks like leaving a threatening note on your windshield and calling you in the middle of the night. Surprised? Yes, Clifford. I had hoped he was something more than just a weak and stupid drunk. I misjudged his character. I instructed him to lure Vanzetti to the mine yard with a promise of inside information about his cousin's land development. Vanzetti thought he had scooped the biggest story in the history of Butte. He told me what he had found. Antonio did a lot of good for this town. I regret having to dispatch him. Sad, really. After I shot him, I drove away. That fool Clifford doubled back with an axe because he thought the cops would link him to Vanzetti. It never occurred to the dimwit that head or not, police might identify Vanzetti by his fingerprints. I don't approve of decapitation, but I must say, it made for hot news in the *Bugle*."

Maguire held his head in his hands and stared at the floor. "Such terrible irony that you were helping me write about the murders. You could have written the entire story yourself."

"I tried to make it look good."

"You tried to kill me in Deer Lodge with a car."

"Not me, Clifford. He followed you. The idiot nearly ruined the story I wanted you to write. Then he ditched it in an alley where the cops found it. Sloppy, that Clifford. He became a liability and paid for it."

"You shot him like the others?"

"Of course. Minutes before Ferndale arrived. I watched from the shadows across the street as they cruised up in that black and white. He and that other cop never had a clue."

"Then Stoffleman tells you to help me write about the murders. We shared bylines. Did it thrill you to write stories about people you shot?"

Nancy ignored his question. "How hard, you know, growing up like that. Mother and I left Butte under a cloud of shame. I planned for years how to make it right."

"Then you became Mary Miller."

"How convenient when the *Bugle* advertised for a reporter. Don't you think? I fit the profile of a society reporter quite well. What a perfect cover, don't you agree?"

"You invested your life in an elaborate ruse to kill people. You're not sane."

"Ah, Maguire, who's to judge the boundaries of sanity? When you told me about your mother leaving you, I understood why you wasted your life writing about how people hurt each other. Are we really that different, Maguire?"

"I never killed anybody."

"Neither had I until I put a round in Kelly's son."

"You belong in Warm Springs."

"I expected more of you, Maguire. The state hospital won't resolve my pain and loss."

"And killing people will?"

"It's not the killings, but the reporting of them, that will honor my father."

"You're a serial killer, Mary. God, look at you."

"Concentrate on the storyline, Maguire. We're long past whatever you think Mary did. It's Nancy, Harvey's daughter, who matters now."

"What do you want from me now in this twisted plot of yours?"

"What I wanted all along, Maguire. For the story to come out. In your case, unfortunately, it might be post-mortem." She pulled a mean gray gun out of her pocket. Maguire stared at the .44 that had killed all the others. The gun looked dull but deadly under the weak light. She pulled back the hammer. Maguire knew what the metallic click meant for him. "I spent years training with firearms," Mary, or Nancy, continued. "I eventually arrived at the understanding that it's not how many times you shoot, but how accurately, that ensures the desired result. I've been quite efficient with my bullets, don't you think?"

"I'm not interested in false praise for murderers."

"Here's what you are going to do, Maguire." She pointed her gun at his heart. "Reach into your coat pocket with your left hand. Drop your weapon on the floor. Then kick it over to me. Do anything else and I will kill you where you sit."

Maguire did as she said, hoping she didn't intend to shoot him after all. Keeping her eyes on him, she retrieved his gun and smiled. "This is a pea shooter, Maguire. You can't bring a firecracker to a gunfight." Nancy tossed his .38 through a broken window. It clattered on the concrete warehouse floor below them. "Now, get over here to the typewriter and go to work. Write the final story, Maguire. For once, try to rise to the example Peter Sullivan set as a flamboyant writer. Tell all those *Bugle* readers how it was, how it really was, in my quest to correct crimes against Harvey Addleston. This will be your biggest story. Your scoop of a lifetime. Leave nothing out."

"The cops will hunt you down after I identify you in print."

"Does it matter, Maguire?"

"Is this how you want your father remembered?"

"That his daughter brought justice to his murder? Yes."

"Vigilante justice, maybe."

"Write it, Maguire. Write it or I will shoot you dead this instant and write it myself. Imagine Stoffleman over at the *Bugle* finding a blood-spattered story under your byline in the afternoon mail. He couldn't resist running it as a monument to his fallen crime reporter. He'd step over your body to print it."

"That's the first thing you've said here that I can agree with," Maguire conceded.

"Get to it. You have a deadline and the clock's ticking."

Maguire dragged the dusty chair behind the desk. He began to type. How thoughtful of Mary, or Nancy, to provide him a couple dozen sheets of paper. She stood behind him. He felt the gun barrel pressing against his spine. He began:

"The daughter of a slain Butte businessman has identified herself as the Purple Rose Killer."

Nancy nudged him with the gun. "Factual, but much too antiseptic, Maguire. You're not writing a church bulletin or another routine burglary story off your crime beat. This is your story of a lifetime. A story involving a woman, of romance, of love. Imagine your last kiss with Mary. Write it with heart."

Maguire rolled a fresh sheet of paper into the typewriter.

"Nancy Addleston grew up aching for her father, a kindly uptown Butte shoe store owner beaten to death over a phony land deal. In the years after his murder, she plotted a series of revenge killings, leaving a trail of purple roses as clues. She returned to Butte under the name Mary Miller, began working as the Bugle's society reporter, and led a secret life as the Purple Rose Killer."

Nancy murmured her approval. "Better, Maguire. If only you wrote your other stories like this. Pour it out, will you?"

Maguire typed for an hour. The keystrokes echoed in the barren room. He wrote from memory, from emotion, from his certainty that she would shoot him if he hesitated. He left nothing out. When he finished, Nancy handed him a stamped envelope addressed to Stoffleman at the *Bugle*.

"It appears I won't be delivering my story in person," Maguire told her.

"It's sad, isn't it? You are a good man, Maguire. Better than I deserved."

"Then you loved me?"

"You're still confusing Mary with Nancy. Hardly matters, does it? I didn't come back to Butte for love."

Nancy pointed the gun at Maguire's head as she moved in front of the desk. She tucked the envelope in her jacket. "We can't let sentiment interfere, can we? I do admit to some sadness at killing Vanzetti."

"You should feel despair at killing them all."

"I feel despair at losing my father."

"If you intended to kill people, why the drama with the purple roses?"

"He raised them. Haven't you figured that out by now? My father said they brought a splash of color to this gray city. He founded the Rocky Mountain Garden Club. Can you imagine a garden club formed to beautify this open sore? On my birthdays, on Easter, he gave me a purple rose. He gave my mother a bouquet of them on their anniversaries. I'm sure you've heard of symbolism, Maguire. What better way for me to honor my father's memory? To give him what this city buried and forgot? Do you know how few people came to his funeral? Being killed in a bar fight leads to disgrace in this town. A hundred men watched what Kelly and Townsend did to my father. You know the Helsinki. Try to get justice in Butte when the union is involved. My father didn't know how to fight. People knew him as a man of sophistication, gentle and caring, a man devoted to his family. Many people loved him. I loved him."

"Maybe so, but you hated everyone else. Your hate prevented you from ever loving anybody, including me."

Nancy raised her gun with both hands. "I'm sorry, Maguire. Don't make this about your own sorry existence. You are a lonely lost man. Mary saw it in you right away. In another life she and you might have made something with each other. You're ghosts of the past, both of you."

"Going to kill me? I need to know, but before you, I've wondered. Where did you grow the roses?"

"You want to add that splash of color to your bleak final moments? Pity you failed ask me when you sat there writing your forever last bylined story for the *Bugle*. The location is beside the point, really, but I suppose you should know. My parents owned a cabin on ten acres back in the woods on Blizzard Mountain. Heard of that area, have you? My father wanted to make it so much more. Then those thugs killed him and his dream. I never forgot our family cabin. It's a bit dilapidated after all these years. I repaired my father's summer greenhouse with carpentry and plastic. You would be surprised how well roses grow so far above sea level."

"Quite dramatic of you," Maguire said, pointing to the typewriter. "How about I write those details into my piece for the *Bugle*?"

"Let's not, Maguire. You're already past deadline on this story." Nancy cocked the gun and aimed it point blank at Maguire's chest. He would die like all the rest, shot through the heart. Maguire wondered whether, in the end, death by murder differed from death by natural causes. Either way Arnie at the Forever More would stretch him naked and drain the last of his blood. That instant before a fatal shot, the worst loneliness Maguire had known, emptied his mind of all thoughts but one.

"I loved you, Mary. I would have married you."

Nancy stared at Maguire. They stood eight feet apart. He saw her blink. A tear rolled down her cheek. In that moment Nancy became Mary again. Maguire closed his eyes. He didn't want to see her pulling the trigger. Not that, not as his last memory. He thought of the smiling Mary. A stranger, yes, but a welcome bright diversion from his humdrum life seeking crime around every dark corner. Oh, Mary.

He heard her whisper, "Not you, Red. You're the better one of us." Maguire pulled himself from his trance in time to see her turn the menacing gun barrel to her chest. It went off with an ear-splitting boom in the small room. He cupped his ears. Nancy staggered backward against the wall. Her eyes, wide open and scared, froze on him for her last breath of life. She slumped to the floor. Dead, Maguire knew. Shaking, stomach churning, he grabbed the desk to avoid falling. The small room reeked of gunpowder and a salty odor of blood. Maguire stared at the woman, his lover, crumpled before him. He needed to alert Stoffleman, and Police Chief Morse, and Arnie Petrovich at Forever More. Soon. They would have to wait. He had a job to do.

Maguire reached into Nancy's coat pocket for the envelope. He felt her hot blood. The bullet had pierced the typed story she intended to send to Stoffleman. "Our story is already outdated," Maguire said to the blank face of Nancy, or the woman he had loved as Mary. "I'll write a fresher one."

He turned to the typewriter. What an improbable place, a murder scene, to write the story of a woman so tortured over her father's beating death that she inflicted the same crime on six innocent people, seven counting Rhonda, eight if Ferndale had died. Maybe the best place. Writing in the heat of the moment made the best stories. Maguire looked at the curious wet newspaper on the desk.

When he unfolded it he found a wilted purple rose. "Meant for me, I presume," he said softly.

He placed the rose on Nancy's body, where it looked quite suitable for the occasion.

Then he began to write.

###

Hello, readers. Many of you have followed me for a long time. Every successful author needs loyal readers to survive in today's competitive publishing world. When you read my books please leave a review on Amazon.com. Doing so encourages other readers to buy my books, which in turn encourages me to continue writing, which means more for you. Thank you for sticking with me. Peace be with you.

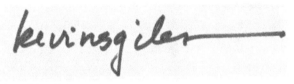

Website: kevinsgiles.com
Email: kevin@kevinsgiles.com
Free newsletter signup: green button at kevinsgiles.com
Facebook: facebook.com/kevsgiles/
Twitter: @kevsgiles
Amazon profile: amazon.com/Kevin-S-Giles

Also by Kevin S. Giles:

Nonfiction:
One Woman Against War: The Jeannette Rankin Story
Jerry's Riot: True Story of Montana's 1959 Prison Disturbance

Fiction:
Summer of the Black Chevy

To order: https://booklocker.com/

CPSIA information can be obtained
at www.ICGtesting.com
Printed in the USA
FSHW011559120920
73664FS